Also by Jay Bonansinga

Bloodhound
Head Case
The Killer Game

THE
SLEEP
POLICE

Jay Bonansinga

A SIGNET BOOK

SIGNET
Published by New American Library, a division of
Penguin Putnam Inc., 375 Hudson Street,
New York, New York 10014, U.S.A.
Penguin Books Ltd, 27 Wrights Lane,
London W8 5TZ, England
Penguin Books Australia Ltd, Ringwood,
Victoria, Australia
Penguin Books Canada Ltd, 10 Alcorn Avenue,
Toronto, Ontario, Canada M4V 3B2
Penguin Books (N.Z.) Ltd, 182–190 Wairau Road,
Auckland 10, New Zealand

Penguin Books Ltd, Registered Offices:
Harmondsworth, Middlesex, England

First published by Signet, an imprint of New American Library,
a division of Penguin Putnam Inc.

First Printing, March 2001
10 9 8 7 6 5 4 3 2 1

Ⓟ REGISTERED TRADEMARK—MARCA REGISTRADA

Printed in the United States of America

PUBLISHER'S NOTE
This is a work of fiction. Names, characters, places, and incidents either are
the product of the author's imagination or are used fictitiously, and any
resemblance to actual persons, living or dead, business establishments, events,
or locales is entirely coincidental.

BOOKS ARE AVAILABLE AT QUANTITY DISCOUNTS WHEN USED TO PROMOTE
PRODUCTS OR SERVICES. FOR INFORMATION PLEASE WRITE TO PREMIUM
MARKETING DIVISION, PENGUIN PUTNAM INC., 375 HUDSON STREET, NEW YORK,
NEW YORK 10014.

For Will

A special thanks to Matthew Snyder, Delin Kormandy, Fred Hunter, Area Six Community Relations, and the men and women of the Chicago Police Department.

"When I hoped for good, evil came; when I looked for light, then came darkness."

—JOB 30:26

PART I

Thumb Suckers

1

Things started going wrong the moment Frank Janus laid eyes on the victim.

"Bambi—? You with us?"

Deep in the recesses of Frank's mind, a cog had jammed suddenly. The warehouse was mostly silent, except for the occasional crackle of a beat cop's radio, the muffled drone of Pakistani music coming through a wall, and the incessant buzzing of greenback flies. They were summer flies. Summer-in-Chicago flies.

And they were busy.

"Earth to Bambi—come in."

The voice was right next to Frank, wowing and fluttering as though underwater, but it might as well have been a mile away. Frank couldn't answer. He couldn't move. His body had stalled, his gaze fixed on that white female victim lying stone dead on the cinders at his feet.

In some adjacent building, the sound of a Vinu and a dholak drum thumped incessantly.

A Vinu is an Indian stringed instrument that sounds like a sitar only lower, and a dholak drum has that hollow ring so common to Middle Eastern music. Together they can really grate on an uninitiated Westerner's ears, especially when coming through cheap walls at a crime scene.

A big meaty hand touched Frank between the shoulder-blades, and he twitched.

"—Whoa there, cowboy, easy does it." The big man was speaking softly in Frank's ear.

Detective Frank Janus tore his gaze away from the corpse, then looked up at his partner. "Sorry, D," he murmured.

"Where'd you go?"

Frank wiped his mouth. "Calcutta, I think."

"You see something?"

"No—whattya mean—the body?" Frank could feel a delicate trickle of sweat under his Bill Blass linen, tracking down the small of his back and into the elastic band of his boxer shorts. Frank Janus was not a large man, but he was well put together. Compact and well groomed. Like a gentleman jock. Tastefully dressed for the Violent Crimes division, with a head full of thick, jet-black curls, which made him look even younger than his thirty-seven years, which was already pretty damn young by Detective Squad standards. Right now he was wearing paper surgical booties over his shoes so that he wouldn't contaminate the black pools of blood. Frank also had a rubber clip on his nose—the kind swimmers and high-divers wear.

Next to him, the big man shrugged. "Yeah, the body, the scene, whatever. You see something?"

Frank said he wasn't sure.

The big man sighed, scanning the crime scene.

They were standing inside an empty, defunct Jewel Foods warehouse in a neighborhood known as Little Pakistan. Loose bricks drifted against the walls, and broken fluorescent tubes dangled from the ceiling, some of them still flickering and humming. Most of the shelves had been removed, leaving ugly whiskers of wires and plumbing sticking out of the floor. But the worst part was the smell.

Cops have all sorts of techniques to mask the smell of a decaying human body. The wagon guys smoke cigars. The lab guys soak cotton balls in Old Spice and stick them in their nostrils. Others smear Vicks VapoRub under their nose. Frank was partial to the diver's clip. But the problem was, the odor would get into his clothes. And into his hair. And it was a bitch to get out. No matter how many times he washed. But today, in this deserted warehouse, the smell was beyond bad. It was incredible. Mostly because it was mid-August, and the temperature outside was edging toward ninety. The warehouse had been stewing in the odors of rotting food and decaying human remains for at least three days. The stench was so pronounced, the detectives seemed to be *swimming* through it. A pair of uniformed officers were huddled in the northeast doorway, bandannas around their faces, trying to siphon a little of the outdoors into their lungs.

"Looks like we got a luncher on our hands," the big detective said under his breath. He had menthol cigarette filters stuck in each nostril to keep the stench at bay. In cop lingo, a "luncher" was a complicated murder case that the cops would probably have to "eat."

The big man was Detective Sully Deets, Frank's partner in the Twenty-fourth for nearly seven years. Somewhere in his midfifties, Deets was a giant pear-shaped Scotsman who favored JCPenneys sportcoats and Ban-Lon shirts. Everything about him screamed cop—from the top of his balding brush-cut down to his scuffed Floresheim wingtips. Deets was the one who had first coined the nickname "Bambi" for Frank. It was "Bambi" because Frank was so polite, so mild mannered, so deferential to absolutely everyone, from his fellow investigators down to the lowliest street skell.

"Definitely a luncher," Frank agreed softly, staring back down at the decedent.

What was going on? The mere sight of the body was rattling Frank like it was his rookie year, like he was some squirt fresh out of the academy looking at his first cadaver. She was just a stiff, for Christ's sake. A little ripe, maybe. But just a body. To a detective in the Violent Crimes division, she wasn't even a person anymore.

She was evidence. But Frank couldn't tear his eyes away from her. In the blast furnace heat, Frank's skin was starting to feel clammy-cold. His gorge was levitating. He felt lightheaded. The shakes were coming.

He quickly reached into his breast pocket and found a plastic drinking straw. He always kept one with him. It was one of those annoying habits he had picked up a few years back when he had tried to quit smoking. Chewing on a plastic straw, for some reason, calmed Frank, comforted him.

He put the straw in his mouth and started gnawing on it, and that's when he heard Deets's voice again.

"Yo, Bambi—?"

Frank looked up. "Huh?"

Deets was looking at him. "You okay?"

Frank nodded. "Yeah, D, absolutely, you bet."

Deets regarded Frank for a moment, then tossed him a container of baby powder.

Frank nearly dropped it. Straw sticking out of his mouth, he fumbled with it for a moment, awkwardly powdering his hands. Then he pulled out his rubber surgical gloves and put them on—a ritual at the outset of every investigation, whether he planned on touching anything or not. Then he pulled out his spiral notebook. He could feel the faint tremors in his hands. He gripped the notebook tightly to hide the trembling from his partner and the other cops. He chewed furiously on his straw. What the hell was happening to him?

He glanced across the warehouse. There was a thin curtain of pale blue smoke rising near the door, coming from the beat cops' cigarettes: another technique to mask the stench. Rays of harsh daylight slanted through the haze. Somewhere on the other side of the wall, the Pakistani music was droning and warbling, the recording hitting a warped section. Frank's chest tightened. He glanced back down at the body, his eyes burning, registering the horror, his stomach muscles clenching.

Deets glanced across the warehouse and motioned at one of the uniforms.

The taller of the two uniforms nodded and made his way across the cinders to the body, stopping about fifteen feet shy of the tape so he didn't step in any of the sticky black pools (and maybe so he didn't have to look at the girl). Dressed in starched navy blue and smelling of rancid Right Guard spray, the cop's name was Steagal and he was first-on-the-scene.

Deets looked at him. "When did you say the call came in?"

"About two-thirty, came in from dispatch, check suspicious smell," Officer Steagal said, keeping the bandanna close to his mouth, cringing at the odor.

Deets wrote in his notebook.

Frank was circling the body now, trying to calm down, chewing on the straw. He hoped that the other cops hadn't noticed his trembling.

"Anonymous call?" Deets was asking Officer Steagal.

"Yeah, but we're thinking it was somebody at the Hindu market or the pawn shop across the alley."

"Nobody's talking, huh?"

The uniform shrugged. "I can't even understand if they're giving me their first names or their last."

"No idea who she is?"

Officer Steagal shrugged again.

A few feet away, Frank was crouching down near the edge of a puddle the color of dark rubies. He clicked his ballpoint open and looked at the body. A cold trickle of ice water ran down his spine. A sitar droned behind the walls, the song of Shiva, the cosmic destroyer. Frank couldn't think of anything to write in his notebook.

Usually, at this early stage, Frank would access the way the body was displayed. Was it covered? Did the killer show remorse? Was it discarded with little concern or discretion? But Frank's mind was a blank all of a sudden. His head was spinning, and it felt like his eyeballs were going to pop out of his skull.

Look at the girl—come on, think—what is it about her?—think, think, think, think, think—what's the matter with you?—you're acting like a goddamned recruit—concentrate!—what is it about the MO . . . ?

Behind Frank, Deets was writing something else in his notebook, then asking Steagal if he could stick around until the crime lab got there.

The uniformed officer nodded, glancing nervously back at the doorway.

"Why don't you wait outside while we do the initial," Deets suggested. "Keep the rubberneckers back."

Officer Steagal nodded again, turned and trotted off toward daylight.

At that same moment, crouching down near the body, Frank Janus raised a rubber-gloved hand and waved the veil of greenbacks off the corpse. The flies billowed up like a blanket peeling away in the wind, revealing the porcelain flesh of the dead woman's face. A fuse popped in Frank's brain.

All at once, Frank realized what was wrong.

The victim was clearly posed—probably postmortem—her nude form placed on its side, curled into the fetal position, legs wrenched up against her tummy. If it wasn't for the bouquet of gore spreading across the floor beneath her, she would have almost looked serene. Her skin was the color of rare Italian marble, her eyes closed in tranquil sleep.

The killer had positioned her thumb in her mouth.

The straw dropped from Frank's mouth and landed on the ground. "Oh Christ," he murmured.

"Whatsamatter, Bambi?—whattyagot?" Deets's voice was very far away.

"Here we go," Frank said, picking up the straw, putting it back in his pocket, his gaze riveted to the corpse. He stood up, wiping his mouth with rubberized fingers, backing away from the pale human remains.

"What is it, Frank?" Deets was standing there with his big hands on his hips.

Frank looked at his partner. "I think we got a serial situation here."

Deets frowned. "What?—this stiff?—this guy?"

"This guy—this MO—we've seen it before," Frank said.

"Whattya mean? Here in the Twenty-fourth?"

"It's a cold case, D—same signature, same thing, same damn thing." Frank was pointing and gaping at the body as though it were a doorway into hell. "I remember it from way back, D, maybe ten years ago."

"You sure?"

"I'm sure as hell, I mean, Christ, the damn thing sent me into the worst funk of my life—"

"Okay, that's gonna go at the top of the GPR—"

"Oh yeah, oh yeah, oh yeah—"

"Okay, Frank, now I want you to do me a favor," Deets said evenly, gently taking Frank's arm.

"What?—" Frank was confused, a wave of gooseflesh washing over him. He looked at the body, then back at his partner.

"Frank, listen to me," Deets said. "I want you to come over here for a second."

The big man ushered Frank away from the body.

Footsteps crunching in cinders, they strode across the warehouse to the opposite wall. Tabla drums and moaning kanjeera vocals penetrated the leprous brick. Fetid heat pressed down on them. Deets made sure their backs were turned so that they were out of ear-shot of the uniformed officers. Frank could feel his pulse racing in his ears, his gut smoldering with nausea. Deets sighed. "Frankie, I think we got a problem."

"What do you mean?"

"You're strung as tight as a banjo."

Frank looked at his partner. "D, I'm sorry—I promise you I got it under control this time—"

"I don't think you do."

"I'm just trying to—"

"You're all jammed up again, Frankie." Deets was speaking in a low, urgent voice all of a sudden.

"I'm just—"

"Frankie, listen to me—"

"D, I'm just trying—"

"We've been through this before! This stiff—if this is a serial thing, if this is the same guy, then fine—we're gonna deal with that. But I'm talking about *you*."

"D, I'm fine."

"I believe you, kid. What I'm saying is, there's a history with this thing, and there's no shame in stepping back for a second. Maybe stopping by Area Six, maybe seeing Pope."

Eyes burning, Frank looked at his partner for a long, awkward moment.

"All right, look," Frank said finally, a little sheepishly. "Maybe I'm a little jacked up, I don't know."

"Nothing to be ashamed of," Deets said.

"I guess maybe I could go back to the house, check the VICAP database, maybe see if Pope's got any time."

Deets gave Frank an encouraging nod. "I'll hold down the fort, do the initials."

Frank nodded, then started across the warehouse, then stopped and turned back to Deets. "And, D . . . I'm not cracking up again. I'm fine this time."

"I know, kid."

Frank turned and made his way across the cinders and out the corner doorway.

The uniforms barely noticed him leaving.

2

Stress Management is in the lower level of Area Six headquarters at the corner of Belmont and Western.

Frank arrived a few minutes before 4:00 and took the main elevator down, his stomach cramping from too many cups of coffee and too little food. He had tried to eat lunch before his appointment, but he had no appetite. He was a bundle of nerves.

The basement level was a recent addition to the headquarters building. A maze of newly carpeted cubicles and private offices, the area was used mostly for administrative purposes, the archiving of crime data and old police business. Inverted lighting gave the corridor a corporate feel, and contemporary Muzak—what the wags nowadays were calling Lite Adult Rock—hummed through speakers embedded in the ceiling. The cool air smelled of new fabric and copy machine toner. Neighborhood Relations had an office down here, as well as Internal Affairs.

At the end of the corridor, a glass door was marked STRESS MANAGEMENT COORDINATOR. Frank entered the modest waiting room and gave his name to a sober-looking woman sitting behind a desk. The woman told Frank that the doctor would be with him in a moment. Frank thanked her, took a seat, and started chewing compulsively on his drinking straw, tearing it to shreds.

Five minutes later, Frank was sitting in Dr. Henry Pope's tiny office, trying to articulate his feelings.

"Tell you the truth, Doc, it's just like last time."

"Dizziness? Shaking?"

"Yep."

"Tightness in the chest, shortness of breath?"

"You got it."

"Thoughts racing? Worried that you're losing your grip, losing your mind?"

"That's about it," Frank said, fidgeting in the Steelcase armchair. The shrink's office was three hundred square feet of folksy clutter. From the bulletin boards plastered with positive messages, family snapshots, and grandchildren's artwork, to the bookshelves crammed with New Age tomes and little figurines urging onlookers to "Hang in there!" and "Keep your chin up!"

Ten years ago, Frank had sat in this same office, agonizing over the same kinds of horrors, the same feelings. The shame, the depression, the dread. Ten years. And now Frank was back looking at the same fingerpaint portraits of Barney the dinosaur, going over the same awful territory.

The doctor looked up at Frank. "And you're convinced these feelings are triggered by the scene itself?"

"Excuse me?"

"What I mean is, you're thinking it was because of the MO? The link to the last one?"

Frank shrugged. "Yeah, I suppose—I don't know—probably."

"Any possibility it was because of the memories, the way you felt back in District Nineteen?"

Frank looked at the old man. "What do you mean?"

"What I mean is, in most cases of Post Traumatic Stress Disorder, there are triggers, and these triggers bring back all these bad feelings—we call it *reexperiencing*—"

"Look, Doc, I understand what you're saying." Frank was sitting forward in his chair. "But when I was back in the Nineteenth, and I saw that first vic—the one with the thumb in her mouth—we never established that I had PTS afterward. I mean, there was never an official diagnosis."

"You're right, Frank, I'm sorry." The doctor wrote something in a manila file folder on his desk. A lanky man in his late sixties with thinning salt-and-pepper hair, Henry Pope wore tortoiseshell reading glasses low on his nose, glancing over them once in a while when something caught his interest. He had a bushy gray goatee and everything about him was stooped: his shoulders, the way he shuffled when he walked, even his kindly hound dog face. He looked like an Old World artisan worn down by life—like an old European toy maker nearing retirement.

On the wall behind his desk were framed diplomas and certificates, and even a patrolman's star mounted on a plaque. Back in the seventies, before he got his PhD, Henry Pope had been a beat cop for a year and a half in Sacramento. Which was probably why the cops liked him so much. He had been one of them. He had ridden alongside them in patrol cars, he had shared their Code-Sevens, he had covered their backs.

Finally Frank spoke up: "I'm not saying you're wrong—about the feelings—I'm just saying, it's not like I went to Vietnam."

The psychiatrist sighed. "I don't know, Frank. You guys in the Violent Crimes Division—you see things. The rest of us would curl up and die."

"It's not as bad as you think."

"But it's pretty bad sometimes—right?"

Frank shrugged again. "The honest truth is, it's part of the job. I don't have to tell *you* that."

"You're right about that, Frank," said the doctor, then wrote something else in the folder. While he was writing, he said, "How about your insomnia? How's the quality of your sleep lately?"

Frank had to smile despite his frayed nerves. "Sleep? That's where people lie on soft things and close their eyes and have pleasant dreams, right?"

Pope looked up. "Still pretty bad?"

"Bad isn't the word."

"You still taking the Restorill?"

"Sometimes," Frank said. "When the going's especially rough."

"How often is that?"

"I don't know—every other night or so."

"And the blackouts? Have you had any recently?"

Frank swallowed hard. "Not for a while. It happens usually when I'm running on no sleep whatsoever. Last year, I went through a fairly rough stretch where I was blacking out every few weeks, but never at work, thank God."

The doctor scribbled in his folder. "What about the nightmares?"

"Once in a while, you know," Frank said.

"Crime scene stuff?"

"Yeah, you know."

The doctor looked at the file for a moment. "How about the noctambulation?"

"The what?"

"Sleepwalking. Night dazes. There was the episode with your wife—?"

"*Ex*-wife."

The doctor raised his hands apologetically. "Sorry. Your ex-wife. How are you doing with that?"

Frank looked at the doctor. "You mean the divorce?"

"Sure . . . and the whole sleepwalking incident. I remember you were devastated by the whole experience."

Frank sighed. "It's all ancient history, really." He paused and thought about it for a second.

Even after all this time, it was still incomprehensible to him that he would physically assault his wife—even if it *was* during a sort of middle-of-the-night fugue state, as she had claimed in the divorce proceedings. Throughout his adult life, Frank had occasionally had problems with sleepwalking. Every few months he would wake up in an unexpected room, or be startled awake, drenched in sweat, wearing an inexplicable article of clothing that he couldn't remember putting on. But he would never strike his wife. Never.

"I guess I've put it behind me," Frank said at last. "Chloe and I rarely talk."

The doctor nodded, then glanced back down at the file. "It's been a few years, Frank, but I remember some stuff about your mother?"

"My mom?"

The doctor looked up at him. "There were dreams that disturbed you, haunted you?"

Frank shrugged. "Yeah, you know. Once in a while I dream about my mom. I'm like most people, I guess."

"We never really got into that last time."

Frank looked at his shoes and managed a wan smile. "I guess we didn't."

The psychiatrist looked over the top of his bifocals. "What's funny? Something about your mother?"

Frank grinned. "I'm sorry, doc, it's just, every time you start talking about my mom I get worried we're gonna start discussing Greek mythology."

Henry Pope took off his glasses and laughed heartily, rubbing his pouchy eyes. "Don't worry, Frank. Oedipus went out of style around here a long time ago."

"That's a relief," Frank said, his smile fading. He glanced down at his jacket sleeve and saw a smudge of fresh ash from the cigarette he had smoked before the session. He rubbed at the stubborn spot. Frank hated stains on his expensive work clothes, and he hated loose ends on the job. And most of all, he hated talking about his mother. As long as Frank could remember, his mother had been one big loose end. Morbidly obese, diagnosed as a mild schizophrenic, Helen Janus had been institutionalized at the Cook County Psychiatric Facility when Frank was a boy, and Frank had never really figured out how to talk about her. Even when Frank was having his initial troubles with the thumb sucker case back when he was a young, green detective in the Nine-

teenth—and Dr. Pope had tried to explore Frank's relationship with his mom—Frank had refused to go there.

"Mind if I have a cigarette?" Frank said finally, reaching for his pack of Marlboros and rooting one out.

The doctor said it was no problem, reached into his
top drawer, pulled out an ashtray, and shoved it across
the cluttered desk.

"Not that I have anything against Freud," Frank said,
fishing in his pocket for his Zippo. He brought the lighter
up to his mouth and realized that his hands were shaking
so badly he couldn't hold the lighter steady enough to
spark the cigarette. The doctor saw this, and without a
word he reached over and held it steady for Frank. Frank
nodded a thank-you, lit the cigarette, and blew smoke
up at the ceiling. At last Frank said, "The problem is—
all due respect to the field of psychology—I just don't
believe you can trace a person's behavior back to the
time they fell off their tricycle."

The psychiatrist was looking at his file. "Let me ask
you something, Frank, and if you don't want to get into
this, just say so."

"You're the doctor, go ahead."

"How old were you when your mother—well—when
she took the Pollock gentleman's life?"

Frank took a drag and blew smoke. "I was—what?—
I was ten."

"And how old was your mom?"

Frank swallowed a nervous lump. "She was thirty-
seven."

"And what are you now, Frank?—thirty-six?"

There was an anguished stretch of silence.

"I'm thirty-seven."

Another beat of silence. Frank felt something turning
inside him.

He looked at the tiles on the floor and murmured, "I
never even thought about that."

"Can you tell me something else, Frank?"

"Go ahead."

"Do you remember when your insomnia started?"

Frank smoked his cigarette for a moment. "I don't know—college, maybe?—no, probably high school."

"High school?"

"Or maybe earlier, I don't remember for sure."

"Could it have been around the time they took your mom away?"

A long pause, as Frank smoked and thought about it. His eyes were burning. He could barely feel the tears welling. "My mom had a thing about sleep," he said in a hushed tone.

"You feel like talking about it, Frank?" the doctor said very softly, very gently.

There was a long pause.

"Frank?"

The pause stretched. Frank was staring at his shoes, thinking about something his mother used to do.

Pope took his glasses off. "Frank? Would you rather not talk about it?"

Finally, Frank looked up at the doctor. "I guess I never told you about the sleep police . . . did I?"

"The sleep police?"

"It was something that my mom used to say to us."

"In what context?"

Frank sighed painfully. "When my brother and I refused to go to sleep."

"Go on."

Frank cleared his throat. "My brother and I were inseparable when we were kids. We'd have these ongoing battles. Try to make each other rack up at Mass, fart sounds under the sheets at night. You know how it is with kids. Always trying to make each other laugh."

"Sounds pretty normal to me," Pope commented. "Especially under the circumstances."

"I'm sure it drove my mom even loonier than she already was, but for the most part she put up with it. Except at night. That's when she couldn't handle it. So she came up with this idea of the sleep police."

"Go on."

Frank took another drag off his cigarette. He was exhausted. Drained. Still shaking slightly. He exhaled a lungful of smoke and said, "She'd come into our room at the end of her rope. God bless her, she was never cross with us, never raised her voice—but she would very softly let us know that it was high time all good boys were asleep because the sleep police would be making their rounds soon."

"That's all she said?"

"No, see, at first, it was just kinda playful. She'd come in and tickle us, and we'd giggle, and she'd say, *'Eeef you boys dohn't be still, the sleep poleeese gonna come and meck you go to sleep forever and ever, jes like Snow White.'*"

"I see."

"But as we grew older, the sleep police got scarier somehow, meaner. I guess it was my mom getting sicker. I used to imagine what they looked like. The sleep police. Big broad shoulders, stone faces. They carried flashlights. But you couldn't see their eyes under the bills of their hats. Something about it really got to me."

The doctor nodded. "I can imagine."

There was another long pause as the doctor consulted his notes, and Frank smoked. Finally Pope looked up and asked Frank about the way the bodies were posed, and whether there might be a significance to the fetal position and Frank's childhood, and the two men talked about this for quite a while.

Before long, it was time to call the emergency meeting to a close.

"Here's what we're gonna do," Pope said, writing something on a small 'script pad on the edge of his desk blotter. "First, I'm going to give you a prescription for a sedative to help you avoid those sleep police, maybe get on a better sleep schedule." He finished writing, tore off the page, and handed it to Frank. "Then, we're gonna meet on a regular basis for the next few weeks, and we're gonna deal with these feelings. See if we can't find you some tools to deal with the stress. Does that sound all right?"

Frank sighed and snubbed out his cigarette. "That's sounds fine, Doc."

"Valerie will work out the scheduling with you," Dr. Pope said. Then he rose to his feet and extended a hand, making it obvious their emergency meeting was drawing to a close. Frank stood up and shook the old man's grizzled hand.

Psychiatrists are like talk show hosts. They can segue out of the most serious discussion, ushering one patient out and another in as though breaking for a commercial.

Frank walked out of the office in a daze.

Somewhere inside him, a seam was beginning to tear.

3

It was long past quitting time when Sully Deets finally went down to the sergeant's office and knocked on the door.

Armanetti's voice: "It's open."

Deets walked into a sterile little office dominated by a bay window view of Warren Park.

"Whattya got, Sully?" Detective-Sergeant Stan Armanetti said from behind his huge walnut desk. A fiftyish man with graying temples, broad shoulders, and a bushy mustache, Armanetti was Deets's immediate supervisor.

Deets tossed the two manila envelopes on the desk. "Jane Doe over in Little Pakistan."

"It's late, Sully," Armanetti said with a sigh, glancing across the office at Krimm, who was standing near the window, gazing out at the dying light. "Gerry's got to get home to his garden."

"Possible serial case," Deets said.

This got Lieutenant Gerald Krimm's attention. He turned and looked at Deets. "The 'S' word," the lieutenant uttered softly, almost to himself.

Deets nodded at the files. "MO looks a lot like an old cold case. It's all in the GPR."

"How about giving us the Cliff Notes, huh, Sully?" Armanetti said with a smile. The sergeant was a buddy-buddy type, a back-slapper who avoided controversy at all costs. Most of the cops in the Twenty-fourth liked him well enough—as long as he stayed out of their faces.

Deets ran down the facts for them: The Jane Doe had been murdered some time early in the morning on the tenth. Judging from her appearance—a tattoo above her left breast, cosmetic surgery scars, trimmed pubic hair, and multiple piercings—she was involved in the sex business. In the parlance of lawyers, she was "high risk." No husband, no boyfriend, no known next of kin. Not the type to be missed by anyone. But the most interesting part of the case was the similarity to the "thumb sucker" from District Nineteen ten years ago. That time, it had been a stripper from the Admiral Men's Club who had been gutted like a Thanksgiving turkey and posed postmortem with her thumb stuck in her mouth.

That case was still open, still as cold as the February turf at Soldier Field.

"You contact media relations yet?" Krimm asked Deets.

"We kept the scene closed until the ME was done, then we gave neighborhood media some bullshit story about a homeless woman croaking."

"How about the Feds?"

"I sent the Special Circumstances file to VICAP and out to Great Lakes. There's one in each of your folders. We'll be contacting Birnbaum for the autopsy."

Armanetti spoke up. "Second and third shifts should get run downs, Sully. They should get copies of everything."

"Sergeant, I'm wondering—"

"What is it, Sully?"

Deets chewed the inside of his cheek. Something was bothering him about this Jane Doe from Little Pakistan. Maybe it was Frank's reaction at the scene, or maybe it was something else. But for the moment, Deets was going by the numbers. At last he said, "In terms of the other shifts, I'm wondering if Janus and I could be primaries on this thing."

There was a pause. Lieutenant Krimm blinked. A thin
and humorless man in his fifties, Krimm wore delicate
little round glasses that had earned him the nickname
"Egghead" from the patrol cops. He was hated by the
rank and file. Right now he was studying Deets. "You've
got a plan, I take it?"

Deets nodded. "Next few days, we'll be canvassing
local titty bars and brothels, working the IR files, reaching out to the boys in the crime lab—"

Krimm raised a hand to cut him off. "You think the
perp is an organized type?"

Deets nodded. "Yessir, I do. The condition of the
body—I mean, assuming all that posing crap is post mor-
tem—this guy needed a lot of time and privacy."

"You think he was making some kind of point?"

"Yeah, I do. It's the same kinda deal back in the Nineteenth ten years ago, same kinda signature."

Armanetti sighed. "This is starting to sound like a 'G'
type of thing to me."

"Boss, we don't have to hand this thing over to the
Feds."

"Sully, I'm sorry, really, I am, but we just don't have
the resources—"

"Look. Boss. I know what you're thinkin. But all due
respect, Frank and I got everything we need to interface
with VICAP. We got the COMPSTAT software, and we
can link up with the National Latent Print Index. I think
we ought to at least be the primaries on this thing while
we're still red line."

There was another pause.

Deets waited as Armanetti and Krimm exchanged a
glance.

At last Krimm looked at Deets and said, "Where the
hell *is* Janus, anyway?"

Deets took a deep breath before answering.

It was a good question, on many different levels.

Where *was* Frank Janus?

*   *   *

The air inside Casa de la Buen Provecho was so ripe with the odors of cumin and smoke, it seemed to cling to Frank's skin as he entered. The nominal light was coming from the flickering table candles and small pots shining through multicolored fabric. And there was a flamenco guitarist way in the back, but the room was so narrow, nobody but the closest couple of booths could hear him.

Frank saw a skinny young man in a denim shirt standing up in back, waving Frank over.

Frank fought his way over to Kyle's table. "How you doing, Boomer?" Frank said.

"Famished, what does it look like?"

The two men embraced. Kyle was the first to let go, an awkward little moment because Frank wasn't ready yet. He kept hugging the younger man tightly, desperately, eyes closed, soaking in the familiar warmth and patchouli smell of his baby brother. Finally Frank let go and slid into the tattered booth across from his brother.

"What a day," Frank said, signaling for a waiter.

"I'm on my third bowl of tortilla chips," Kyle said, feigning exasperation. "The waiter's getting suspicious I might have a tape worm."

"Sorry I'm late," Frank said.

"You okay, Francis?"

"Never better, don't worry about me," Frank said unconvincingly. The waiter came, and Frank ordered a nonalcoholic beer.

When the waiter was gone, Kyle said, "NA beer? Aren't you homicide detectives supposed to be heavy drinkers?"

"I'm partial to the hard drugs myself," Frank said, then pointed at his bother's left ear. "The extra earrings are a nice touch."

"You like 'em?" Kyle brushed his fingertip across the row of delicate little silver rings pierced through the outer edge of his ear. A slender, pale, bookish young man in his early thirties with a mousy beard, Kyle Janus had Frank's dark curly hair, and he wore it long, tied back in a pony tale. Behind his wire-rim glasses were the eyes of a brilliant wounded soul. "Multiple earrings are de rigueur with the teaching assistants nowadays," he added with a little grin.

Frank grinned back at him. "You're gonna need more than that to get laid on an assistant professor's salary."

"My brother, the Philistine," Kyle muttered under his breath.

"What happens if I pull on them?" Frank said, pretending to grab at the earrings. "Does your nose fall off?"

Kyle shoved him away, and they wrestled for a moment, and they were laughing all of a sudden like they were in grade school again, and people were watching them, and then the waiter came and the Janus boys quieted down. Frank ordered a taco salad. Kyle ordered a combination plate. Both men paid close attention to the prices. Finally the waiter left, and Kyle got serious.

"So what kind of abomination-of-nature have you guys been cleaning up lately?"

"Oh, you know, the usual," Frank said. "Society's flotsam and jetsam, you know."

There was a pause, as Kyle Janus regarded his older brother. "You sure you're okay?"

"I'm fine—why?—I'm doing great."

"You sure?"

"Yes, Boomer, I'm sure, you can stop worrying about me," Frank said with a stiff smile. The image flickered suddenly in his midbrain: a marble-fleshed corpse curled in the fetal position. His stomach clenched.

Kyle plucked a chip from the basket and chewed it gloomily, gazing off toward the smoky end of the restaurant.

Frank watched his brother. "What's the matter, Boomer?"

Kyle looked at Frank. "I got a call from Dr. Hemphill today."

Frank bristled at the name.

Dr. Gloria Hemphill was the administrator at the Clarendon Psychiatric Hospital where Helen Janus was currently being warehoused. Since 1989, Helen had been a patient at Clarendon after serving out her time for voluntary manslaughter at Cook County. For a while, Clarendon had seemed a humane answer to Helen's needs. She was allowed to work in the gardens, and she was allowed contact with other patients, and she was treated with dignity. But then Hemphill had taken over the directorship, and the woman had proven to be a fascist disciplinarian. The doctor had not taken kindly to Helen Janus's quirks. Social hours were cut, medication was increased, and Helen started to decline.

"What's the problem this time?" Frank said. "Mom's pilfering toilet paper again?"

"She's deteriorating, Francis," Kyle said flatly, staring at the chips as though they were dead rats.

"What do you mean—deteriorating?"

"She's psychotic again, and this time they think it's complicated by Alzheimer's."

Frank swallowed hard. "The combination platter."

"She's in a bad way, Francis."

"What did Nurse Wretched say?"

"Hemphill wants to move her."

"Move her where?"

Kyle stared at the chips. "God only knows—some kind of nursing home for vegetables."

There was a long pause, as Frank thought about it, the delicate sound of flamenco guitar warbling out over the din of voices and steaming skillets of shrimp *fajitas*. The smell of death on Frank's linen jacket.

"Okay, well, we're not gonna do that," Frank said, nodding to no one in particular.

"Francis, we don't have a—"

"No, no, no . . . we're not gonna do that," Frank said again. "We're not."

"Francis, do we have a choice—?"

"We're not going to put her in some hell hole," Frank said. His voice was raw. His eyes burning.

Kyle stared at him.

The flamenco guitarist strummed.

"We're not," Frank murmured, then picked up a plastic straw from the water glass and started chewing on it.

4

2:30 A.M.

Another sleepless night.

A single library lamp on a cheap desk, thin ghosts of cigarette smoke curling upward, a tumbler of tepid milk nearby. Frank in his boxer shorts, hunched at his computer.

The apartment was a typical shotgun bungalow on Chicago's north side—the best Frank could do on his 50K salary after his divorce from Chloe. And right now Frank was in his cluttered living room, his dark-rimmed eyes locked on the home page of the VICAP Website. VICAP stands for Violent Criminal Apprehension Program, and it's operated by the National Center for the Analysis of Violent Crime just outside of Washington, DC. VICAP is the largest single source for tracking unsolved homicides.

An FBI insignia flashed at the top of the screen.

Frank clicked through the police message boards, entered a brief description of the thumb sucker signature, and told the index to search for matches in the Great Lakes area. A moment later, a window appeared informing Frank there were only two Special Circumstances files available with similar signatures. One was dated 8–12–00—today—and the other was 2–16–90.

Both files were CPD.

Frank sighed and lit another cigarette. It looked as though Deets had been busy today, filing the latest

thumb sucker on all the data bases. Frank opened the
SC file dated 1990, and all the pertinent forensics from
that first thumb sucker case blinked on screen. Frank
scanned the luminous blue lines of text, and for an instant he was cast back to that desolate, litter-strewn alley
off Wacker Drive. It had been midwinter, and the pavement had been black ice, and the girl's body had been
tucked behind the Dumpster. Her porcelain face was serene and empty.

Dead cold lips closed around a slender thumb.

Frank picked up his milk and spilled a little bit on the
keyboard. Was he shaking again? *Reexperiencing?* He
wiped the keyboard with his shirttail, set the milk down,
and took a nervous drag off his cigarette.

The warm milk was one of the countless insomnia remedies he had tried over the years. He had also tried ripe
bananas, cold turkey, melatonin, valerian root, white
noise generators, and even bizarre folk remedies like putting an onion in a jar and sniffing it at bedtime. Nothing
worked. Even the heavy tranquilizers were a wash—
Frank would simply wake up in the middle of the night
with a raging headache. Over the years, Frank had seen
a slew of specialists, and had been diagnosed with a
mouthful of maladies, including parasomnia (severe insomnia), mild episodes of somnambulation (sleepwalking), frequent pavor nocturnus (night terrors) and
daytime transitory syncopal attacks (brief fainting spells
or blackouts). But nobody seemed able to help him get
a good night's sleep.

Frank reached over and flipped his printer on.

Then he printed out the links that had come in over
the last few months.

He closed the VICAP site and went on to other sites.
He checked the National Crime Information Center,
then punched into the Illinois Bureau of Investigation
Website, then took a look at the Violent Crimes Linkage
Analysis System. He didn't find much. He went into the
search engine—a phrase that Frank had always relished,

feeling like a search engine *himself* from time to time—
and the screen flickered for a moment. Then an unusual
window came on his screen.

Frank blinked.

At first, Frank thought the computer must have crashed.
iMacs were notorious for crashing and freezing, and
Frank's computer had certainly experienced its share of
glitches. But this was no warning window. This was different. A two-by-three-inch square in the center of the
screen with yellow borders and black-on-white type inside it.

The type style was simple Geneva, a common font for
most Macs:

> Walk away from the thumb sucker case—shut it
> down—forget about it.

Staring at the screen, his eyes watering, his brain fuzzy
and his mouth dry from the medication, Frank was frozen in his chair for a moment.

The announcement had come out of nowhere, like an
annoying pop-up advertisement or "buddy" message . . .
but that was impossible. Frank had customized his e-mail
and search engine to block all unsolicited incoming ads
and junk mail. Besides, this thing was meant specifically
for Frank.

"Okay, Deets, hardy-har-har, you can stop goofing
around," Frank grumbled at the computer, his body relaxing slightly as he realized it must be a gag. A bad
joke. Deets must have been trying to cheer him up.

He pressed the escape button and nothing happened.
All at once, Frank remembered how inept Sully Deets
was with computers. The big man would never be able
to engineer a surprise message over the Web. In fact,
Frank wasn't even sure it was possible to send a message
window through the Internet to a single terminal. He
pressed the delete button.

The message stayed on his screen, the words trumpeting in his brain:

> Walk away from the thumb sucker case—shut it down—forget about it.

Suddenly Frank was shaking again, his heart starting to pump a little faster. What if this was some kind of message from the perp himself? What if this guy was a player, a smart ass, a goof like Son of Sam or the Zodiac killer? What if the perp were initiating some kind of communication with Frank, making the first move in a bizarre game of chess?

Frank's skin tingled on the backs of his arms as he stared at the luminous message.

Out in the kitchen, a sudden noise.

Frank jumped.

He spun around and glanced over his shoulder at the swinging saloon doors leading out into his little kitchenette. It was dark in there. Once in a while, on hot nights, when the AC was running hard, the old linoleum would crackle. But Frank wasn't sure if that's what he had heard. It had been a faint creaking noise, as though something had shifted its weight out there.

And that's when the panic and the realization washed over Frank all at once. The noise in the kitchen . . . the unexpected message on his computer . . . the luminous window that could have only been generated from *his own keyboard!* Somebody was *inside* his apartment, fucking with his Mac.

Somebody familiar with the thumb sucker files.

Frank snapped off the light and dropped to the floor immediately.

He crawled as silently and quickly as possible across the dark living room. His head was throbbing, full of cotton from the Dalmane, but the panic was piercing the fuzz like a sharpened knife. His heart was racing. The rug burned his knees, but he didn't feel it.

He was focused on getting to his bedroom.

His service weapon was hanging on the hat stand next to his closet, still tucked in its braided black leather holster. Frank sprang to his feet and raced over to the gun, yanking it out of the sheath and quickly checking the cylinder. Then he swallowed the fear and slid back out the door.

He gripped the revolver in classic police "tripod" stance, and scanned the living room.

Nothing there.

He listened for the cracking sound out in the kitchenette, trying not to make a sound as he backed along the wall toward the swinging doors. His heart was beating so loudly he wondered if the intruder could hear it. His hands were white-knuckle tight around the handgun. It was a Charter Arms Bulldog, a .44 Special designed for maximum punch. Six-inch barrel. Five rounds of modified hollowpoints.

Some cops call the Bulldog the Paranoid Special, because it's the maximum-sized side arm that a city policeman is allowed to carry. But Frank didn't care what they called it. He just needed the peace of mind.

He shoved the swinging doors open and pointed the Bulldog at the empty kitchen.

Even in the gloom it was clear that there was nobody lurking in there.

Frank let out a pained sigh of relief.

He spent the next ten minutes searching the rest of the apartment with his gun raised and ready. He looked in the bathroom, behind the shower curtain, and in the linen closet. He looked under his bed, in his closet, and behind the book shelves. He looked in the pantry and out in the living room behind the video cabinet.

He even looked out in the main corridor.

There was nobody there.

Finally Frank went back to his computer, printed the message window and saved it on a disk. He shut the computer off and sat down on the sofa.

He stared at the printout for a long time. He lit a cigarette and stared at it some more. He found a plastic straw in his pencil holder, and he started chewing on it, but no matter how hard he tried, he could not tear his gaze from that unexpected message:

> Walk away from the thumb sucker case—shut it down—forget about it.

5

Dawn came to Rogers Park on a whisper of hot lake breezes. The threads of brilliant sunlight spindled down through the high-tension wires and elm trees, and the smell of garbage promised another blast furnace of a day. Early morning traffic mingled with the ubiquitous buzz of cicadas.

Frank arrived at the Twenty-fourth well before the third shift had knocked off. He was greeted in the coffee room by the night crew—Detectives Bozelli and Jeffers—and the three men stood around for a while, chatting idly about the thumb sucker, commiserating over the new union steward and the lousy HMO plan. Frank did his best to hide his trembling. Freshly showered and shaved, dressed in a crisp new jacket, he felt a little better now that he was at work, and even though he was running on zero sleep—and was still rattled by the mysterious message on his iMac—he was anxious to get back on the case.

The medical examiner's report was sitting on Frank's desk blotter when he sat down.

He opened the report and scanned the findings.

No ID yet on the second thumb sucker. Time of death was estimated at sixty to sixty-five hours before discovery, which meant the girl had been killed on Sunday morning, some time between 2:00 and 5:00 A.M. There were bits of undigested tortilla in her stomach. Lividity in the upper body cavity indicated that she had been moved postmortem. Elevated serotonin levels suggested that she had died from blood loss. Official cause of death: massive hemorrhaging due to a sharp force trauma to the abdomen.

Frank lit a cigarette and thought about the nut job who did this.

You need time. Don't you? You need privacy. You need a cozy place to be alone with your toys. Don't you? Everything has to be just right . . .

Frank looked back at the report.

High histamine levels indicated that the victim was conscious when she died. Usually an indication of struggle or torture. Tests confirmed that she had high levels of the sedative pentobarbital in her bloodstream. Probably to keep her manageable. There were defensive wounds across the palms of her hands, and there were minor, unexplained lesions across the platysma muscle of her neck, although there were no signs of strangulation. A cadaveric spasm at the time of death explained the retention of the "pose."

Frank looked across the squad room. The morning shift was starting to filter in. A couple of secretaries, a tactical officer picking up his radio gear. Frank took a drag off his cigarette and thought of the strange message flickering on his iMac. He knew he should report the message right away, put it in his GPR and tell Deets about, maybe get the tech guys to look at his computer. But something told him to wait, to keep it to himself for the time being. Was it hubris? Did he think that the message was going to help him solve the case?

Walk away from the thumb sucker case—shut it down—forget about it.

Frank closed the ME report.

There was a manila envelope sitting in his in-basket marked A/V DEPT., full of forensic photographs and Polaroids from the crime scene. Frank opened it and spread the photographs across his desk. He arranged the black-

and-white shots of blood patterns into a mosaic. He stared at it, and he smoked, and he imagined the sequence of events. He extrapolated from the blood drop trajectories, and the drag marks, and the blossoms of arterial spray on brick walls. He used the profiling techniques that the FBI had taught the unit years ago, after the first thumb sucker had stymied them.

You get the drugs into her early. Don't you? Then you get her inside the doorway. Where it's dark. Right there. And you give her the same speech you gave the last one.

"Bambi!"

The voice nudged Frank out of his reverie. He glanced up and saw big Sully Deets ambling toward him. "Top of the morning, Mr. Investigator," Frank said with nod, gathering up the photos and stuffing them back into the envelope.

"Lookin' chipper this morning," Deets said, shrugging off his rayon sport coat and taking a seat at his cluttered desk, which was adjacent to Frank's. He already had damp spots under his Ban-Lon armpits. "You see the man yesterday?"

Frank nodded. "Had a good talk, yeah, thanks."

"That's good."

"Thanks, D."

Deets shrugged. "Hey, shit happens to everybody. You see the ME report?"

"We got a pharmacist on our hands," Frank said.

"Yeah, I already checked on the drug. It's strictly over-the-counter."

Frank nodded, then pulled a Marlboro out of his pocket and sparked it. "You talk to Armanetti?"

"Yeah, he's got us primary on this. For the time being at least. Krimm was in his office at the time."

Frank nodded, then took a nervous drag off the cigarette. "SC file says there was no mention of the sedative on the first thumb sucker."

"Maybe the guy's getting more careful. I talked to Birnbaum on the way in this morning," Deets said.

Frank let out a sigh. "When's he taking over?"

"We got a couple of days. Birnbaum's gonna send his lab guys out there this afternoon, whatever good it'll do 'em."

"No prints whatsoever, huh?" Frank said.

"No prints, not even a partial," Deets said with a silent belch, snapping his gum distastefully. "Pathologist tried the girl's fingernails, teeth, even her eyeballs."

"Gloves?"

"Definitely."

All at once, Frank noticed someone coming down the hallway with a lunchbox.

"Excuse me, D, one second," Frank said, pushing himself away from his desk.

Frank got up and chased after the kid in the T-shirt and laminated security pass. "Johnny! Hold up!"

Johnny Trout paused outside the property room door. "Morning, Frank."

"Hey, Johnny, how ya doing?"

"Not bad, Frank. What's going on?" Prematurely bald, his smooth pate sunburned as red as a lobster, Johnny Trout was the resident tech-head around the squad house. He was in charge of the property room, the dispatch equipment, the wireless beat radios, the video gear, the computers, everything around the Twenty-fourth that might require more than a *Reader's Digest* knowledge of electronics. He also knew more about Bruce Lee movies than a healthy person really should.

"Got a question for ya," Frank said. "It's a little convoluted. I'm just wondering, is it possible—I got an iMac, okay—is it possible for somebody to hack into my computer through the Internet, and then make a message come on my screen that looks like it came from my own keyboard?"

The bald kid licked his lips for a moment, thinking. "Um . . . you mean simple text?"

"Actually, I'm talking about a message window."

"A message window?"

"Yeah. You know. A box with edges, and background, and text inside it."

"Over e-mail?"

"No, actually, I'm talking about while I'm online, looking at a Web site."

Trout took a long, deep breath, then said, "I guess it's possible, but it's highly unlikely."

"Yeah?"

The kid shrugged. "You can't control a rig's internal default parameters from outside that rig."

"Yeah? Okay, thanks a lot, Johnny, I appreciate it." Frank started to turn away.

"You want me to show you what I'm talking about?" Trout said, gesturing with his thumb back toward his office.

"No thanks, Johnny, I'm swamped today, I appreciate it." Frank turned and hurried back to his desk.

Deets was already putting on his sportcoat, preparing to go back out into the heat. "You ready to go ID this vic?"

"Lead the way, D," Frank said, grabbing his jacket and notebook, then following the big man toward the exit.

Frank and Deets were in the show room of the Little Red Rooster Lounge when the beeper went off.

"Son of a bitch," Deets grumbled, digging under his coat, grabbing the beeper off his belt.

"Sorry," Frank murmured to the dancer, his stomach twisting in the smoky, blue gloom. Frank was trying to keep the interview light and breezy, trying to keep the girl relaxed. It wasn't easy.

"Am I in some kind of trouble, Detective?" the dancer asked nervously, her silk robe tented by massive artificial breasts. Her peroxide blond hair gleamed in the low light. Her lips were outlined in thin, black eyeliner. Somewhere nearby, in some other room, the bass-line from Steve Miller's "Abracadabra" thumped through a wall.

The room smelled deodorized, like the inside of a cab.

"No, Miss Jamison, not at all," Frank said with a contrite smile. He was nauseous and exhausted. "We're just trying to locate a girl. If you could just tell us exactly what your friend told you, that would be fabulous—"

Deets was growling to himself, "Piece of shit is impossible to read in this dump." He was trying to read his beeper in the dim light, fishing in his pocket for his reading glasses.

Something was bugging Deets. Frank had noticed it from the very first interview. He was all cranky, and he was being nasty to the girls, and he was acting like a bully, which wasn't like Deets at all. It was making Frank uncomfortable. Frank liked to treat people with respect.

"All I can tell you is what I heard Tiffany say last night," the dancer said. She was frightened. Frank could tell by the way she was blinking, like she had something in her eye. "Tiffany said there was talk among the other dancers that we should be careful, that we should have the bouncers walk us to our cars."

"Okay, no problem," Frank said, writing in his notebook. "You think Tiffany would mind chatting with us for a second?"

"Son of a bitch!" Deets barked, reading the tiny liquid crystal numbers.

"What is it, D?" Frank said, looking at his partner.

"One-eighty-seven over in Albany Park," Deets said, starting toward the door. "Come on, Frank."

"Thanks a lot, Miss Jamison," Frank said, handing the stripper his business card. "Like I said, my name's Detective Janus, and if you hear anything else, if you have any problems, don't hesitate to call me."

Deets was pausing near the door, turning and pointing a finger at the stripper. "I want statements from you and your girlfriend on the record! You can put them on video down at the Twenty-fourth District Headquarters!"

The stripper chewed on her fingernail, said nothing.

"You hear what I said?!" Deets yelled.

"Yeah, sure, I can hardly wait," she muttered, staring at the floor in exasperation.

"You got a problem with that?!" Deets barked at her.

"No, sir," the dancer replied.

Deets stormed out of the club.

Frank followed him into the humid sunlight, eyes blinking at the glare. "What's wrong, D? What's going on?"

Deets marched across the gravel lot to the unmarked Crown Victoria which was parked near a chain link fence. He opened the driver's door and got in. Frank followed, got in the passenger side and shut the door. The car was hot enough to bake bread. Deets started it up and got the A/C blasting.

"Talk to me, D—what's the matter?" Frank asked again, as Deets pulled out of the lot.

"I hate these flesh pits with a passion," Deets said over the rush of the air conditioning.

"What's the deal with the one-eighty-seven?" Frank asked.

"It's gotta be a match-up, and they're calling us in to consult."

"Another thumb sucker?" Frank could feel a shiver of ice on his neck.

Deets nodded, then called into the house to get the lowdown on the Albany Park scene.

Fifteen minutes later they were pulling up in front of a boarded-up bodega cooking in the sun at the corner of Lawrence and Seimens. An ancient, cracked hard-shell sign over the door said FOOD & LIQU R, and a profusion of weeds fringed the foundation and sidewalk. Yellow crime-scene tape was drawn across the front, and a clutch of CPD vehicles were parked at haphazard angles across the litter-strewn parkway: a patrol car, a couple of unmarked squads, and a crime lab wagon.

Deets parked near the side lot and got out of the car. Frank joined him.

"You gonna be okay?" Deets asked.

"Yeah, D, absolutely, thanks. This one a popper?"

"No, actually, it's a fresh one. You sure you're okay?"

Frank managed a smile and patted his coat pocket. "Better living through chemistry."

Deets tossed him the baby powder. They put on their rubber gloves. Put their shields on their pockets. Got out their notebooks.

Then they stepped under the tape and slipped inside the half ajar plywood door.

Thin shafts of daylight sliced through the dust motes, barely illuminating a narrow, abandoned store full of empty shelves. Air ripe with animal droppings. A motor drive buzzing, a strobe light flashing. Six dark suits in the back, huddled near a forlorn little bundle of flesh on the floor.

A blood pool as dark as black strap molasses.

"Thumb sucker," Deets said under his breath as they approached the scene.

Frank felt lightheaded. He fought it. He gripped his notebook white-knuckle tight.

"Sully Deets?" One of the Albany Park detectives, a beefy black gentleman in wrinkled polyester, was glancing up at the newcomers.

"Look who's here," Deets said, approaching the group, extending his hand.

The black man grinned and the two men shook hands, their rubberized palms squeaking faintly. "They still let you play detective up there in the Twenty-fourth?"

"Last time I checked, we had better closure rates than the Seventeenth."

"But we can still beat your asses in softball," the black man said with a twinkle in his eye.

"You remember Frank Janus?" Deets gestured at Frank.

Frank said hello to Detective Roy "Smokey" Harris, and the black detective introduced the other men, the detectives, the lab people.

"Whattya got, Smokey?" Deets said at last.

The black man shrugged. "You tell me. Saw your SC file and figured this might match up."

Frank stood his distance, staring at the dead woman on the floor. She was nude, as pale and thin as a greyhound, with old needle tracks on her arms. She was lying on her side, her legs pulled up against her ravaged abdomen. Entrails glistened beneath her. Her right arm was tucked inward, her thumb inserted into her mouth.

"—local bangers found her," Harris was saying. "Found her wallet tucked neatly into that bundle of clothes over there. Name's Irene Jeeter. Streetwalker, worked down on Cicero."

Frank took a deep breath and tried to focus on his job. He opened his notebook.

"—We got some great stuff off the scene. No prints yet, but we got a heel mark, and the lab guys say we got a hair that doesn't belong to the lady—"

The strobe light flashed.

Something fell out of Frank's notebook.

He glanced down and saw it was a piece of paper. He knelt down and picked it up. It was a piece of white typing paper, carefully folded to a quarter of its size. Frank had no idea where it had come from, and evidently nobody else had seen it hit the ground, because the others, including Deets, were still concentrating on the scene.

Frank stood back up.

He unfolded the paper, and he saw the message hastily scrawled in ballpoint.

The same color ink as the ballpoint in his pocket.

Stop investigating the thumb sucker case! It's a dead end!! It cannot be solved! Give up!

Frank started backing toward the boarded door, his head swimming, his pulse racing.

"Frank?" Deets was looking at him now.

"I gotta—I need to—I gotta go check on something," Frank was stammering.

Frank turned and hurried out the narrow channel between the worm-eaten plywood and the doorjamb.

Stumbling out into the furious sunlight, blinking fitfully, head full of cotton, he tried to breathe, but he couldn't, he couldn't get a decent breath. He still had the note in one rubber-gloved hand and the notebook in the other. He staggered across the parkway, then down a narrow alley running between the building and a deserted loading dock.

Dark spots obscured his vision.

He managed to make it over to a large, moldering peach crate, and he flopped down on it. His heart was hammering against his sternum, and his eyesight was wavering, like a dark storm cloud was moving across his field of vision. He tried to read the message, but a sudden shockwave was bolting through him.

Then everything went black.

Frank woke up somewhere else.

He was still in the alley, but he wasn't slumped on the peach crate anymore.

Sharp pain stabbed up his lower back, so profound it wrenched a groan out of him. He felt a cold wet sensation on his ass. He tried to open his eyes and look around, but his vision was still clouded. The sound of Deets's voice was coming from somewhere to his left, and he saw the ground, the grease marks, and the scabrous pavement of the alley.

"Bambi—?!"

All at once Frank realized he was on the opposite side of the alley, on the ground, his back pressed against the wall. He couldn't feel his legs. The folded paper was gone. His notebook was gone. His rubber gloves were gone, and his hands—as well as his sleeves—were soaking wet, saturated with some unidentified fluid. His feet were alseep. A terrible ammonia smell hung in the air around him.

"Bambi!—you okay?!" Deet's voice: a little panicky now. Footsteps coming fast.

Frank tried to straighten up, but he quickly realized his lower extremities were asleep. Needles of numbness tingled in his joints. Cold panic suddenly trickled down his spine, the realization shrieking in his mind.

"I'm—I'm all right—" Frank managed, pulling himself up into a sitting position against the alley wall.

Deets was approaching with a couple of plastic Ziploc bags under his arm. "What the hell happened?"

"Nothing—I got a little dizzy."

Deets gave him a hand, helping him up. "Been looking all over for ya."

"Sorry, D, I'm okay," Frank said, trying to get his bearings. He was drenched in sweat. His mouth tasted of bitter almonds. He was terrified: the realization.

"Lab guys are done," Deets said. "I was getting worried—you sure you're okay?—what happened to your gloves?"

"I'm fine, D, really." Frank rubbed his wet hands on his damp jacket. "Little dizzy spell, you know. Must have fallen in a puddle."

"Friggin' heat probably," Deets said, unconvinced, then raised a plastic bag. "Got some goddamn physical evidence for once."

Frank could barely focus on the bag. "What is it?"

"Fresh cigarette butt," Deets said. "Found it near a heel mark, behind the door. Perp is getting careless."

"That's fabulous, D," Frank said, trying to stand on his prickling, numb joints.

"Come on, Bambi, let's get you outta this heat," Deets said, putting an arm around Frank, ushering him toward the street.

Frank hobbled along as best he could . . .

. . . but he could not stop thinking about the fact that—before awakening—he had been curled into a fetal position on the dirty cement.

6

Henry Pope was not even close to being finished when the sound of chirping came from across the room. It was coming from inside Frank Janus's sportcoat, which was currently slung over a chair near the door. A cellular phone: one of life's little modern conveniences that always made Henry long for the days of rotary dials and the *Fibber McGee and Molly Show*.

"Okay, Frank, let's bring you back up now," the psychiatrist said very evenly, adopting the gentle, mellifluous tones he had perfected for therapeutic hypnosis.

Frank was lying back on a divan adjacent to Henry's chair. Eyes closed, body relaxed, shirt buttons loosened around his neck, left arm elevated in midair, Frank was in a deep trance. "Yes," he said softly.

"Can you hear me, Frank?" Henry said.

"Yes."

"We're going to get back on that imaginary elevator now. Can you see it?"

"Yes."

The cellular kept chirping.

"That's good, Frank, and now I want you to get back on that elevator, and we're going to start rising back up to consciousness now . . . okay, Frank?"

"Yes."

"Good, now we're rising up one level to the basement,

and you're still feeling good, and you're not afraid. Do you understand? Can you hear me, Frank?"

"Yes."

"Great, okay, and now we're rising up to the ground floor level, and you're almost back to consciousness, and you're feeling good, and you're refreshed, and when I snap my fingers at the count of one, you'll be able to sleep at night, and you won't have any more nightmares. Do you understand, Frank?"

"Yes."

The cellular continued beeping.

"And every morning you'll wake up refreshed, and you'll be alert during the day, and you won't let the crime scenes bother you anymore, and you won't have any more blackouts. Are you ready to come back, Frank?"

"Yes, I'm ready."

"All right, here we go—five, four, three, two, one." Henry snapped his fingers.

Frank's eyes fluttered open. He looked around for a moment, disoriented, his eyes glassy. The sound of the cellular tittering hadn't registered yet.

"Welcome back, Frank," Henry said with a smile. "How do you feel?"

Frank licked his lips. "Um . . . good. I feel . . . pretty good. How did I do?"

"Came through with flying colors, Frank, as usual," Henry said, his heart aching for this poor young man.

Frank was glancing toward the chirping sound. "Is that—?"

"Yeah, Frank, it's your phone." Henry nodded. "I thought I should bring you back so you could answer it."

The detective went over to his coat, fished through the pocket, and grabbed his phone. He flipped it on and said, "Hello." He listened for a moment. "Yeah, this is he." His expression hardened. "I'm sorry, you said she did what?"

Henry watched with concern. There was something

wrong, and it was tearing the doctor apart to see this poor kid dealing with so much life-stress. The detective reminded Henry of his youngest son, Mitch. Mitch was a sweet kid just like Frank. Why did the good always seem to suffer more than the evil?

Frank snapped the cellular off and put on his coat. "Sorry, Doctor Pope, I'm gonna have to cut the rest of the session short," he said.

"I understand, Frank," Henry said. "I hope it's not serious."

"It's my mom," Frank said, his expression bloodless and terrified all of a sudden. "She accidentally took too many sleeping pills."

"Oh no," Henry uttered sadly. "I'm sorry to hear that. Is she—okay?"

"Barely," Frank said. "I apologize for running out on you like this, I promise I'll be in touch." And then he walked out.

The door closed with a resounding click.

Frank sat on one side of the bed, and Kyle sat on the other, both men staring at the obese crone lying unconscious in the nest of sheets and IV tubes. Helen's flaccid, liverspotted face was oddly serene, her translucent eyelids so thin and wrinkled you could almost see her eyeballs through them. A tiny metal heart-rate cuff was clipped to one of her plump, arthritic fingers.

The room was institutional green, the air close with disinfectant, filled with the pinging, electronic breathing sounds of vital monitors.

"Hemphill says Mom's a DNR," Kyle murmured, his goateed face resting on his clasped hands as he gazed at his mother.

"DNR?" Frank said.

"Do-not-resuscitate."

"What?" Frank swallowed a wave of nausea. "I don't remember seeing that in the paperwork."

"Well, *somebody* put it there."

"You think Mom wrote that in?"

Kyle shrugged. "I don't know. I don't know what her legal status is."

"What do you mean?"

Kyle sighed. "Is she still considered a convict?"

"What do mean? She was never a convict—"

"She was—what?—not guilty by reason of insanity? What is that?"

"Let's not get into this again, Boomer, come on," Frank said with a weary hitch in his voice. He was sitting on a stiff vinyl armchair next to a sputtering air vent that smelled of must and refrigerant, and he was starting to get dizzy again. His head felt like a faulty gyroscope. His stomach was levitating again, threatening to bring up his lunch. He needed a cigarette and a cup of coffee. He had changed out of his damp suit and into a fresh one, but he felt worse than ever. His eyes ached. His body ached. His soul ached.

Kyle was gazing sadly at his mother. "Look, I'm starting to think maybe—I don't know—maybe Hemphill's right."

"What?!" Frank couldn't believe his ears. "You mean about pulling the plug?!"

Kyle looked at his brother. "No, no, no. Look. All I'm saying is, we should look at the humane side of things."

"Meaning what?"

"I don't know," Kyle said and looked back at Helen. She was breathing low, thick breaths, her mouth gaping open. Her eyebrows furrowed suddenly, as though she were having some kind of troubling dream. One of her hands clutched at the sheet, an involuntary reflex probably. Kyle watched this for a moment, his face crestfallen. Then he said, "I just don't want it to get to the point where she's unmanageable."

Frank felt his heart breaking like a clock jamming inside him, his eyes welling. "I understand what you're saying," Frank said softly.

"She was a piece of work, wasn't she?" Kyle said, his voice faint now, barely audible above the monitors.

"Still is," Frank said.

Kyle nodded, looking at the woman for another moment, a single tear tracking down the younger man's face.

Frank saw the bead glistening on his brother's cheek, and the sight of it made Frank mist up a little. Frank pressed his hand against the bridge of his nose. A wave of vertigo fluttered through him.

"Hey, Francis, I just thought of something," Kyle said.

Frank looked up.

Kyle's face was wet. He tried to smile but his face wouldn't allow it. "*We're* the sleep police now," he said, nodding at his mother.

"What?" Frank wasn't sure he had heard him correctly.

"The sleep police? Remember?" Kyle pointed at his mother. "We're mom's sleep police now."

Frank swallowed. "Yeah, Boomer . . . sure."

Then Frank turned away and tried not to let his brother see him cry.

Deets's desk was inundated with paper. You couldn't see his blotter anymore. You couldn't even see his overflowing ashtray. There were bundles of GPR forms in descending chronological order on the left. And there were stacks of missing person data sheets on the right, each one clipped to a black-and-white of a smiling girl. And there were crime scene diagrams, ME reports, and autopsy notes from the Wacker scene and the Devon Avenue Jane Doe. There were also packets of polaroids from the Jeeter scene, shots of blood drip patterns, and numerous angles of a single heel mark.

Deets was on the phone, holding a pink WHILE-YOU-WERE-OUT phone message in his left hand, listening to his wife's voice on the other end of the line.

"It's already six-thirty, Sul, for Chrissake," Margie was saying. A hard-as-nails South Sider, Margie Deets had a voice like rusty barbed wire, and she did not suffer work-aholic husbands lightly. "When the hell are you coming home? I got a letter from Wendy today, and we need to talk about it. She needs money, Sully."

This got Deets's attention. He dropped the slip, gripping the phone a little tighter. "You got what?"

"A letter from Wendy, and we need to talk about it. She needs money, Sul."

"I told you—"

"She's still your daughter, Sully."

There was a pause. Deets sighed. His twenty-six-year-old daughter had left home when she was eighteen to become a stage actress in New York. Instead she became a phone sex operator. This was by far the worst thing that had ever happened to Sully Deets. "I don't have time for this right now," he said finally through clenched teeth.

"Sully—"

"I gotta go, Margie, I'll see you in an hour," he said, and hung up the phone.

He sat there for a moment, stewing in his own slow-cooked anger. A secretary strolled by, and she said hello, and Deets didn't even hear her. He was too busy brooding. Not only for his wayward daughter, but for the suspicions that were festering inside him. The cigarette butt from the Jeeter scene, the heel, the hair follicle. What began as a vague, troubling knot in his belly was now metastasizing into something hard and cancerous. He picked up the note and looked at the hastily scrawled note from the technician: *The collapsed filter belongs to a Marlboro regular, still working on possible DNA match.*

"Fuck it," Deets grumbled, pushing himself away from his desk, standing up on sore legs and putting on his jacket.

He made his way down the corridor.

Before leaving the squad house, he stopped by the men's locker room.

The air inside the locker room was peppery with BO

and hair tonic, and there were three other detectives in there, over by the sinks, talking basketball, discussing whether the post-Jordan Bulls were ever going to get their act together. Deets nodded a greeting to them and then went over to his own locker and sat down on the wooden bench in front of it. He pretended to untie his shoes. He waited. A few moments later, the other detectives filed out and Deets went over to the last locker on the right. There was no padlock.

The name stenciled at the top said JANUS, DET. F.

Deets opened the metal door and looked inside. There wasn't much. A gym bag on the top shelf, a box of plastic drinking straws, a bottle of Maalox, an empty shoulder holster with an extra speed loader. There was also a fresh sportcoat—one of Frank's high fashion jobs—and a pair of shiny Lagerfeld loafers on the shelf. Deets picked up one of the shoes and looked at the heel.

Then he put the shoe back, closed the locker, and wandered out of the locker room.

Deets left the squad house in a dark mood, unaware that he had missed a carton of cigarettes on the top shelf of Frank's locker, behind the box of straws.

They were Marlboro regulars.

7

The Twenty-fourth late at night. Quiet. The sounds of janitors down the hall. Power buffers humming. And Frank Janus, the insomniac, slumped in a folding chair by a bank of video monitors, half asleep, a zombie hypnotized by the blue flicker of a TV screen.

Frank bolted upright suddenly, gasping, blinking fitfully at the screen.

Had he been asleep? He couldn't remember. He couldn't even remember sitting down in this folding chair. The last thing he remembered was standing over by the window, shuffling through the witness statement videos. Now he was sitting across the room, and a strange voice was crackling out of the tiny speaker on the side of the monitor—

"—Girls turn up dead, sure, but like, a lot of dudes I see, they're on a death trip anyway, so it's like, what do you do? There was this one guy, he figured out how to file his teeth down, I mean, I shit you not, he filed them down like razor sharp, and he kinda looked like a fish, you know, with these razor teeth, like a fucking shark—"

On screen was a greasepaint harlequin, a broken-down streetwalker masquerading as a Goth, her white face sporting a spiderweb around two bloodshot eyes. Her voice was cured by smoke and booze. She sat in a chair against a light blue cardboard backdrop—the standard departmental backdrop—and she spoke right into the lens, like she was at ease with cameras, like she had done this before, and she spoke in dreamy tangents, dampened by years of drugs and degradation.

"*—and his thing was, he wanted to bite my nipples off and eat them. I swear to God. It was like, he had this kit with him, these fucking bandages and alcohol, so my tits wouldn't get infected, I mean, what kind of fucking shit is that—?*"

Frank hit STOP.

He swallowed hard, running fingers through his hair. These statements were ridiculous. They were getting him nowhere. Jittery and dizzy, his chest tight with tension, he looked around the room again, listening to the silence for a moment, listening for any signs of life out in the squad house, but all he could hear was the whirr of a vacuum cleaner and a distant fax machine chittering.

Where the hell was everybody?

He went out into the main room and saw one of the third-shift guys—Randy Jeffers—over by the vending machine, rattling a lever, trying to get a candy bar to spit out. Frank waved at him. A thin, light-skinned black man, Jeffers looked up, nodded, then went back to the lever.

Frank went over to his desk.

Out of the corner of his eye, he saw Deets's desk across the aisle. It was a disaster area, the in-box brimming with forms waiting to be filled out, the blotter covered with a spray of bulging manila files. And everything was exactly as it had been thirty minutes ago—

—except for a mysterious unmarked package sitting on top of the folders.

"What the heck is this?" Frank said, walking over to Deets's desk and picking up the package, taking a closer look.

Cops are not the least bit shy about checking out each other's interoffice mail, especially partners.

The package was about the size of a paperback book, and weighed only a few ounces, and the brown wrapping

paper had been neatly sealed with invisible tape. There
were no labels on it. Frank frowned. Somebody other
than the interoffice mail boy must have dropped this
thing on Deets's desk.

But why leave it blank?

"What the hell?" he said, his gaze glued to the object.

All at once a flutter of panic traveled up his gorge,
dizziness coursing over him. He thought of the message
on his computer, the note in his notebook: *Walk away,
shut it down, forget about it.* Pipe bombs were small these
days. There were metal detectors downstairs, near the
door, and most of the mail was routinely scanned. But
what if this thing had slipped through? Maybe Frank was
being paranoid. Maybe it was the lack of sleep. But there
was something wrong with this picture.

He glanced over at Jeffers. "Hey, Randy! Did you see
who it was, dropped this thing on Sully's desk?"

The black detective looked up from the vending machine. "What's that?"

Frank waved the package. "This package—you have
any idea who put it on Deets's desk?"

"Sorry, Frank, no," Jeffers said. "Call the mail room."

Frank waved a thank-you.

He couldn't call the mail room right now because the
mail room was closed. He looked at the package. He
rattled it. Something was loose inside it. Like a pea or a
rock or . . . what? . . . a detonator? Frank took a deep
breath. He glanced over at Jeffers. The black detective
was wandering off toward the break room with his candy
bar. Frank was alone now.

Frank put the package down, a spurt of adrenaline
juicing through his veins.

He reached for his phone.

There was supposed to be somebody down in Tactical
right now, at least one third-shift officer. Frank remembered the number from a couple of weeks ago when he
and Deets needed assistance on an arrest over at Loyola.

Frank dialed the four-digit interoffice number with a trembling hand.

A voice answered on the second ring. "Twenty-fourth Tactical, this is Porterly."

"Jim, it's Frank Janus upstairs."

"Frankie—how ya doin'?"

"Great, I'm doing great. How's Kim?"

"Meaner than ever. Finally made me get rid of that fucking German shepherd."

"That's too bad, Jimmy."

"What's up, Frank?"

"Not much. I was just wondering—um—you got anybody from Special Units on tonight?"

"Special Units?"

Frank was trying to sound low-key, trying not to sound spooked. "Yeah, you know. Like Haz Mat or ECU."

ECU stands for Explosive Control Unit. In the wake of the '68 Convention, as well as subsequent incidents at O'Hare Airport, the Chicago Police Department created a fulltime bomb squad that still operates today. Officer James Porterly was one of the few neighborhood tactical people who had any experience working for the unit.

"I got some hours in ECU, Frank," Porterly was saying. "You need somebody?"

"Yeah, well, we got a package up here—um—I don't know. Maybe it's nothing."

There was a pause. Then Porterly's voice: "You mean, like, a suspicious package?"

Frank took a deep breath. "I don't know—yeah— maybe it's a little suspicious. It's unmarked."

"It's unmarked?"

"Yeah, it just turned up—"

"Wait a minute, wait, you're saying it's in the house right now?"

"That's right."

"And it's unmarked?"

"Yeah."

"Where is it right now?"

"It's on Sully Deets's desk."

Another pause. "And he brought this thing in with him?"

"No, no, see, Deets isn't even here," Frank said, his throat scratchy and dry all of a sudden. He could not stop staring at the package. "The thing just turned up on his desk. I was working some overtime hours, looking at some tapes in the property room, and I came out, and there it was."

"You mean somebody put it on Sully's desk?"

"Yeah, that's right."

"What's it look like?"

Frank let out a tense sigh, then told Porterly what the thing looked like.

While he was describing the package's dimensions, Frank could see out of the corner of his eye a figure at the end of the hallway, peering out the break room door. It was Jeffers. He was listening now with some interest.

Jeffers started toward Frank.

"And it rattled when you shook it?" Porterly was saying now on the other end of the line.

"Yeah, that's right, like a hollow rattling sound."

"Are you holding it right now?"

"No."

"I wouldn't."

"Okay."

"I wouldn't rattle it anymore, either."

"Okay, no problem," Frank said. "What do you want me to do, Jim?"

There was a long pause, and Frank waited, his heart thumping. Jeffers was standing next to him now, staring at the package.

Finally Porterly's voice said, "It's probably nothing, Frankie. They're usually nothing."

"Okay," Frank said and looked at Jeffers. Jeffers was staring at the package.

"Just to be safe," Porterly added, "why don't you clear everybody out of there."

Frank glanced at Jeffers. "You want me to clear everybody out?"

Porterly's voice: "Yeah, just go around and tell everybody not to panic, tell 'em there might be a gas leak or something. No big deal."

Frank swallowed hard. "What if—uh—what if I—miss somebody?"

Another pause. "Tell you what. Why don't you go ahead and pull the fire alarm. Like I said, it's probably nothing. We'll tell Media Relations it's a possible gas leak. There can't be that many people in the building."

Frank let out a breath. "Okay, Jim. If that's what you think we should do."

"It's probably a waste of time," Porterly said. "I'll take the thing out in a containment basket."

"Okay, Jim."

"You can meet me in the back lot. Like I said, it's probably nothing."

"Okay, Jim, that sounds good."

Frank hung up.

He looked at the package, then looked at Jeffers. "Come on, Randy. Let's go have a cigarette."

On his way out, Frank pulled the fire alarm.

8

Making his way through the maze of desks on the second floor, lugging the portable bomb basket and a duffel bag full of gear, Jim Porterly was sweating. He always perspired like crazy when he had the bomb suit on, especially when he had to carry equipment. A heavy coverall made from Teflon-filled panels, the bomb suit resembled a deep-sea diving rig, but was more unwieldy.

Through his helmet, Porterly could hear the muffled screech of the fire alarm buzzer. He could see Sully Deets's desk straight ahead.

The small brown-wrapped package was still sitting on the desk blotter.

Porterly carried the bomb basket over to the desk and gingerly set it down. The basket looked like a large iron kettle in which you might cook stew for about a hundred people. On top was a pressurized hatch that you open like the top of a submarine. The vessel was rated at a maximum of ten pounds of C-4 explosives. Porterly opened the hatch.

He used a mechanical reacher to pick up the unidentified package. He swung the package across the width of the desk very carefully, keeping his eyes on a fixed point between the package and the top of the bomb basket, just as he had been trained to do. The inside of the basket was as black as a stag's heart. Porterly carefully lowered the package through the opening and into the vessel.

Then Porterly very gently closed the top of the bomb basket, sealing the pressure lock.

He let out a long sigh of relief. His scalp itched inside his helmet, but there was nothing he could do about that right now. He still had to get the thing out of the building, and then get the thing disarmed if necessary. Porterly still believed—especially after seeing the package—that it was nothing. But he couldn't take any chances.

The fire alarm kept buzzing.

Carefully picking up the basket, Porterly carried it down the hallway to the elevator. He pressed *G* for ground floor, and the doors closed, and Porterly rode down breathing hard, the sound of his breaths like a huge bellows in his ears. He was hyperalert. He could hear the clang and rattle of the elevator pulleys just under the muffled din of the fire alarm. His mouth was dry. His eyes were watering.

He reached the ground floor and proceeded down the hallway to the loading dock exit.

When he finally made it outside, he allowed himself another faint sigh of relief. The night sky was huge and hazy above him, the humidity hanging low like a shroud. The lot was sparsely occupied by a few patrol cars, a couple of unmarked squads, and some civilian vehicles.

Frank Janus and Randy Jeffers were standing about a hundred yards away, near the corner of the building, nervously smoking cigarettes, watching. Porterly waved at them. They waved back. There were a couple of other onlookers—some guys from Property Crimes—perched on an adjacent parking viaduct. In the gleam of the vapor lights, they looked like owls all lined up for the evening's meal. Or maybe buzzards looking for carrion.

Porterly carried the basket out to a safe zone in the center of the parking lot.

Under the sodium lights the containment vessel shimmered with a dull gleam, like a cast-iron skillet that had just been scrubbed. It looked slightly ominous. Porterly dropped his duffel bag next to it and took some deep breaths. The next few seconds were always the most critical. Porterly wanted to finish this thing quickly, with as little drama as necessary.

In the duffel bag Porterly had brought along a portable X-ray scanner, an electronic stethoscope, and some hand tools. He also had a specially designed coil of rope that the bomb guys referred to as a "jerkus rope," one of the indispensable low-tech items in his arsenal.

He took out the jerkus rope and carefully threaded it through a rubberized opening in the vessel. Then, peering through a tiny window, Porterly looped the end of the jerkus rope around the package and gently pulled the slack out of it.

Then he backed away from the bomb basket, letting out rope as he went along.

The other cops were riveted. The parking lot seemed very quiet all of a sudden.

Porterly flipped up the helmet visor. "You guys probably ought to take cover," he called out to his colleagues. "Just to be on the safe side."

The cops ducked behind the telephone poles and concrete ramparts on the edge of the lot.

"Like I said, it's probably nothing!" Porterly called out, flipping the visor down. He was maybe fifty yards away from the bomb basket.

He yanked the rope.

Nothing happened.

Porterly could almost hear the collective sighs of relief from Frank Janus and the other cops in the shadows behind him. Even the crickets and the distant noises of the city seemed to sigh, resuming their normal drone of ambient noise.

It was always an odd moment, when a device turns out to be nothing.

Porterly felt a secret twinge of disappointment.

"One more item on the agenda," he murmured to him-self, his voice loud inside his helmet.

He went over to the duffel bag and pulled out a device that looked like one of those radar guns used by state troopers. About the size of a video camera, with a six-inch-wide window on one end, the portable X-ray ma-chine was an invaluable part of the bomb squad field office. It was the only way to tell for sure if something was wired.

He knelt down and opened the vessel.

He scanned the package, and he watched the window flicker with a luminous blue image.

Porterly smiled. The object inside the package was im-mediately recognizable.

9

Frank was watching Porterly hunching over the iron container, when Porterly's voice suddenly rang out across the lot. "Come on over, Frank, we're clear!"

"Excuse me?" Frank called back.

"Come on over," Porterly said, taking off his helmet, rising to his feet. The tac officer turned and waved Frank over. "Come over and take a look at your explosive device."

Frank looked at Jeffers, and Jeffers gave Frank a confused look, and then Frank made his way around the edge of the building and across the lot.

"Take a look, Frank," Porterly was saying, climbing out of his bomb suit.

Frank approached cautiously. Gravel crunched loudly beneath his feet. His eyeballs felt too big for his skull. He was so dizzy the lot was beginning to spin slightly in his peripheral vision. He looked down at the X-ray gun.

The ghost of a rectangular object glowed on the tiny display screen.

"It's a videotape?" Frank said.

"That would be my educated guess," Porterly quipped, peeling off his huge Teflon-lined trousers.

Frank stared at the display. "You're kidding me."

"Nope."

"Just an ordinary videocassette?" Frank said incredulously.

"That's what it looks like, Frank."

"Jesus, I'm sorry about all the trouble."

"Don't worry about it. You did the right thing, Frankie. It's my job, it's what I do."

Jeffers was approaching, glancing over Frank's shoulder. "What the hell is it?"

Frank turned and gave Jeffers a sheepish look. "I think it's what you would call a false alarm."

Jeffers took a closer look at the X-ray. "That looks like a fucking—"

"It is, Randy, it is," Frank said with a sigh. "It's a videotape."

Jeffers stared at the glowing image.

The other cops were coming now. One of the older guys—a graying, crew-cut sergeant in Property Crimes named Grasso—was staring at the X-ray with a grin. "Whattya got there, Frank? 'Debbie Does Dallas'?"

Porterly smiled, wiping his face with a handkerchief. "No, it's probably home movies of Deets's daughter."

The cops all had a big laugh at that one.

"Gotta admit, it's not one of my prouder moments," Frank said with a sheepish, apologetic smile.

"Don't worry about it, Frankie," Jeffers said, giving Frank a conciliatory pat on the back. "Probably would have done the same thing myself."

"Hey, Jimmy," Grasso spoke up, "you gonna let us go back inside now or what?"

Porterly was gathering up his gear. "Go ahead, fellas," he said. "Just be on the lookout for any dangerous porno."

They all laughed and made their way back across the lot toward the entrance.

Frank watched them filter back into the building. The fire alarm had gone silent.

"—So whattya think it is?" Jeffers was saying.

Frank turned and looked him. "Excuse me?"

"The videotape," Jeffers said, pointing at the black iron bomb container.

Frank shrugged. "Probably nothing. Probably another witness statement."

Porterly reached down into the hold, grabbed the package and lifted it out of the basket. He loosened the jerkus rope and handed the package to Frank. "Happy viewing, Frankie," Porterly said.

"Thanks, Jim, I appreciate all the trouble," Frank said, looking down at the package. The plain brown wrapper was torn on one side from the pressure of the rope.

"Don't mention it, Frank," Porterly said, then slung the duffel over his shoulder, grabbed the bomb basket, and started across the parking lot.

Jeffers gave Frank one last pat on the shoulder, then followed Porterly across the lot and into the building.

Frank stood there for a long moment, clutching the videotape, feeling ashamed, woozy, lightheaded. His stomach was still tight with tension. What was happening to him? His life was falling apart. He looked down at the videotape, and he felt compelled to hurl it across the lot. Watch it hit the side of the building and shatter into a million pieces.

He stared at it for a moment.

Curiosity got the better of him, and he carried the package back inside the building.

On his way back up to Violent Crimes, Frank passed the public information and complaint desks, the watch commander's office, the briefing room, and the holding cells. The graveyard shift folks were still finding their way back into the building, making their way back to their desks—about a half a dozen As and a couple of desk sergeants, all chatting about the bogus fire alarm and all the excitement—and it made Frank feel like an idiot, like a problem child.

He avoided their gazes.

When he got back to his desk on the second floor, he couldn't resist opening the package.

Sure enough, it was a videotape.

The trouble was, it was also unmarked. No box. No label. Nothing stamped on its plastic shell. Just a generic unmarked videocassette, relatively new, its black styrene cartridge still gleaming, factory-fresh. For some reason, Frank shook it again. It seemed like the appropriate thing to do. The cassette rattled slightly, the tape hubs loosely grommeted inside its contours. But nothing else out of the ordinary. Just a generic, black, plastic, unmarked videocassette.

Frank knew that Deets was not the type to give a damn if Frank looked at it.

Frank took it into the property room, went over to the VCR near the window, and ejected the tape of the white-faced prostitute. Then he popped the mystery tape into the machine, and he pressed PLAY.

An image flickered on the screen.

Frank became very still.

The image of a solitary man, alone in a room, staring into the lens of the camera. The room was very familiar to Frank. The man looked very intense, maybe even a little exhausted. He was seen in medium close-up, and his eyes had the strangest look—both glassy and intense at the same time. He was trembling faintly. It was obvious he was about to say something very important— maybe even frightening—into the camera lens.

Frank's entire body rashed with gooseflesh, and not merely because it was obvious that Frank was about to learn something terrible . . .

. . . but also because he was looking at an image of someone he thought he knew fairly well.

10

"Okay, heads up, Deets . . . I want to make a statement."

The image was poorly framed, the sound hollow and tinny, the lighting harsh, as though a bare light bulb were shining just out of the frame, throwing an awkward glare on the side of the on-screen face. The background was the faded blue cardboard backdrop of the interrogation room. The voice was hoarse and slightly strained.

"This is regarding the thumb sucker case, and I'm only going to do this once, so get your notebook out, Deets. Sharpen your pencil. And listen closely."

There was a pause then, the man on screen staring feverishly into the lens.

In the world of television production, there's a thing called the "talking head." It's an all-purpose catch-phrase for the kind of bland close-up you see on the nightly news. A single on-camera personality, their face filling the frame from roughly midchest up to a few inches above their head, the talking head is usually the best medium for the objective dissemination of information, news, and educational content.

Right now, the talking head on the battered CPD Trinitron was Frank Janus.

It was Frank.

And he was speaking into the camera in hushed, measured tones.

"Now I'm sure you're probably wondering: Why would

my partner send me a videotape like this? Why not just talk over a cup of that shitty squad coffee, right? Well, there's a good reason I'm making this statement on video, Deets, and I'll get to that in a minute. But first, I want to get to my statement. I want to do this properly."

Across the room, Frank stood very still, a rivulet of cold sweat spidering down the hollow of his back. He was staring at a talking head of *himself*, and he had no memory of videotaping it. He had no memory of making *any* videotape of himself. His mind reeled for a moment. Was this some elaborate video notebook that he had made and forgotten? Why the hell was he addressing Deets with such an obvious attitude?

The Video-Frank was talking into the camera lens.

"This concerns the Wacker Jane Doe from ten years ago, the Jeeter case, and the Pakistani Jane Doe. Are you listening, Deets? All those theories you had about the MO . . . the methodology, the signature . . . the privacy, the amount of time it takes to alter the bodies postmortem, the state of mind of the killer, all that stuff . . . you were right, Deets, about everything. You want to know how I know this? Because the guy we're hunting for—the thumb sucker killer—is me."

Another pause.

Frank felt his stomach seizing up, his pulse racing in his neck, the dizziness washing over him. What in God's name was going on? Was this a joke? Some kind of gag Deets was working on? But how could it be? It was Frank on screen. *Frank.* Frank was watching himself.

He couldn't move, and he couldn't tear his gaze from the monitor.

"You heard right, Deets, I'm the guy. I'm the perp. I killed that stripper down on Wacker Drive, and I killed that Jane Doe in Little Pakistan, and—"

All at once Frank lunged at the VCR, slamming the PAUSE button.

The image froze.

Footsteps were coming. Just outside the door. Somebody striding down the corridor toward the property room. Frank quickly pressed the INPUT switch, and the screen went blank, filling with electronic snow.

Randy Jeffers appeared in the doorway. "So what did the mystery tape turn out to be?" he asked, sipping coffee from a paper cup.

"Take a look," Frank said, pointing nervously at the monitor.

Jeffers entered the room, walked over to the Trinitron and glanced at the screen. Jeffers's face fell like a little boy at the end of a party. "Blank?"

"Yep." Frank nodded.

"You gotta be kidding me? After all that?"

"Typical, huh?"

The black detective shook his head. "Hell, at least it coulda been Marilyn Chambers."

Frank managed a fleeting smile. "Yeah, just my luck."

"There is no God," Jeffers said, staring at the snowy screen.

"Tell me about it," Frank said.

Jeffers shrugged, then walked out.

Frank stood there for a moment, his heart hammering.

He rushed over to the door, carefully closed it and twisted the deadbolt.

Then he went back to the VCR and pressed PLAY.

"—and I killed Irene Jeeter. But it's not what you think. It's very complicated, Deets. Which brings me to the reason I made this videotape. You see, I'm not Frank Janus right now. Not exactly. I'm what's known as an alter personality. I live inside Frank Janus, and I only come out when Frank's asleep."

There was another pause.

Standing in front of the monitor, fists clenched like tight little stones, Frank was paralyzed. This had to be a joke. It had to be. There were all sorts of gizmos out there on the market nowadays that enabled home computer enthusiasts to fuck with video images. Gizmos that would have made George Lucas drool ten years ago. You could get them down at the local Radio Shack. But the more Frank grasped for feeble explanations, the more the image on the screen drew him in, terrified him. The face was his, and it was pumped up with adrenaline and madness.

It was like looking into a fun house mirror.

The on-screen Frank's eyes were glinting.

"It's pretty amazing, how it works. It's like I live in a cocoon, and I turn into a butterfly every few nights when Frank finally drifts off to sleep. And Frank's not even aware of it. At least, I don't think he is. He might suspect something's going on, I don't know. But he's been blacking out so much lately, it's pretty easy."

Frank made a sound—hardly audible above the sizzle of the TV's speaker—a little, anguished, breathy sound.

He stared at the TV.

"I've lived inside Frank for most of his life, but I only started coming out about ten years ago. I know it's a big bite to swallow, Deets. I realize you're an old pragmatist, but try to understand: I kill because I have to. I don't have a choice. Most guys, they have a choice. They're evil. But I'm not like that. I'm doing God's work. The work has to be done."

Another pause.

Frank let out a tense sigh and looked away. "Somebody's fucking with me," he whispered to himself, and then shook his head and tried to laugh. But no laughter would come out of him. No laughter would come.

His image kept flickering on the screen.

"Admit it, Deets: These past few days, you were starting to look at Frank a little more closely. Each successive case within a five-mile radius of Frank's apartment at the time of the killing? Remember that little ratty brownstone Frank lived in down on Grand? That was six blocks from where you found the first victim. And then there's the cigarette butt—Frank's brand—and the ligature marks around the victims' necks. I think if you check, you'll find that Frank is left-handed."

Frank was gaping at the screen now, his eyes burning, the icy dread seeping into his gut.

This was real. This was no joke. This was no fake. This was him.

Or at least, some facsimile of him.

"Anyway, that's about all I wanted to say, Deets. I'm tired of this life. I've done my part for God, and now it's time to retire. I realize after this tape gets around, they'll put us away for a long, long time, and that's probably the best thing."

Another pause.

Somewhere in the hidden, shadowy recesses of Frank's mind, a warning alarm was sounding. The ME reports had described lacerations across the necks of each victim. Frank had agonized over those forensic photos, the macro close-ups of strangely similar papery cuts on the left side of each victim's neck. Now he was standing in the dusty property room, staring down at his left hand, staring at his nicotine-stained thumb, staring at his thumbnail. He wore his nails long, but he bit them compulsively. His thumbnails were always jagged.

Without even being aware of it, Frank was edging slowly away from the TV now, backing toward a small metal typing desk in the far corner of the room, toward the lower left-hand drawer where Johnny Trout kept a secret stash of Johnny Walker in a pint bottle, swaddled in newspaper and rubber bands. But Frank couldn't take his eyes off that dusty TV screen. His video image had a shimmer of something like madness in its eyes. Or maybe it was simple exhaustion, or perhaps even disgust. It was hard to tell. The picture was very contrasty and softly focused, the trademarks of a cheap, consumer-grade video camera.

"Oh, I almost forgot. You might be wondering who I am, whether or not I have a name . . ."

Frank was reaching down without looking, opening the bottom desk drawer, rooting around for the bottle. He lifted it out of the drawer and set it on the desk. He unscrewed the plastic cap and took a swig, his gaze riveted to the TV screen.

"... *I call myself the Sleep Police.*"

All at once the image turned to snow, the recording coming to an abrupt end.

Frank chugged the remaining contents of the Johnny Walker bottle.

The only sound in the room now was the hissing of blank tape across playback heads.

And the feverish voice echoing in Frank's mind, about to change his life forever.

PART II

Frank's Final Act as a Policeman

"What other dungeon is so dark as one's own heart! What jailer so inexorable as one's own self!"
—NATHANIEL HAWTHORNE
The House of the Seven Gables

11

Frank hurried through the turnstile, his stomach stitched with panic. He grabbed a basket and headed for the rear of the drug store.

The twenty-four-hour Walgreens was jumping with early morning traffic, the aisles blazing with fluorescent light. There was an old blue-haired woman at the photo counter, thumbing through coupons, a couple of suits standing behind her in the checkout line, cradling plastic-wrapped muffins and self-serve coffee. There was a teen-age stockboy over by the cosmetics counter, stamping price tags on boxes of Clairol rinse treatments. The rear of the store was a labyrinth of medications and personal hygiene products.

Frank rushed along the back wall, past the antacids, past the laxatives, past the cough drops and cold tablets, until he found the sleep-aid display. He scanned the bottom shelf. Beneath the boxes of Nytol and Sominex, were the stimulants. Frank started tossing boxes into his basket: Caffedrine caplets, Ultra Pep-back with Eleveine, No-Doz, Maximum Strength Awake, and Stay-Up by Miles. Just to be safe, he went over to the cold-relief shelf and grabbed some Sudafed. Then he went over to the diet bin and picked up some Dexetrim and Acutrim. Anything that would keep him awake.

Anything to keep him from cracking apart again.

On his way back to the checkout counter, he grabbed

a couple of bottles of Vitamin B$_{12}$ and a six-pack of Jolt Cola. He had plenty of coffee at home, and if the need arose, he would stop at a Starbucks on the way. He was not going to black out again. He was not going to fall asleep until he figured things out. In front of him, the line at the cash register had grown. There were a couple of black matrons in tank tops and summer hats standing behind the suits.

Frank fidgeted, waiting for his turn, his mind churning like an engine with broken bearings. He felt damaged. He felt filthy, like a leper. He felt as though his face were deformed, as though the people around him were trying not to stare. Could he have another personality inside him—a parasite feeding off the damaged cells of his brain—and not even be aware of it? But the worst part—the part that he wouldn't let himself think about right now—was the pathology.

The thumb suckers.

"Must be pretty damn tired," a voice said, shaking Frank out of his rumination.

Frank looked up at the checkout girl. "What?—oh—yeah."

"All this stuff, must be awful damn tired," the girl commented as she scanned each box. A heavyset black girl in a purple Walgreens pinafore, she seemed only mildly interested.

"You have no idea," Frank said, pulling his credit card from his wallet. His gaze fell on his driver's license, then his detective shield and his county ID badge—the tiny thumbnail mug shots of a young Greek cop staring earnestly into the camera, the same face that had just glared out at him from that statement videotape. All at once his whole identity seemed corrupted, fractured.

Who was he?

"Total's $57.16," the clerk mumbled.

Frank swiped his card on the self-service reader, signed the receipt, grabbed his bag of stimulants, and left in a hurry.

*   *   *

The voice was crackling over the line: "And you're sure there's no way you made this thing and forgot about it."

"Absolutely positive."

"Maybe some kind of profiling technique? Getting into the killer's mindset?"

"No way."

"Some kind of process you dreamt up?"

"Believe me, Doc, I would remember."

"Fair enough. I've just got to ask the obvious questions."

"I understand," Frank said, wiping the sweat from his brow with a trembly hand. He was standing in a phone booth at the corner of Western and Peterson, and the Plexiglas-encased coffin was like a pressure cooker. The morning sun was beating down on the booth, and Frank could smell his body odor like spoor. "I just keep thinking, it looks like me, it sounds like me, but it isn't me."

"Do you think it's something you might have made during noctambulation?" asked the voice.

Frank thought about it. "You mean sleepwalking?"

"Exactly."

Frank shrugged. "I guess. But Jesus, I mean, the video is so blatantly—it's so—what's the word—it's so *insinuating*."

"I understand," the doctor said. "But this kind of condition is complex and fluid."

"Jesus," Frank uttered under his breath. He was thinking of his mother. He was thinking of that over-boiled look in her eyes the day she killed the teacher, and the way Frank's own eyes looked on that obscene videotape.

"Okay, Frank, I want you to do something for me," the voice said.

"Sure, okay," Frank said.

"I want you to try and stay calm, and we'll work through this thing together," the doctor said.

Frank took a deep breath. Even the simple presence of Henry Pope's voice in his ear made him feel better.

Frank had called the doctor at home—amazingly, Pope's number had been in the book—and luckily the doctor had not yet left for work. Frank had expected Pope to be upset about having to deal with a frantic patient at this early hour, but the psychiatrist had been monumentally courteous and accommodating. It was as though Henry Pope were a life preserver tossed out over the phone lines to a drowning Frank. At least now Frank would be able to keep his head above water and think.

"I hear you, Doc, I'm trying, I'm trying to stay calm," Frank said.

"Call me Henry."

"Okay, fair enough," Frank said. "Henry it is."

"I want to ask you something else, Frank," the voice said.

Frank took a deep breath. "Go ahead."

"This isn't going to be easy to answer."

"Fire away."

"Is it possible—what I mean is—is there any possibility that the tape is authentic?"

A cold current jolted through Frank's gut. "What you mean, authentic?"

"What I mean is, do you think there's any possibility—and I'm not saying there is—but do you think there's any possibility that this other personality actually exists?"

"What?—no—I mean—*Jesus*—no."

"Do you understand what I'm asking?"

Frank swallowed air. The tape was resting inside his jacket pocket, a black plastic tumor radiating dread. "Yeah—I mean—yes, I understand what you're asking, and no, no way, there's no way."

"I gotta ask the question, Frank."

"I understand what you're saying, but, I mean, how would it be possible for a man to have—you know what I'm saying—how would it be possible?"

"It's pretty darn near impossible, Frank, to be honest with you."

Frank let out a pained sigh. "At least I got *that* going for me."

"The only reason I'm even getting into this right now, Frank, is because, you know, there are deaths involved."

"You're talking about the thumb suckers."

"The cold cases, yes."

Frank was nodding. "And this tape, this videotape, it amounts to a confession, basically."

There was the briefest of pauses. "I'm not saying that, Frank."

A car horn trumpeted in the distance, making Frank jump slightly. The caffeine pills were already starting to work on him. He mopped the sweat from his brow and took another deep breath.

A few minutes ago, at the beginning of the conversation, Frank had reminded Henry Pope of the doctor-patient confidentiality oath. It was specified in both the union bylaws and the group policy's small print that a psychiatrist cannot reveal anything spoken in confidence under the aegis of a patient's therapy. But when the commission of a crime is involved, the lines of discretion get a little blurry.

"All I'm saying is, you've got to look at all sides of this thing, Frank," Henry Pope was saying on the other end of the line. "Let's just say for a minute this other personality is authentic. Hypothetically."

Frank wiped his mouth. "Tell me again what you mean by authentic."

"Okay, look, lemme ask you this: Is it you on camera? Are you absolutely certain it's you, and it's not a fake?"

An inexplicable chill traveled through Frank as he remembered staring into his own eyes. "I don't know—yeah. I guess I'm pretty sure it's not a fake."

"Okay, then, if it's not a fake, and it's really you, then that narrows down the explanations. Would you agree?"

"Yeah. I guess. Yeah."

"Then the real question is, what if it's more than some kind of ambulatory trance state?"

"Ambulatory what?"

"Another form of sleepwalking, sort of like you're act-ing out some nasty anxiety dream. Does that make sense?"

Frank stared at his distorted reflection in the chrome faceplate of the pay phone. "I guess, yeah."

"Then you've gotta look at the other possibilities as well."

"Right."

"And whether the guy on the tape is real."

"The other personality."

"That's right."

Frank shivered again. He felt as though he were run-ning a temperature. "Go on," he uttered.

"All I'm saying is, there's a way to deal with this kind of thing."

"You mean when there's a crime involved," Frank said.

"That's exactly right, there's a way to deal with this when there's a homicide involved."

"You think it's possible I've got another personality?"

There was another brief pause. "That's impossible to answer, Frank."

"But you've got an idea how to deal with this?"

"Look, I'm not saying I think you're at this point yet," the voice said.

"What point?"

"I'm not saying I think you should do this."

"Do what?"

"I guess you'd call it?—what?—voluntary commit-ment?"

Frank closed his eyes for a moment. "I'm not ready for that yet."

"I understand—"

"I just don't think I'm ready for that yet."

"I understand, Frank, and believe me, I wasn't im-plying—"

"I've gotta go."

"Frank—"

"I really have to get going. I'll call you back. I've gotta figure this thing out."

"Frank, wait—"

"I'll call you back, I'm sorry," Frank said, then hung up the receiver.

He shoved the booth door open, and stumbled out into the Chicago morning.

12

The sun slanted down hard through the miniblinds across Frank's front window. The heat was horrible. A single rotary fan clattered and swayed back and forth across the bay window, a woefully inadequate addition to the single window-unit air conditioner in the rear.

Frank's living room was a stifling, airless tableau, the faded floral-papered walls sweating old odors of stale cigarettes and boiled cabbage in the heat. There were little numbered evidence flags everywhere—in the sofa cushions, in the oriental rug, in the back of the TV, under the window overlooking the fire escape.

As an investigator, Frank's job was all about observation. And now he was observing himself, his own environment. Buzzing with caffeine-induced adrenalin, eyes burning with emotion, he was struggling to look at his world, to find some trace, some clue of another personality. He was still hanging onto the slim hope that the videotape was a fake, or a fluke, or some kind of elaborate scam. But if it wasn't—and Frank was truly cracked—then Frank wanted to be the one to find out first. And that was why he had called in sick today, and that was why he was treating his apartment like a crime scene.

Click!

He snapped off another Polaroid of the window by the fire escape. Then he went over to his makeshift bulletin board leaning against the wall by his TV. He thumbtacked the photograph next to a bunch of others lined up in sequence.

Under the Polaroids were index cards scrawled with entries taken directly from Frank's diaries. Over the past few years, whenever his blackouts had flared up, Frank had recorded them in his journals. He figured that the documentation might help with future medical treatment or therapy. But now they were forming a mosaic of clues.

Frank stared at the photograph of the window, as the Polaroid developed, going from milky to darker, richer colors. It was easier for him to be objective when looking at photographs. It was how he had been trained. It was the way of the crime lab. When Frank looked at the real objects, he sometimes missed things. But now he was staring at a shot of his own kitchen window, the congealed paint around the sill, the crank lock in the lower right hand corner.

Something clicked in his brain.

In the picture, through the dusty vinyl blinds, Frank could see the fire escape ladder leading down to the back alley, and the battered metal garbage Dumpster down in the shadows. Frank glanced over at the index card next to the photo. Fever-chills spidered up his back.

He went over to the window and opened the crank lock, then swung open the hinged pane. He looked down at the weathered iron steps leading down to the cracked pavement, the mounds of soggy newspapers and trash.

"Wait a minute," Frank murmured under his breath.

He strode back to the bulletin board and looked at the picture, and then read the journal entry underneath it, scrawled in his cramped handwriting. It was a recent entry, from only last week.

Can't sleep again tonight! Dizzy as hell, nerves fried... What's wrong with me? What's wrong with me?

Turning away from the bulletin board, panic squeezing his chest, he tried to think back to that night five days ago when he felt so dizzy. He remembered going into the bathroom and throwing open the medicine cabinet, looking for his Verapamil for his heart murmur. And then he remembered going into the kitchen, and making himself a sandwich.

But he had never gotten a chance to eat it. He had blacked out on the kitchen floor.

And he had awakened in another part of the apartment, his bare feet filthy, cracked, and bloody.

"Wait a minute, wait-a-minute, wait-a-minute," he muttered, his heart jittering. He went over to the VCR, his pulse thumping in his ears. He pressed the PLAY button and watched the TV screen, the image flickering for a moment, then locking onto the mysterious talking head.

"—only come out when Frank's asleep—"

Frank punched the FAST-FORWARD button, then pressed PLAY again.

"—I'm doing God's work—"

Frank hit the PAUSE button again glancing at the window, the anger seething inside him. He pressed the FAST-FORWARD button, then hit the PLAY button again.

"It's pretty amazing, how it works. It's like I live in a cocoon, and I turn into a butterfly every few nights when Frank finally drifts off to sleep—"

Frank slammed his hand down on the PAUSE button, the monstrous version of him frozen on the TV, eyes glowing with tiny orange specks of light.

Like cinders smoldering.

"Son of a bitch!" Frank cried, then spun away from the TV and kicked the bulletin board as hard as he could, and the blow cracked the cheap corkboard down the middle, jarring the photographs and note cards loose, sending them fluttering to the floor.

Then he turned to the bookcase and swiped his hand across the contents of the shelf. Tapes, paperbacks, and LPs careened to the floor. An old cracked, yellowed photo album fell open on the rug. Frank stood there for a moment, staring down at the photo album, his fists clenching.

It had fallen open to a boyhood photograph of Frank and Kyle in snowsuits, circa early seventies.

Frank knelt. He picked up the album, holding it with trembling hands. He rubbed his fingertip across the yellowed plastic protective layer. It was a snapshot of him and Kyle on a toboggan at Garvey Park, a few blurry figures in the background. One of the figures was the Old Greek, the boys' guardian, Uncle Andreas, his big, bushy handlebar mustache barely visible under the hood of his parka.

Frank turned the page.

And he stared.

And somehow, deep down, Frank knew exactly what he had to do before he even saw the picture.

It was another grainy black-and-white snapshot—this one showing a heavyset woman in a housedress with dark circles under her eyes, smoking a cigarette, leaning against a cheap formica counter in some low-rent Chicago bungalow. She was smirking at the camera, half embarrassed, half defiant. There was a plastic Flintstones cup next to her on the counter, alongside a sixteen-ounce can of Colt 45 malt liquor.

It was one of the most indelible memories Frank had of his mother. The way she drank her beer out of that silly Flintstones cup.

Frank knew what he had to do even before he laid eyes on her picture.

It took Frank five and a half hours to make it up the dark river of asphalt called Highway 94 to the outskirts of Green Bay. Blinded by the passing lights of long-haul semis, head buzzing with the Dexedrine drone, Frank was driving a '96 Honda Civic that badly needed new plugs and points, and when it got up around seventy-five it vibrated furiously. But it had a good stereo, which helped Frank think and stay awake.

He reached Clarendon at around midnight.

A state facility, comprised of about fifty acres of desolate wetlands and aging brick buildings, Clarendon Psychiatric Hospital had always enjoyed a long-term reciprocal agreement with the Cook County Psychiatric Association, housing many of Chicago's overflow mental patients. At night, the winding two-lane that led up to the main building was fairly imposing, a narrow channel shrouded by hemlock and black pine, broken only by the occasional reflector pole or errant deer.

Arriving through a cloud of fog, Frank steered the Civic up the snaking access road, his vision blurred from lack of sleep and night blindness. He parked in the visitor's lot and went into the main building through the side entrance.

The place smelled of misery, old urine, disinfectant, and overcooked gruel. Frank checked in with the central reception desk, flashing his detective's shield in order to get in after hours. He was directed to Dr. Hemphill's assistant. Frank thanked the nurse and strode down the main corridor, by-passing the assistant's office and heading straight for the special care ward.

Helen Janus's room was number 177–B, which was the last room on the right. Frank had to go through two security doors, and flash his badge at twice as many orderlies in order to get to his mother. When he finally reached her room, his palms were sweating. He gently opened her door, expecting to see her unconscious, hooked to IV tubes, mouth slack, eyes rolled back in her head as she had been before.

But when he stepped inside the private room, he was greeted by one very noisy, very hungry surprise.

13

"You zee pudding man?"

The old woman's voice croaked out across the room on a burble of phlegm. Amazingly, Helen Janus was sitting up against her headboard, eyes open and awake, staring directly at Frank, the loose flesh beneath her chin jiggling. She had bandages wrapped around her wrists.

"Mom?"

"Veneeela pudding—I order eet hours ago!"

"Mom, it's me, it's Frankie," Frank said softly, coming over to her bedside. He was shaking furiously now. He didn't know what to do.

"I order eeet hours ago!"

"I'm not the pudding man, Mom, I'm your son, Frank, Frankie, your son."

"Vat does a girl need to do to get pudding around here?"

"It's Frankie, Mom."

She waved a plump, arthritic hand, the fat under her massive arm swaying. "Eeet's no use," she said, and then she put her face in her ruined hands.

Frank cautiously came around and put a hand tenderly on her shoulder.

And that's when he saw the cup.

The cup.

It was sitting on her bedside tray. Someone must have gone down and fetched it from her personal trunk in the

basement storage room. It was empty, dry as flint, the
cartoon characters long faded off its side. You could
barely see Fred Flintstone's trademark yellow animal-
skin tunic, Wilma's bouffant. It probably still smelled of
rancid Colt 45.

It was Helen's security blanket.

Something about that Flintstones cup sent Frank reeling backward in time . . .

. . . and for one long excruciating moment, he saw
his mother's whole sad life flicker across his mind like
a nickelodeon.

America in the 1950s.

A lonely Levittown tract home.

*Hiding from the world, barely able to speak English,
newlywed Helen Janus finds herself living the life of a
recluse, while her husband, Constantin, travels the eastern
seaboard in his beat-up Nash as a Fuller brush salesman.
Conny Janus is a heavy drinker and a womanizer, and
he takes advantage of every opportunity to stray. Along
the way, he acquires not only emphysema and cirrhosis
of the liver, but a major case of gonorrhea. Meanwhile,
Helen is gaining weight and becoming the town flake. She
papers her windows with the covers of movie star maga-
zines, and she talks to voices, and she dresses in men's
slacks, which is highly scandalous to the neighbors. But
her illness is just beneath the surface, buried in eccentrici-
ties. The undiagnosed schizophrenia becomes an integral
part of her life, like a wooden leg or a set of dentures.*

*By the time the children come, the Januses are living in
Chicago, their marriage teetering on the brink. Constantin
is drinking a quart of port wine every day now and avail-
ing himself of the local prostitutes on a regular basis.
Helen balloons to nearly three hundred pounds and starts
taking phenobarbital for her "nervous spells." She is also
talking to pictures of Jesus Christ and Sophia Loren. It is
a miracle the boys are born healthy. Little Frankie comes*

first, in the spring of '64, and a couple of years later, little Kasos (aka Kyle) is born.

Helen is strangely galvanized by motherhood. It touches off some deep instinct within her, and she showers the kids with affection. The children become her *raison d'être.* Her solitary purpose on this earth. She loses sixty pounds, and her schizophrenia goes into a sort of remission. Unfortunately, the stress of raising two little boys is too much for her marriage. One morning, Constantin just ups and vanishes. No note, no sign that he had ever lived in their little brick bungalow other than a few empty drawers and the lingering smell of stale cigars and Aqua Velva aftershave.

Helen is left to fend for herself and her children.

She does the best she can under the circumstances. She gets a job in a sweatshop on Damen Avenue sewing tent canvas, and she starts dating a succession of single men around the neighborhood. Frankie and Kyle get used to seeing a different "uncle" in their mother's bed every night. Money is tight, and sometimes the neighborhood kids tease the boys about their "crazy mom," and once in a while the voices plague Helen late at night. But mostly things are okay because Helen Janus adores her children with every fiber of her being.

Even on the night of the murder, the boys know that their mother adores them.

It's Frank who first stumbles upon the bloody scene. Only ten years old, his bare feet cold on the hardwood floor, he peers into his mother's bedroom and sees the blossom of deep scarlet on the curtains. He sees the school teacher's body splayed across the bed, half naked, the flesh marbled in blood. He sees the schoolteacher's head lolled backward, the left eye a tiny black pocket of gore. And Frank sees his mother, sitting on the edge of the bed, murmuring under her breath, conversing with one of her voices, her enormous breasts dangling inside her robe, her plump fingers gently cradling the .38 special in her lap as though it were a lost kitten.

*She glances up at Frank then—gazing through a blue
veil of cordite smoke—and she says in her thick Greek
accent, "Jez ree-membeer thet I luff you, Frankie."*

*And even after the cops come and take Helen away,
and the courts send the boys downstate to live with their
Uncle Andreas and Aunt Nikki, and the system all but
banishes Helen to a lifetime of institutions . . . those words
continue to fester in the recesses of Frank's burgeoning
mind. I love you, Frankie. What does she really mean by
that? What does it mean for a mother to love a child as
furiously as Helen? Does it mean people have to die? Is
it all Frankie's fault?*

*These questions will haunt Frank Janus for the rest of
his days.*

*Especially late at night. Especially when he can't get
to sleep.*

"Mom, please—"

Back in the here and now. Frank kneeling next to
the bed. Moonlight spilling on hospital sheets, a plump,
rheumatoid hand clutching the linen.

"It's Frankie, Mom, please, listen to me, it's important—" Frank was leaning toward Helen's headboard,
his lips only inches away from her liver-spotted ears. He
couldn't stand it anymore. He had to ask her the question. Whether she understood or not.

He had to ask her.

"Mom, can you hear me?"

Her lidded eyes gazed up at him. "You're not zee
pudding man."

"No, Mom, I'm not the pudding man, I'm your son—"

"My—?"

"Your son, Mom—*Frankie*—it's Frankie."

Eyes blinking, creases around her mouth deepening.
"Frankie?"

"I need to ask you something," Frank said, his throat
filling with a lump, his eyes moistening. All of a sudden
he felt nine years old again, and it was late at night, and

he had wet the bed again, and now he had to ask his mommy to clean him up. "It's very important," he said.

"Frankie—"

"That's right, Mom, it's Frankie, and I have to ask you something very important. Do you understand?"

"My baby," she said, and her hand fluttered around his face like an injured bird.

"That's right," Frank said, his throat squeezing his words, his voice breaking. He had to get the question out before he broke down. "I need to ask you something, Mom, something about me."

"Some-zing about my little Frankie?"

"Think hard, Mom, it's important."

The old woman's face warmed, her eyes glistening, filling with affection. "Vot's the matter, Frankie? Tell me vot's the matter."

A tear broke and tracked down Frank's cheek. "Am I sick, Mom?"

"You are not feeling well, honey?"

"No, Mom, it's not that," Frank said, wiping his eyes. He was fighting the tears with everything he had. "What I want to know is, am I ill? Like you? Am I mentally ill? Did you ever notice anything? When I was growing up? Later? Anything at all?"

The old woman pressed a palsied hand to Frank's cheek. "You are my baby boy," she said.

"I know, Mom, but—"

"You are zee sweetest child I ever saw," she said, her big dark eyes shimmering. "Never gave your mudder any problem, always the sweetest boy."

Frank closed his eyes and wept.

"Frankie?" Helen's voice was like a rustle of dead leaves in the silent room.

Frank swallowed all the blackness and pain. For a moment, he couldn't find his voice. His knees ached from kneeling. He felt as though he were taking some kind of horrible communion.

"Frankie?"

Frank opened his eyes and looked at her.

She was grinning, showing her yellowed teeth and crumbling bridgework. "I know vot you are doing," she said with a smirk.

"What?"

"You cannot fool me," she said.

"I don't understand, Mom, what are you talking about?"

The old woman pointed a pudgy, bent finger at him. "You're trying to fool me into letting you stay up."

"Excuse me?" Frank wiped his eyes, wiped his mouth. He was nonplussed.

"You ought to be in bed, Frankie," she said.

"Mom—"

"Look at zee time, Frankie, ees way past your bed time."

"Mom, I'm trying to—"

"You know vot happens to boys who stay up past their bedtimes," she said.

Frank didn't answer.

The old woman wagged her trembly sausage finger at him. "Zee sleep poleeese come and get you, Frankie."

Frank stared at her yellowed eyes. A cool tremor knitted down his spine.

After a long moment, he said very softly, "You're right, Mom."

"To bed you go now, Frankie. Okay?"

"Okay, Mom, I will."

She smiled, patting his hand. "Turn out zee light on your way, huh?"

"I will, Mom. I love you." Frank stood up, leaned over the bed and kissed her forehead. She smelled like body odor and Minute-Rub.

Frank started for the door.

Helen's voice trailing off behind him: "And ask zem, vot's a girl got to do to get some pudding around here?"

On his way home, the hallucinations started.

He was on the Edens Expressway, a few miles south

of the Illinois border, chewing a caffeine tablet, his denim shirt damp with sweat, his eyes burning from fatigue and overworked tear ducts. His mind was a broken kaleidoscope of fractured memories and half-formed fears. He was staring at the flickering white lines in his headlights, the sky just starting to bruise a pale blue predawn glow on the horizon, when the first image flashed up at him—

(—*his own fingers manipulating a syringe*—)

—and Frank slammed his eyes shut, nearly losing control of the Honda.

The car jagged across the center line, kissing the gravel shoulder and sending a spume of dust up into the night. Frank wrestled the steering wheel. His heart leaped in his chest. And he just barely avoided sideswiping a guard rail before pulling the car back in line.

He swallowed the urge to scream and felt a tide of dread rising in him as black and poisonous as cancer. The vision had popped out of the dark passing forest like a jack-in-the-box, and now it had touched off something inside him. Old emotions were flooding through his veins. Like when he and his brother had to go live with his Aunt Nikki, and Frank had acted out his anger by burning down the toolshed. The guilt had been unbearable. Denatured, hundred-proof guilt, flowing through him, making him sick to his stomach.

Now he was drowning in guilt for something a million times more savage.

He gripped the wheel tighter, and he concentrated on nothing but the road for several miles, as the dawn lightened the sky, melting from a dull gray to a faded salmon color. The approaching day was making Frank's head pound. He was up to seventy-two waking hours now without much more than a few scattered blackouts of sleep.

He was reaching for the cigarette lighter with trembling hands when the next hallucination jumped out at him from the dashboard—

(—his own hand clutching a curved hunting knife, thrusting it into the soft pale meat of a woman's belly—)

Frank cringed, and the car swerved as the dread spurted through his arteries.

Shame flowed through him. Self-loathing coursed through his marrow. How in God's name could he have done these things? Even with an alter personality, how could Frank have done these things with his own hands? He wanted to kill himself. He wanted to yank the wheel and careen across the median into oncoming traffic, but that would only raise the tally of victims who had died at his hand.

He managed to make it all the way back to the North Shore without passing out.

Later, Frank would remember driving off the road near the B'hai Temple in Wilmette. He would remember his hands going numb on the steering wheel, and his vision clouding, and the Honda cobbling over a sidewalk, then sliding down an embankment and into a deserted construction site.

The last thing he would remember—before blacking out—was coming to a rest near an abandoned Porta Potti and trying to get his door open. It was futile. He had nowhere to go, no place to hide. And besides, how does a person hide from their self?

But the worst part was just before Frank passed out: The feeling smoldering deep down inside him, a tiny glowing ember of hope that he was innocent . . .

. . . a tiny glowing ember that was slowly but surely being extinguished.

14

A dog barking.

Eyes fluttering open, the cool grit of old linoleum pressed against Frank's cheek.

Frank tried to move, but he found his body as brittle and immovable as deadwood, and when he tried to tilt his head to get a better look at his surroundings, the light seemed to close in around him, the shadowy tunnel ahead of him shifting and stretching away like a spyglass turning inside out. He could smell the oily, black odors of resins and burning rubber. Spanish *Vato* music played through cheap speakers somewhere.

He managed to sit up, his head spinning, sudden pain shearing along his spine. His stomach was scoured empty, and there was dried vomit along the front of his denim shirt. He looked around and realized he was in the filthy back hallway of a greasy little body shop somewhere in the city. He could hear the whine of power drills behind him, rowdy voices speaking in Spanish, metallic hammering noises. Yellowed *Playboy* calendars hung on the walls above him, and sunlight slanted in from an open garage doorway about twenty feet away.

Frank looked down at his watch. It was almost noon. How long had he been out?

He turned toward the open doorway, the glare of sunlight making him blink. He rubbed his eyes and tried to focus on the outside. Through the doorway he could see

another innocuous alley, the pavement stained with
grease, the far wall emblazoned with graffiti. Somebody
had written "SUCK MY COCK" in orange Rust-Oleum
spray paint, and a page of newsprint was tumbling by on
a noxious breeze.

There was an object resting on the cement near the
open doorway.

Frank's heart began to flutter as he gaped at the object. His muscles were seizing up all of a sudden, his
mouth fast-drying. The object was obviously meant for
him. A special delivery from a ghost. He managed to
rise to his feet. He barely noticed his joints screaming
with pain, or the dizziness washing over him, or the fact
that his skull felt as though it had been bashed in with
a baseball bat.

He was too fixated on the tiny package sitting on the
pavement near the door.

He walked over to it, knelt down, and picked it up. It
weighed about the same as the other unmarked package,
and when Frank shook it, the sound of grommets rattled
loosely. It was most certainly another videotape. But this
time, there was an additional layer of cruelty. An extra
element of sick humor that was turning Frank's stomach.

The thing was all wrapped up like a birthday present,
with pastel confetti paper and a neat little pink bow.

The sun was hot and angry on the back of Sully Deets's
neck as he trudged up a flight of stone steps leading up
to the threshold of Frank Janus's apartment building.
All around Deets, the Chippewa Park neighborhood was
bustling with activity. The air smelled of tar and exhaust,
and the sound of a distant jackhammer grated on
Deets's nerves.

The sad fact was, Deets was about to do something
that he never dreamed in a million years he would have
to do as a homicide detective. Sure, he had been in the
shit now and again over the years. He had seen domestics
that would make *Night of the Living Dead* seem like a

Disney movie. And one time he had even been forced to fish a severed head out of the Chicago River with a bamboo pole. He had seen everything. But he had never ever expected to question his own partner in a series of gruesome serial murders.

He reached the front porch and paused, pulling out a hankie to wipe his neck.

Just a few minutes ago, Deets had gotten word from the Cook County Coroner that they had finally identified the Jane Doe from Little Pakistan by running the corpse's fingerprints through the National Automated Fingerprint Identification System. She was Sandra Louise Dreighton, thirty-three years old, formerly residing at the Heart of Chicago transient hotel. Also known as Jennifer Juggs, she was a former house dancer down at the Treasure Chest on Wells Street. She had been in and out of the Gateway Treatment Center three times over the last decade for cocaine addiction, and she had a five-year-old daughter currently residing in a foster home. Maybe poor Sandra Louise had been trying to clean her life up at the time of her death. Maybe not. Deets would never know.

Deets stared at the row of metal mailboxes. Frank's was the last one. Deets paused, gazing at the doorbell button below it. A fly buzzed and ticked nervously against the transom over the door.

They didn't pay Deets enough to deal with shit like this, especially since he had only been given three merit raises in over twenty years on the job—first as a uniform, then in Property Crimes, and then in Homicide. And now *this*. A mere three years away from his pension, standing in the heat outside Frank Janus's place, sick to his stomach, about to give the third degree to the best partner he ever had.

Over the course of his tenure with the CPD, Sully Deets had seen all types, from the good to the bad to the plugugly. On more than one occasion, Deets had heard of cops going off the track and turning violent. But Frank Janus was unlike any other cop Deets had

ever encountered. Frank Janus was gold. Frank Janus
was a mensch. Sure, he was a little delicate, a little edgy,
but God damn it, there was nobody Deets would rather
have watching his back.

Unfortunately, Deets could no longer ignore the hunch
that had been twisting around in his gut for days. It had
started with the strange behavior Frank had exhibited at
the scenes. And it had grown as the evidence mounted.
The heel imprint from a high-fashion loafer that matched
Frank's, the hair follicle that matched a hair taken off
Frank's desk, the fragment of a Marlboro cigarette that
Deets had finally connected to Frank's own brand, and
the series of fibers found under Sandra Louise Dreighton's fake nails that matched fibers from Frank's locker.
And then there was the weird incident with the bomb
squad, and whatever was on that videotape. And finally,
the realization that all three thumb suckers had resided
within a three-mile radius of Frank's apartment.

Deets had run out of options.

He sighed, and he was reaching for the door buzzer—
in fact, his hand was literally poised in the air over the
button—when a shrill sound suddenly chirped from his
pocket.

His beeper.

Deets dug the device out of his pocket and looked at
the display. It was a dispatch number with the 187 suffix
at the end. There had been another murder somewhere
in Deets's sector, and Deets was needed.

Relieved, Deets turned and hurried back down the
stone steps.

Saved by the bell.

Frank took a CTA bus north along the lake shore with
the birthday gift tucked under his arm, his mind writhing
with panic. He felt the stares of other passengers. He
looked atrocious, wrinkled and pale and sick.

He made it back to Wilmette by 1:00 P.M., and he
found the Honda in a tow-lot near the north edge of the

Northwestern University campus. He flashed his shield at the cashier, and he got his car back without much of a problem.

He headed straight home, the birthday gift burning a hole on the passenger side.

When he arrived back at his apartment, he didn't even bother to change out of his clothes or go to the bathroom. He went immediately into his living room and switched on his VCR and TV. He looked down at the birthday gift clutched in his hands, and noticed something was wrong. It felt wet. He looked at his hand and saw blood.

He dropped the gift.

His palm was smeared with blood. Deep, scarlet blood, as thick and shiny as thirty-weight oil.

Dizziness yanked at him, threatened to knock him off his feet. His knees wobbled. He brought his hand up to his nose and smelled the unmistakable coppery aroma. He rubbed his fingers together and felt the silky texture of the blood. His guts were as tight as a noose, his bowels burning. He looked down the floor and saw the birthday gift.

Tiny droplets of blood had spattered the carpet where he had dropped the gift.

"Christ," Frank uttered with horror. "Christ—*Christ*—"

He managed to reach down and grab the gift off the floor. Then he stumbled into the kitchen, ran water in the sink, rinsed his hands and wiped the package with a paper towel. A dab of blood was beaded on the end of the faucet, a few drops in the seams and cracks of the counters. Frank madly wiped it away, mind in a frenzy.

Whose blood was it? Frank's cop-instinct was sending up warning alarms through his brain. There was blood all over his apartment now. Somebody's DNA was in the cracks of his kitchen counters, spotting the rug in his living room. Now Frank was having a hard time drawing a breath, his chest squeezing tighter and tighter. It felt as though his heart was about to explode.

He opened the birthday present with wet, trembling hands.

He stood there for a long moment, frozen in terror as he stared at the contents of the package.

There were two items. One of them was another unmarked videotape, another malignant shell of plastic just waiting to infect Frank's life with more poison. And the other item—the source of the blood—was wrapped in a thin membrane of sodden Kleenex.

Frank carefully opened the Kleenex and gazed down at the grotesquely flattened object.

It was the severed remains of a human ear, with a row of delicate little silver rings pierced through it.

15

The whir of the videotape, the hollow click of the play-back heads . . .

Standing in front of the TV, absolute horror constricting his throat, flooding his eyes, squashing his heart, Frank felt his entire world contracting into a tight black tunnel around that cathode-ray tube in front of him. The flicker of blue light filling the tunnel for a moment, a series of electronic spurts and crackles coalescing into an image . . .

(A shaky, hand-held view of an empty apartment, the camera moving through familiar rooms, glimpses of scarred hardwood floors, and walls spattered and smeared with blood. The image bounces and jags toward the bathroom, as though the camera operator is merrily walking through this deadly-still apartment. The sound of breathing can be heard.)

A single tear began to track down Frank's cheek as he gaped at the terrible video. He was shaking now. He knew what was coming next.

(The camera enters the modest little bathroom, shakily panning across a porcelain sink to a claw-foot bathtub in the corner. A black plastic curtain is drawn. Blood droplets stipple the tub and the walls behind it.)

Frank recognized the bathroom. The magazine rack filled with literary quarterlies. The toiletries lined up along the back of the toilet.

Clenching his fists so tightly his fingernails began to dig into the flesh of his palms, Frank didn't want to see what was coming next, and yet he could not tear his eyes away.

(The camera settles on the commode, and then a figure steps in front of the lens: It's Frank. The Bad Frank. The Angry Frank. Dressed in a painter's coverall splattered with congealed blood, he stares into the lens, breathing hard. He looks like a man trying to control his raging temper. His eyes are rimmed in red, as though he's been crying. He takes a deep breath, then says, "You fucking prick, you had to watch that videotape. You had to stick your nose where it doesn't belong—")

Frank watched in horror, his knuckles turning white from the pressure of his fists.

(The on-screen Frank twitches with anger and says, "You want to see what happens when certain cops refuse to mind their own business and don't stop being so nosy?" Then he reaches behind himself, and he shoves the shower curtain aside, revealing the surprise guest lying in the tub.)

"Ah-Jesus-no," Frank moaned in agony, his body seizing up at the sight of his brother.

(The camera holding for one excruciatingly long moment on the dead body.)

Frank slammed his eyes closed, the terror and revulsion erupting in him.

It wasn't possible, it couldn't be, it just couldn't be, not like this . . .

Frank managed to look back up at the screen, the abomination screaming at him, and the image of his own face leering back at him like an obscene gibbous moon. It was too much for him. He tried to scream something at the screen, but his voice got tangled up in his throat. And finally all the bile and horror rose up in him, and he lurched forward, collapsing to his knees.

He roared vomit all over the rug.

(On the screen, Frank's brother Kyle is lying stone-dead

in the tub, curled into a fetal position, his thumb in his mouth, the side of his face a bloody pulp.)

Frank heaved the rest of his guts out, then managed to wipe his face.

The Video-Frank was saying something else into the camera—something clever and cruel—but Frank could hear nothing now but the rushing jet-engine sounds in his ears. Perhaps it was the sound of his own sanity swirling down the drain.

"WHY?!"

Frank lashed out at the TV, shoving it with all his might backward off the shelf.

The monitor bounced off the back wall, then tumbled forward to the floor. The tube shattered on impact, making a horrendous cracking noise, followed by a fizzing high-voltage pop that seemed to envelop the TV for a moment. Frank cried out in garbled, inarticulate rage, as a thick metallic odor of burning circuits filled the room.

Sobbing, choking on his own rage, Frank lunged at the VCR. He tore the videotape out of the deck, then rended it to pieces with his bare hands.

"WHY?!"

He hurled the pieces to the floor and stomped on them.

Then he collapsed again.

Face buried in his hands, body convulsing, Frank sobbed uncontrollably on the bloodstained Oriental rug for several moments. He kept repeating Kyle's nickname—*Boomer-Boomer-Boomer*—and then—*"I'm so sorry, I'm so sorry, I'm so sorry, Boomer"*—and the horror and revulsion were pressing down on Frank like a gigantic invisible hand of an angry god, and he sank to the floor.

Darkness closed in around him, along with the vile tide of self-loathing. He could hardly breathe, the shock was so overwhelming.

And he lay there like that for several moments.

Until he heard the sounds.

*   *   *

A pair of sedans skidding to a halt, almost simultaneously, against the curb outside the Chippewa Park building—an unmarked Crown Victoria and a black-and-white beat car, radios crackling. A big man wearing a cheap rayon sportcoat, his sidearm bulging beneath the hem, emerged from the Ford. Two uniformed cops emerged from the black-and-white.

"I'll take care of the formalities," Sully Deets said to the uniforms. "You two just stay in the background, back me up if you have to."

Deets started up the stone steps.

The uniforms followed him, unsnapping the safety straps off their service revolvers as they came. They had to hustle to keep up with the big man, who was striding up the steps two-at-a-time, his big fleshy face all grim and set. The younger of the two uniforms—a kid named Foley, only eighteen months out of the academy—sensed something was going on. Not only were they about to put the collar on one of their own—a decorated detective yet—but their honcho, Deets, was real conflicted about the whole thing. Something was very wrong with this picture, and it was making Foley nervous.

A dispatcher's voice suddenly sizzled out of Foley's hip radio.

Deets shot the kid a glance on his way up the steps. "This is my partner we're dealing with here, not some skell. I don't want anybody hard-nosing, or anybody flashing any iron. You got that?"

Foley and his partner nodded.

Deets reached the top of the stairs, pausing to fish in his pocket for a skeleton key. "I'll do the talking," he said, glancing back at the other two.

As if there was any question as to who would be doing the talking.

Prostrate on the floor, engulfed in a haze of grief and shock, Frank could hear the crackle of a police radio outside, nearby, and the sound of it did something to Frank.

He sat up, his ears ringing, his whole body feeling galvanized, as though it had suddenly undergone a transformation from one element to another. He stood up, the image of his brother dying like an animal vibrating in his head. Frank shuddered, his eyes pressing shut, trying to will the image out of his brain. "I'm so sorry, Boomer," he uttered under his breath.

The police radio was getting closer. It was in his building now, downstairs, in the front foyer. And all at once a series of realizations were streaming through Frank's mind: the Thumb Sucker Killer was inside him, a parasite who had killed his own brother, a monster, a sideshow attraction, and Deets was too smart a cop not to figure it out, and now Frank's life was over, it was over, and there was really only one last opportunity to take responsibility for his sickness.

One last chance.

Outside his door, in the hallway: footsteps, the sizzle of a dispatcher's voice.

Frank rushed over to the closet, threw open the door and tossed aside the hanging coats and plastic-wrapped dry cleaning. He found the shotgun clipped to plastic brackets against the back wall. It was a Remington Model 870 from Frank's patrol days, a cutdown version with a nine-inch barrel, a seven-round magazine and a pistol grip—the same kind of weapon carried by the presidential protection detail of the Secret Service. Frank tore it off the brackets.

The shotgun was mostly for home defense nowadays, especially since the mere sound of the pump-action slide was enough to scare off any burglars. But right now Frank needed it for insurance. Insurance that he would be given a chance to do the right thing. That's all he wanted.

One chance.

There was a knock on the front door—loud and fast—and then a voice.

"Bambi?"

Frank's spine straightened. It was amazing how fast his world was coming unraveled.

He went over to the door, gripping the shotgun tightly, wiping the tears and snot off his face onto his shoulder. He tried to talk. "That you, D?"

Through the door: "Yeah, Bambi, it's me."

"How ya doin', D?"

"All right, I guess. You know. Things could always be better."

Frank sniffed back his tears and tried to focus. "I'm gonna open the door, D."

"Okay."

"I'm opening the door now, D," Frank said, raising the shotgun, aiming it at the gap, hands trembling wildly. He unlatched the deadbolt.

Then he cracked the door a few inches.

Outside, in the hallway, the three cops stiffened at the sight of the shotgun, looking like cats arching their backs: Deets frozen, wide-eyed, the two uniforms behind him instinctively reaching for their Smith & Wessons.

Deets shot his hand up. "It's okay, we're all friends here. It's okay."

"How's it going, D?"

"No complaints, Bambi, you know how it is."

"Who'd listen, right?"

"Exactly."

The cop named Foley suddenly drew his gun.

Frank yanked the pump back with a loud clang.

"Put it away, Foley," Deets said, his gaze riveted to the barrel of Frank's 870.

Foley started to say, "But—"

"PUT THE GODDAMN PIECE AWAY, FOLEY!"

The younger uniform reluctantly holstered his gun. The heat in the hallway was tremendous. Faces were already glistening with sweat.

"Sorry about all this, D," Frank said finally.

"Don't worry about it, Bambi."

"I'm not doing too good," Frank said.

Deets nodded. "I know."

Frank swallowed a lump of grief. "You're here to tell me about my brother, right?"

Deets chewed the inside of his cheek for a moment. "I'm still a little unclear on what's been going on."

"You and me both, D," Frank said.

"They tell me I'm supposed to take you down," Deets said.

"That's what I figured."

"I'm sorry, Bambi."

Frank looked at him, tried to keep the tears at bay. "You got something solid off my brother's scene?"

Deets nodded. "Yeah, actually, we got a couple of things. Some more fibers, some handwriting."

"Handwriting?"

Deets looked ill. He sighed. "Stuff written in blood. On the walls."

Frank looked at him. "On the walls?"

"Yeah."

Frank flashed back to the smears of blood in the video, or perhaps he was flashing back to an actual memory. He swallowed hard. "You mind telling me what it said, D?"

"Something about sleep."

"Sleep?"

"Yeah, something about the 'sleep police.' It was in your handwriting, Bambi."

Cold liquid streamed down Frank's spine. "Crime lab guys figured that out at the scene?"

"I recognized it," Deets said softly.

Frank nodded.

"Got all kinds of prints, too," Deets went on. "Did a rapid check at the scene, just to make sure. Got a hundred and eleven matches."

"Okay, D, I see what you're up against," Frank said.

One of the uniforms put his hand on his gun.

Frank raised the shotgun.

Deets put a hand up. "We're just talking here, fellas, no need to get ornery over this thing."

"Sorry," the uniform muttered.

"I can't let it go down like this, guys," Frank said. "I'm real sorry."

"What do you need, Frank?" Deets asked.

"It's just—" Frank paused, wiping his tears with his shoulder.

"You name it, Bambi, we'll do what we can."

"I appreciate it, D, it's just—" Another pause.

"We're here for ya."

"Okay. Look. Um . . ."

Pause.

Deets was licking his lips thoughtfully, sweat shimmering on his forehead. "Whatever it is, Frank, we'll do our best to get it for you."

"Okay, here's the thing," Frank said. "Would it be okay if you guys waited here for one second? I need to go get something, and I'll be right back. Okay?"

There was a tense pause, as Deets exchanged glances with the other cops.

Frank watched them. "I won't do anything crazy, guys, I promise."

After a moment, Deeds nodded. "Go ahead, Bambi, we'll be waiting right here."

16

Frank shuffled backward into the kitchen, keeping the shotgun raised and aimed at the front door.

Frantically scooping the severed ear off the counter with his left hand, gripping the Remington with his right, he moved as swiftly as possible. He grabbed a towel and laid the ear in it. Then he tore open the freezer and grabbed a few ice cubes, then wrapped the ice in the towel.

He was in some kind of a horrible zone. Woozy with shock, reeling with rage and terror. Maybe he wasn't thinking clearly, and maybe he was—it didn't matter anymore. He was long past caring.

He returned to the front door with the bundle tucked under his arm.

Out in the hallway, Deets and the uniforms were drenched in sweat and losing their patience.

"Talk to me, Bambi," Deets said.

"I need you to do two things for me, D, if it's all right," Frank said, his eyes welling.

"I'm listening."

Frank handed the bundle to Deets. "If you don't mind, I'd like you to return this to my brother's body."

Deets looked at the bundle quizzically.

Frank explained, "It's my brother's ear."

A pause as the cops stared.

"If it's okay," Frank went on, "I'd like you to give it to the coroner so he can reattach it."

There was another pause, as the cops looked at the bundle and then at Frank.

"What's the second thing, Bambi?" Deets said.

"The second thing," Frank said, his voice cracking, "is that I'd like to see Pope."

Deets nodded. "We'll have him waiting at the Twenty-fourth when we get there."

"Um, actually, D, what I need is, I need to see Dr. Pope here."

"Here?"

"That's the way I'd really like to do it."

Deets looked at him. "You want us to bring him here?"

Frank nodded, holding the shotgun. "If it wouldn't be too much of a problem."

Deets breathed in a long, pained breath. He glanced at the other cops. Foley, the younger one, was getting very antsy. He shook his head in disgust and whispered something like, "Jesus Christ . . ."

"PLEASE! PLEASE!" Frank was aiming the shotgun at the younger cop, screaming at the top of his lungs, "I'M ASKING YOU GUYS TO DO THIS ONE THING FOR ME! THIS ONE THING! *PLEASE—!!*"

"Okay, Bambi, okay, okay, okay, easy, it's all right," Deets was saying, holding his hands up in surrender.

A pause. Frank was breathing hard, his finger on the trigger.

"Everybody just calm down," Deets said.

"I'm sorry, D," Frank said, cringing at the bolt of pain jabbing up his spine.

Another pause.

"Okay, everybody, let's just take this one step at a time," Deets said.

"I promise you, D, if you make this happen I will make things right."

Deets pursed his lips, thinking, agonizing. Finally he

said, "Okay, here's what we'll do. We'll have to post uniforms in front and in back."

"I understand," Frank said.

"And we'll have to do this quickly, before IAB or Media catches wind of it."

"I agree, D, that's absolutely right," Frank said, wiping another tear off his face.

"Okay, Bambi, here's the deal: You stay put, and I go try to track down the good doctor."

"I really do appreciate it, D."

Deets looked at Frank. "You gotta promise me, though. Some reason I can't find Pope, or he's indisposed, or whatever—"

"I'll come peacefully, D, I swear to God."

Deets let out a long, pained sigh, nodded at the other two cops, then started down the corridor toward the stairs.

Frank watched them leave, then shut his door and shoved the deadbolt home.

He went back into the living room, pulled an armchair across the shards of broken videocassette and sat down facing the front door. He kept the shotgun across his lap, his hand clutching the grip, ready for action.

Then he began composing a speech in his mind.

It was Henry Pope's day off, and when Deets tried to reach the doctor at home, all he got was the doctor's answering machine. So Deets hopped in his Crown Victoria and made a mad haul up Sheridan Road.

By the time Deets arrived in Kenilworth—Pope's neighborhood—word had spread across the entire CPD that one of their own detectives had blown a gasket and was the primary suspect in a series of high-profile, unsolved killings. It had started in the county coroner's lab, after Deets had dropped off the severed ear, and it had spread like a house on fire. Deets's cell phone had rung at least a half a dozen times with frantic inquiries from Armanetti, Krimm, Internal Affairs, and even people from Mayor Daley's office. His radio was boiling with frenzied dispatches, and the Media division was going into overdrive, trying to deal with the so-called "stand-off" that was occurring at this very moment at Detective Janus's apartment building. It was all making Deets's ulcer flare up with a vengeance.

And that's why it was especially incongruous to find Henry Pope at home that day, in the study of his old Victorian painted lady, dozing with his half-glasses on the end of his nose, and a book tented over his potbelly. He looked so peaceful there, like a retired grandfather, slumped in his Hepplewhite armchair, a glass of ice tea and a box of Nilla Wafers next to him.

"Doc?! Hello?!" Deets was standing outside the study's window, gazing through leaded glass at the slumbering doctor. A moment ago, Deets had tried unsuccessfully to get somebody to answer the front doorbell, and now he was knee-deep in impatiens and daffodils, frantically tapping on the window pane.

Through the glass, Pope was stirring.

"Doc! Doc!" Deets tapping madly on the glass.

"Who is it?" Pope mumbled, blinking, coming awake with a start. All around him were countless framed photographs of grand kids. Little porcelain Hummels of children and cherubs, and bronze figurines of babies.

"It's Sully Deets, Doc! CPD! District twenty-four!" Deets was waving outside the window like an idiot.

The old man struggled out of his chair, groaning, setting his book on the coffee table. "What in God's name?" he murmured, shuffling over to the window.

"It's Deets, Doc! Sully Deets!"

"Deets? What the hell are you doing in my window well?" The psychologist was squinting to see through the glass. The sun was glaring.

Deets motioned toward the south, toward the city. "Got a major situation, needs a psych evaluation."

The old man looked nonplussed. He was still half asleep, blinking fitfully.

"*Frank Janus*, Doc," Deets said, glancing at his watch. "Poor guy's having a meltdown, needs a pro."

Pope was blinking at the sun. "Greenthal is on call today, Sully."

"He asked for you, Doc. Come on out, I'll explain the whole thing on the way."

The old man frowned. "On the way? On the way where?"

"I'll explain the whole thing in the car. Come on, Doc. Please. This is a major situation going down here. Frank trusts you. I'm asking you to do this one thing."

There was a pause. The old man took a deep breath, glancing around his study. Finally, he let out a long, pained sigh and turned back to the window. "All right, Sully, let me get my other glasses."

Frank was in his bedroom, trying to rip the floor-length mirror off the back of his door. At the same time, he was clutching the shotgun in his free hand, aiming it at the windows just in case some Tactical guy got heroic.

The mirror wouldn't budge. It was bracketed to the door with plastic screws, congealed with years of paint and grime. Frank finally gave up and searched the room for a tool. He found a metal shoehorn in his dresser drawer and proceeded to pry the edges of the mirror until the corner broke and the whole thing toppled to the floor.

Miraculously the mirror didn't shatter; it only cracked down the middle.

Frank picked up the mirror and hauled it out into the living room.

Working quickly, soaked with flop-sweat and fatigue, holding the shotgun under his arm, he propped the mirror against the wall, near the front doorjamb. He angled it so that it was facing the center of the room, where the broken shards of videocassette and ruined television lay scattered on the faded Oriental rug. Then Frank took his place in front of the looking glass.

Out in the hallway, more police radios were crackling. Reinforcements had been coming for the past hour, ever since Deets had left. There was a boatload out there in the corridor now—uniforms, Tactical people, even a couple of ATF guys. Frank had been watching them arrive every few minutes through his drawn venetian blinds.

The street in front of his place was also buzzing. There were at least a dozen beat cars down there, several unmarked squads, a couple of Tactical wagons and even a media van from one of the local TV affiliates. Yellow crime-scene tape cordoned off the building's entrance, and it wouldn't be long before there was more media. Word had gotten out about the fruitcake holed up in his northside apartment.

Let the freak show begin.

But Frank didn't care about any of that. He had too much to think about now. Crouched down on his living room floor, shotgun under his arm, Frank could feel his brother's spirit worming inside him—betrayed by his own flesh and blood, taken prematurely from this world in a spasm of horror. What kind of terror had poor Kyle known just before dying at the hand of his big brother?

Frank shuddered.

Out in the hallway: Frantic whispers, the sound of several service-issue shotguns cocking.

Frank braced himself, lifting the shotgun, aiming it at the front door. He was prepared for the very real possibility that Deets would not return, that he would not be able to find Dr. Pope, that the SWAT guys would run out of patience and storm Frank's apartment. After all, there were no hostages to worry about—at least none that walked around with a discrete body of their own.

In the cracked mirror next to the door, Frank looked at his hostage: *himself.*

In the mirror, fractured by the spider vein running down the length of the glass, Frank saw his reflection—a frightened, confused, desperate man, wearing a drenched denim shirt, crouched on an Oriental rug with a shotgun and wild eyes. But beneath the surface of the reflection was the Other. The shadow self. The dark alter ego who had crawled out of a hellish corner of Frank's psyche to turn his world into a festering hell.

"Fuck you," Frank said calmly to his reflection.

There was no answer.

"Come on out, you fuck," Frank said. "The world is waiting, we're all waiting."

Still no answer.

Frank swallowed back his terror, and he aimed the shotgun at his own fractured image.

He half expected his face to subtly change when addressed in this fashion, summoning his alter ego to the surface. He wasn't sure exactly how these things worked, but he had seen enough movies. He remembered Lee J. Cobb summoning the alter personalities out of Joanne Woodward in *The Three Faces of Eve*, and he remembered Sally Field summoning her kaleidoscope of personalities in *Sybil*. But those were only movies. This was terribly real. This was a pearl of sweat tracking down the small of Frank's back as the sound of an Ithaca twelve-gauge shotgun chucked and clanged out in the hallway.

"Come on and show your filthy—" Frank stopped suddenly when he heard a familiar voice out in the corridor.

"Frank?"

Frank straightened like a child hearing his father's voice, his hands tightening on the shotgun. It was Henry Pope. Thank God.

"Doc?"

The muffled voice replied, "Yeah, kid. It's me. What's going on?"

Frank let out an anguished sigh. At last, he could finish this thing once and for all . . .

. . . and perform his final act as a policeman.

17

Frank rose up slowly, then hobbled over to the front door. His hands were slick on the butt of the Remington. A droplet of sweat touched one of his eyelids. "I apologize for dragging you down here," he said to the door.

"Tell me what's going on, Frank," the muffled voice said, penetrating the door, sounding monumentally professional. Just a faint flutter of nerves.

"I'm going to open the door now," Frank said. "I'd appreciate it if everybody other than the doctor would step away from the door."

The old man's voice: "Hold on a second, Frank."

There were shuffling sounds, whispers, boots squeaking on the stairs.

"Okay, Frank, it's just me," said the voice.

"I'm going to let you in the apartment," Frank explained, "but before I do that, I want to warn you about a couple of things."

"Go ahead, Frank."

"I've got a shotgun," Frank said.

"I understand," the voice said.

"To be perfectly honest, Doc, it's just to keep everybody at bay until I figure things out."

"Okay."

"I think I got things figured out now."

"Okay, Frank."

"Don't be alarmed by it," Frank said.

"Okay, Frank, fair enough."

"The other thing is, I'm going to open the door quickly, and I'd appreciate it if you would come in with your hands where I can see them. Okay?"

"No problem, Frank."

"Okay, here we go. You ready?"

The voice: "Ready when you are, Frank."

Frank released the deadbolt, then carefully opened the door.

Henry Pope was standing on the threshold, dressed in a corduroy sportcoat, his arms raised, his eyes full of nervous tension behind his bifocals. His grizzled chin was shaking faintly, and his big arthritic hands were trembling above his head.

Frank could feel the scopes of ATF agents on him, the suspicious gazes of Tactical cops boring into him from the far end of the corridor.

He gently grabbed Pope's lapel and pulled him into the apartment.

"I'm sorry to put you through all this, Doc," Frank said, carefully shoving the psychiatrist against the wall next to the mirror.

Then Frank slammed the front door closed, chucking the deadbolt.

"What's going on, Frank?" the old man said. He looked rattled.

"If you don't mind, Doc, I'd like you to keep your hands up for a second." Frank patted the psychiatrist down, searching for suspicious bumps or wires. "Okay, that's great, Doc. You can put them down now."

Pope took a deep breath, trying to calm himself. His hands would not stop shaking. He glanced at the broken mirror, and the pieces of videocassette and busted TV. "Looks like things have gotten a little out of hand," he said softly.

"Yeah, they sure have," Frank said. "Can I ask you to stand over there by the window?"

The doctor nodded, and took his place in front of the venetian blinds.

"Thanks, Doc," Frank said, then stepped back to the center of the living room.

Frank stood facing his reflection. The heat was weighing down on him, heavy and oppressive. Sweat tickled down his forehead, down his chest. He stared at his reflection. His reflection glowered back at him.

"Frank?" Pope's voice pierced Frank's daze. "Can you tell me what's going on?"

"I ran across another videotape," Frank said, his gaze locked on the broken reflection.

Pope nodded.

Frank said, "This time it was my brother."

"I heard," Pope said softly. "I'm sorry, Frank."

Frank felt his guts twisting, the tears like broken glass on his face. "He was only thirty-two years old."

The doctor nodded, didn't say anything.

Frank's nose was running now. "He was working on a novel. Did I mention that? He was halfway through it."

The doctor didn't say anything.

Frank closed his eyes and wept for a moment, and then: "They loved him up at the college."

"I'm sure they did, Frank," the doctor said.

Frank dabbed his eyes on his shoulder, then glared at the cracked looking glass. He raised the shotgun, and aimed it at his broken face.

"Frank?" Pope said nervously.

Frank stared at the mirror, aiming the gun.

"Frank, let's try to cool down a little," Pope said. "All right? Will you do that for me?"

Frank kept staring.

"Frank?"

No answer.

"Frank, will you do me one favor? Will you talk through this thing with me?"

Still no answer.

"Frank, please." Pope's voice was thin and reedy, uncharacteristically tense. "Will you talk to me? Will you do that?"

After a long pause, Frank said, "I've been going over this in my mind."

Another pause.

"That's good, Frank."

"I've made a decision about what I'm going to do."

"Good."

"I'm going to turn myself in."

Pope nodded. "I will help you in any way that I can, Frank, I promise you that much."

"Voluntary commitment," Frank said, staring at that cracked mirror.

"That's fine, Frank."

"Just like you said, Doc."

Pope nodded again, looking faintly relieved. "That's probably the best thing."

"I'll hand myself over to you, Doc, and only you," Frank said.

"You will be treated with respect, Frank. I give you my word on that."

"There just one thing, Doc," Frank said. "Before I turn myself over. I need you to witness something."

There was a pause.

"What is it, Frank?"

Frank looked at his reflection. "You're under arrest," he said, speaking directly to the mirror. "For the murders of Irene Jeeter, Sandra Louise Dreighton, and Kyle Janus."

Then Frank pulled the trigger—

—and the Remington barked—

—and the sound was enormous, a metallic depth charge that tore open the stillness of the little apartment.

The kickback nearly dislocated Frank's shoulder, the blast gobbling a hole in the center of the mirror, sending a thunderhead of dust and debris and silver fragments everywhere, and out in the hallway, the sound of stunned Tactical officers hitting the floor was like a series of drumbeats, the rhythm broken only by startled cries. Then the sounds of pump slides cocking in unison, footsteps hurrying toward Frank's door. The sound of a battering ram thumping into the door.

"WAIT!" Pope's voice was ragged, his face turned away from the concussion. "IT'S OKAY!"

Ears ringing, Frank pumped the Remington, sending a plastic shell casing bouncing across the floor.

Suddenly there was a huge thud, as the battering ram slammed a second time into the door.

"WE'RE ALL RIGHT!" Pope cried out. "PLEASE! GIVE US A SECOND! WE'RE OKAY!"

Frank aimed the shotgun at the shattered mirror. "You have the right to remain silent," he told his reflection, breathing hard and fast.

Pope was trembling. "Frank, please—"

"Anything you say can be used against you in a court of law," Frank informed the alter. A drop of sweat ran into his eye, and he blinked it away.

"Frank, come on—"

"You have the right to consult an attorney before questioning," Frank told his reflection, aiming the shotgun with trembling hands.

"Frank—"

"You have the right to have your attorney present with you during questioning," Frank told the mirror.

"Frank, don't—!"

"If you cannot afford an attorney," Frank went on, breathing hard, aiming the gun, "one will be appointed for you at no expense to you!"

"Okay, Frank, that's good, you made your point."

Pause. Breathing heavily. Glaring at the shattered glass. Clutching his shotgun. "You may choose," Frank said to his reflection between desperate breaths, "to exercise these rights at any time."

Now a long, agonizing pause. Dr. Henry Pope stood there with his back pressed against the wall, his gray face moist, his eyes watering with panic.

Ten feet away, Frank stood there with the shotgun in his sweaty grasp, chest rising and falling, gaze fixed on the ruined mirror by the door. In the webbing of broken glass, his reflection didn't change. It didn't answer. It didn't do anything but stare.

A moment passed.

Then Frank began to weep. He could feel the sobs building in his gut, then rising up his gorge and shaking him. He dropped the shotgun, and the tears poured out of him. He dropped to his knees, and he wept like a baby. His whole body convulsed with sorrow and anguish.

He felt old, arthritic hands on his shoulders, then a skinny arm around his back.

"Let it out, Frank, it's okay," Henry Pope was softly murmuring. The old man had knelt down next to Frank, and was now holding Frank with both arms.

Frank collapsed into the psychiatrist's arms and let the grief wash through him.

"It's okay, it's okay," Pope kept murmuring.

Frank barely heard the pry bar snapping the deadbolt open across the room, or the first of the black-clad Tactical officers shuffling into the apartment in their heavy flak suits and helmets, their assault weapons at the ready.

They came in two-by-two. They systematically secured the room, kicking the shotgun across the hardwood and motioning at each other.

In his watery peripheral vision, Frank saw them descending on him and the doctor. "It's okay," Doctor Pope uttered softly, more to the Tactical guys now than to Frank.

Before long, Frank had cried himself out.

And he huddled there on the floor next to Pope for quite some time, his body numb, his eyes stinging. He was trying to get his bearings back. He was spent. His brother was dead. His life was over. And now all that he had left was a fading sense of responsibility. For his own destiny, his own genetics. His own sickness.

Frank managed to stand. There were fifteen other cops in his apartment now, half of them with their weapons drawn. Frank could smell the leather and machine oil and BO. He looked around at all the faces shimmering with perspiration. He recognized a few of them.

"How ya doing, Tommy?" Frank said to one of the Tac guys standing in the back.

The cop named Tommy nodded sheepishly.

"You okay to walk?" Pope asked Frank.

Frank nodded. "Sure, Doc, absolutely."

The doctor nodded at the other cops, and one of the Tactical guys—a young man with thick glasses named Hazlett—came over and gently patted Frank down. Satisfied there was nothing concealed anywhere, Hazlett carefully escorted Frank across the room and out the door.

In the hallway, Frank paused.

The other cops looked at him.

"You know what, guys," Frank said softly, his voice strained to a near whisper. "You probably ought to cuff me."

PART III

The Endless Night

"We wake from one dream into another dream."
—EMERSON, "Illusions"

18

Dusk closed around the city like a fist.

It was an ugly sunset, the sky turning a dirty, mossy green around 8:00. The air was so still and muggy that phone booths and car windows started fogging with condensation, and trees seemed to droop like tired old dowagers along Michigan Avenue. An angry summer rain was closing in. It rumbled along the horizon to the south, veins of lightning flickering over the steel factories of Gary and Hammond, Indiana.

That's how summers are in Chicago. Passive-aggressive. One day everything's lovely, dry and sunny, and then the weather just gets pissed off and dumps a whole bunch of misery on the lakeshore.

Sitting in the back of an unmarked minivan, heading south on Sheridan Road, Frank watched the first scattered raindrops hitting the windshield. Plink! Plink! Plink! He was shackled now, the two stainless cuffs around his wrist connected to a leather belt, which connected to a chain running down to his ankle cuffs. His joints were stiff and sore, as though he'd recently been electrocuted, and his head was full of cement. Doctor Pope sat beside him, softly talking on his cellular to a hospital administrator. A couple of federal marshals were in the front seat, one of them driving, the other shuffling through a leather portfolio. But all Frank could do was stare at that front windshield, and the drops coming faster and faster.

Plink! Plink-plink-plink!

How did Frank feel? In one sense, the pain was still too vast to get his mind around; the gravity of what had happened had still not completely sunken in, and the twenty milligrams of Trilofan that Pope had given him were only serving to keep Frank calm. He could still think. His mind was still working. And that was tearing him apart. The truth was, he wanted more than anything else to be punished, which, in turn, would punish his alter ego. He wanted to go through incredible hell. He wanted to suffer. Not only for killing his own brother, but for all the selfish, narcissistic things he done in his life. For neglecting Chloe all those years. For neglecting his mother. Frank wanted the rest of his life to be a living hell, full of loneliness, humiliation, and shame.

He was about to get his wish.

They took him to Cook County Hospital for preliminary evaluation and observation, as dictated in the Chicago Police Department protocol. They took him around back to the service entrance in order to avoid the press. By this point, the rain had arrived, and it was coming down in sheets across the crowded parking lot. And much to the marshals' dismay, there were at least half a dozen TV vans and a cluster of hungry crime reporters huddling under the loading dock roof, waiting to pounce on the story. Someone had tipped the media, of course, and the two marshals had to muscle their way through the crowd with Frank shuffling along in his chains like Quasimodo.

Inside the hospital, Frank was deluged by psychiatric staff, police attaches, IAB people, deputies from the mayor's office, and other cops simply trying to lend support. Deets was there as well, with Tom Leavens, one of the city's top criminal attorneys, ready to take on Frank's case. Frank was overwhelmed. He could barely talk.

Dr. Pope made a concerted effort to usher Frank

through processing with a minimum of hassles. They ended up in a starkly furnished interview room in the violence wing—stained white walls, acoustic tile ceiling, two-way mirror, bars on the windows, fortified locks on the door, and the two beefy marshals standing watch. For nearly an hour, Frank sat in that institutional white room on a metal folding chair, smoking cigarettes with his trembling, shackled hands, telling the story of his split personality and murderous alter ego—essentially his confession—to Pope, a county administrator, and a video camera.

Eventually, they made all the notes they were going to make and took Frank to a second interview room.

This second room was only slightly less institutional, with a carpeted floor, blazing fluorescent lights, and drapes drawn across the windows. Frank was shackled to the base of a straight-backed armchair, and given a cigarette. Then he was subjected to a series of formalities. He was interviewed by an old friend, Agent Birnbaum of the FBI, and he was questioned by Sergeant Armanetti and Lieutenant Krimm of the Twenty-fourth. He was allowed fifteen minutes with Tom Leavens, attorney-at-law. A well-groomed, delicate man in a Brooks Bothers suit, Leavens excitedly told Frank about the automatism defense.

In U.S. Common law, sleepwalking is considered a form of automatism (or involuntary behavior). This dictates that criminal acts performed during the condition of sleepwalking can be construed as either unconscious or governed by a form of psychosis, therefore forming the basis of a plea of not guilty by reason of insanity. Or, as the criminal code more succinctly states: *"Subject to the provisions of this Code relating to negligent acts and omissions, a person is not criminally responsible for an act or omission which occurs independently of the exercise of his will or for an event which occurs by accident."*

It didn't matter. Frank was going to take full responsibility for his alter ego's actions, regardless of whether they occurred while Frank was blacked out, asleep, or dancing around, whistling "Dixie." A part of Frank had done these killings, and that meant the whole organism was infected. The whole organism was sick. Frank didn't care whether they gave him the lethal injection or sent him away to an asylum for the rest of his days. That was for others to decide. Frank was just a cop. He had solved the thumb sucker case, and now his life was over.

Tom Leavens took it fairly well. The lawyer assured Frank that he didn't have to make up his mind tonight. There was plenty of time to put together a defense. Leavens was pleasant, courteous, and professional. He left his card on the table next to Frank.

Around ten o'clock they brought Frank some dinner. Baked chicken, peas, mashed potatoes, and apple sauce. Frank was surprised by his own appetite. He ate nearly all of it while the rains droned outside the window. Finally, Frank asked politely if they could bring him a fresh pack of Marlboros.

Five minutes later, Doctor Pope returned with the cigarettes, a worn leather portfolio, and a smile. One of the marshals lingered by the door.

"How they been treating you, Frank?" the doctor asked, sitting down next to Frank. He lit Frank's cigarette.

"Very decently," Frank said.

"You're well liked."

Frank shrugged. "I don't know about that."

"Seriously, the guys around the Twenty-fourth are devastated by all this."

Frank smoked and nodded.

"How are you feeling, Frank?"

"Tired."

Pope looked at him. "You want to sleep?"

The thought hadn't even occurred to Frank. He was so exhausted, he was almost too tired to sleep. "I'm not sure I can," he said.

"I can give you something for the trip," Pope said.

Frank looked at him. "The trip?"

"Yeah, I mentioned it earlier, you probably forgot. We need to transport you to Gale tonight, hopefully under the radar of the media."

Frederick Gale Memorial Psychiatric Hospital was a state facility on the South Side of Chicago with a long-standing relationship with the criminal courts. The facility offered emergency/crises services on a twenty-four-hour basis, as well as a huge, secure campus with a wide array of buildings. Gale was one of the only hospitals of its kind that featured a state-of-the-art wing for high-risk patients. These were people who used to be known in the old politically incorrect days as "the criminally insane."

Frank took a drag off the cigarette and looked at the psychiatrist. "More tests?"

Pope sighed. "The drill goes like this: You'll be kept there until bond is set, and you'll be evaluated again by a team of forensic shrinks. I'm not sure how long the process will take, but I'll be along for the ride. Don't worry about it. The key is, you want to be honest and upfront with everybody, especially yourself."

Frank nodded, smoking.

"You okay, Frank?"

Frank nodded again.

The psychiatrist sat there for a moment with a look of weary concern on his haggard face, a laminated pass clipped to his jacket, his big gnarled hands clutching the leather portfolio. He looked like a nervous father, and on many levels he *was* Frank's surrogate father. "I can give you something," Pope said at last. "Knock you out for the trip, wake up tomorrow morning in your own private room."

Frank thought about it for a moment. Was he ready to sink into that black ocean of dreamless sleep yet? Was he ready to face the emptiness? Something in the back of his mind told him that was a bad idea. Something in the recesses of his brain urged him to stay awake. Was

128 *Jay Bonansinga*

it the Other? Was Frank still being manipulated by his alter ego like a puppet attached to invisible strings?

Maybe it was the sleeplessness working on him now, the latter stages of his insomnia where the world mutates into one giant hallucination.

Frank had experienced every conceivable phase of sleep deprivation, from the irritability and trancelike staring jags of the early stages, to the raw nerves, slurred speech and hallucinations of the later phase. The longest he had ever gone without sleep was four days, and that was back when he had tried to wean himself off the Halcion tablets he was taking. He remembered the fourth day, walking around like a zombie, no appetite, incapable of focusing on the simplest task, his nervous system so jacked up his own footsteps were capable of making him jump. But that was right before he had passed out in the employee lounge at the Twenty-fourth.

Tonight was different. Tonight he was closing in on four days of sleeplessness, and he was still buzzing with nervous tension, still hyperalert. Was it the shock? Things seemed unreal, but it was a different kind of unreality than he remembered from his last binge of insomnia. Tonight the world around him seemed so clearly focused, so crisp, it almost looked artificial. The harsh greenish quality of the fluorescent light glaring off Pope's face. The sound of the marshal's thick, mucousy breathing across the room. The dead flies behind the barred window panes. The sound of rain on the rooftops. Something was happening to Frank.

"I think I'd rather stay awake, Doc," Frank said at last.

"You're sure?" Pope asked.

"Definitely."

There was an awkward pause.

"Okay, Frank." Pope rose on his creaking knees. "In a few minutes, the marshals will be back in to get you ready. I'll hang around and ride over there with you. Okay?"

Frank nodded. "That sounds fine." Then he put his hand out. "I really appreciate all you've done for me, Doc."

The two men shook hands.

Then Pope turned and walked out.

19

They dressed Frank in hospital whites. They let him keep his leather shoes on. But they took everything else. His personal effects, his denim shirt and Ralph Lauren corduroys, his shield, his belt, everything. They sealed his things in a paper box—like a gift box—and filed it away for safekeeping.

They replaced his original shackles with new ones made of some shiny alloy. The wrist cuffs were connected to a leather belt around his waist, and the ankle cuffs were connected by a short chain. The shackles forced Frank to take awkward baby steps when he walked, and the chain made delicate jangling noises.

It was nearly midnight when they took him out the rear and into the night.

The cool mist felt good on Frank's face as they led him across the loading dock. There were four escorts. The two marshals, walking on either side of Frank, and Doctor Pope, shuffling along behind him, holding an umbrella over Frank like he was some kind of ragtag dignitary, and a beefy black orderly named Goodwell bringing up the rear. The air smelled of earthworms and car exhaust. The rain had settled into a steady billowing curtain, the dirty water sluicing down the gutters along Ogden Avenue to the west.

The parking lot was nearly empty now, the intermittent lightning flashing like a photo-strobe, illuminating graffiti-stained ramparts and lonely streets. There were two uniformed cops waiting at the edge of the dock near an idling transport van, their faces shrouded by the hoods of their rain slickers and the bills of their hats. A beat car was parked nearby, its headlights cutting twin swaths through the rain, its engine idling above the noise of the rushing water.

"We're gonna pause here for a second, Detective," said the older marshal, a ruddy-complected man named Curless, gently taking Frank's elbow and stopping him near the ramp that connected up to the back of the van. The splash of rain was moistening the bottoms of Frank's togs, and Pope adjusted the umbrella over Frank as the younger marshal, a skinny man named Briggs, checked the ramp and unlocked the back of the van.

There was a strange sort of respect and courtesy being paid to Frank by the other officers. Mostly because of Frank's reputation for being a good cop, a standup guy. Murder or no murder.

"Just one more second," Curless said.

"How you doing, Frank?" Henry Pope asked.

Frank told the doctor he was doing fine, and thanks very much for asking.

Fifteen feet away, on the edge of the ramp, Briggs was opening the back of the transport van and revealing the interior in a sudden flicker of lightning: Filthy corrugated iron floor, metal benches on either side, a waffled metal screen separating the front cab. Something troubling sparking in the back of Frank's mind: (—they'll put us away for a long, long time, and that's probably the best thing—)

"You okay, Frank?"

Pope's voice next to him. Steadying him. Giving him courage.

Frank sniffed the air as though it were smelling salts. "Yeah, Doc, I'm fine."

The younger marshal came up the ramp and nodded at his partner. Curless took Frank's arm. "Here we go,

Detective," he said, and started Frank down the ramp, then into the transport vehicle.

The inside of the van smelled like fear. The sharp garlicky aromas of body odor and greasy hair and nerves. Frank could smell the emotions clinging to the rusty metal walls. He sat down on one side, the bench hard and cool beneath his ass. His heart felt like a stone. There was an Ithaca clamped to the wall across from him. The shotgun gleamed in the rays of streetlights slanting through the back.

"Mr. Curless and Mr. Goodwell are both going to ride back here with us, Frank," Doctor Pope said.

Frank said that was fine.

The orderly took a seat opposite Frank.

"I'm gonna have to secure your shackle to the floor," the older marshal told Frank.

Frank said that was no problem.

Curless knelt down near Frank's feet and fiddled with a set of keys, while Briggs stood outside the rear doors watching.

"Closing the doors now," the younger marshal said, and Frank glanced over his shoulder at the rear of the van. The dim illumination from sodium-vapor lights faded away as Briggs swung the doors shut.

The doors clanged with a strange finality.

(—*put us away for a long, long time*—)

Frank closed his eyes.

"Frank?"

"I'm okay," Frank said, looking over at Pope, who was sitting on the bench next to him.

The older marshal pulled the shotgun off its clamps, then took his place near the rear doors, squatting, checking the Ithaca's breech. In front, the cab door slammed, the engine revved, and the van surged away from the dock.

"I got something for you," Pope was saying over the whoosh of the tires on wet pavement.

Frank looked at the psychiatrist. "I'm sorry—what?"

"I got something for you," Pope said again, fishing around in his jacket pocket.

The van was swaying gently, pulling out onto Ogden Avenue and heading west toward Roosevelt Road, the wiper blades slapping in rhythm with the bumps. Through the waffled grating in front, Frank could just barely make out the red-blue flash of the escort car's lights reflecting off the van's windshield. He turned to the psychiatrist.

Pope was digging in his breast pocket. "It's here somewhere," he was saying. "Ah! Here it is."

Pope pulled something shiny from his coat. He dangled it across Frank's shackled hands.

Frank looked down and saw a gold chain with something attached to the end. He took a closer look. It was a gold crucifix about two inches long. Frank looked up at the psychiatrist. "I don't understand."

"The psychiatric community gets a bum rap sometimes for being antispiritual," Pope said.

Frank was confused.

Passing headlights were slithering across the inside walls of the van, momentarily illuminating the doctor's weathered face. "It was my mother's," he said, a sad glint in his eyes. "Remarkable Scots-Irish woman. Married for sixty-five years to the same man—a cop. Had seven kids. The day I got out of the academy, she went to mass and made a deal with God. Said she'd give the force one of her seven kids, but she wanted the rest to be civilians."

The van hit a bump, and Frank looked back down at the crucifix. It was old, the gold dull, the chain slightly oxidized. The center of the cross was a bulbous sacred heart, big enough to contain a photo. "I still don't—"

"I just thought it might give you a little comfort," Pope said.

Frank was vexed. He was an agnostic. He had prayed maybe twice in his whole life. He looked up at Pope. "I appreciate the gesture, Henry."

The psychiatrist shrugged. "I just thought, all that stuff about doing God's work, you know."

Frank stared at him. "Pardon me?"

"The tape. On the tape. Your alter ego said he was doing God's work."

An icy finger brushed the back of Frank's neck. "Excuse me?"

"The tape, the videotape, the first one." A slice of a passing headlight slid across the doctor's face. "The other personality had said he was doing God's work. Right? And I thought you might find comfort in prayer."

Frank froze.

The passage of time itself suddenly seemed to seize up inside the dark, swaying van.

Frank tried to speak, tried to act as though nothing had happened—as though they had just exchanged some meaningless bit of encouragement—but it was difficult, it was difficult hiding his shock.

"What is it, Frank? What's wrong?"

The other men were looking at Frank now—Goodwell, the orderly, his chiseled black face almost blue in the darkness, and Curless in back, the old veteran, clutching his shotgun. Something was wrong.

"Frank—?"

All at once the realization struck Frank hard, a tidal wave of emotion crashing down on him.

It couldn't be. It was impossible. *Impossible.* But there was no other explanation. No other explanation. All at once, the night had turned to day, and good had turned to evil, and Frank's world had turned inside out, the sheer abruptness of the revelation choking the breath out of him—pure white-hot rage slamming into sudden relief, mixing with paralyzing fear and utter disbelief.

He was innocent.

The van took a tight turn, the g-forces pressing Frank against the wall. Frank tensed.

Pope stood up, and Goodwell sprang to his feet. "Looks like he's having a seizure," the orderly said.

"I'm—I'm—"

An idea flickered suddenly in Frank's mind, and he acted on it almost immediately.

"Frank, what's wrong?" Pope said urgently, reaching down for Frank, but it was too late.

Frank had suddenly acted out the very condition he had been suffering for most of his adult life, and he did an extremely convincing job of it, his movements perfectly capturing the telltale symptoms—his body slumping, his head lolling back and his eyes rolling back into their sockets.

And he slid sideways until his shoulder landed hard on the bench and his shackles went taut.

And he pretended to pass out.

20

He felt Pope's palsied, sandpaper fingertips on his neck, searching for a pulse, and suddenly the old man's touch was no longer benign, no longer softly paternal. It was scaly and gritty now, like the back of a snake. Frank could hear the others gathering over him, and he heard Curless saying something into his radio, probably signaling the escort car.

"Two-twenty, stand by," the older marshal was saying. "Got a possible ten-thirty-three with the prisoner. Stay on course. Will advise."

"Pulse is elevated," Pope was saying, his hands pressing down on Frank's forehead. "Feels like he's running a temperature."

"What's going on?" The sound of Briggs's voice from the front.

"Keep following the squad!" Curless yelled.

Eyes closed, heart thumping, mind swimming with panic, Frank tried to think. The drugs had mostly worn off, but Frank was still pretty woozy, pretty dazed. This phony blackout would only buy him a few minutes of time, but it would be time well spent. He would only have one chance.

One chance.

"What's the matter with him?" Curless demanded.

"I think he's having another syncopal attack," Pope replied.

"A what?"

"A fainting spell," Goodwell informed him.

Frank continued feigning unconsciousness, letting his body go limp against the bonds while the others hovered over him. The shackles were digging into his ankles. He could taste blood in his mouth. He tried to visualize his next move, like an athlete visualizing a big play, relying on one specific piece of good luck.

A long shot.

If Frank let enough drool bubble out of his mouth, and he twitched a little bit, then maybe . . . just maybe . . .

"Take the shackles off, Curless, quickly!" Pope ordered all of a sudden.

"We're not supposed to—"

"I think he's preconvulsive! Please! Do it now!"

Eyes locked shut, Frank was shivering and twitching. He could feel Curless fumbling at the ankle locks. Within seconds he was completely free of all the cuffs, and he could feel Pope and Goodwell lifting him up into a supine position on the bench, steadying him gently. Frank allowed one eyelid to crack open just enough to see his target: Curless's Ithaca, tucked under the marshal's arm, gleaming in the dim light. Frank's heart was racing.

Pope reached down, and pushed open Frank's eyelid. "That's strange," the doctor said.

All at once Frank sprang from the bench—

—and chaos erupted.

It all happened in the space of an instant, but to Frank, as he lurched toward Curless, it seemed as though time was mired in slow motion, like a nightmare.

The marshal was caught off-guard—as was Goodwell, as was Pope—and Frank slammed into Curless with everything he had, like a linebacker putting a solid hit on an unsuspecting tight end. Pain shrieked across Frank's collarbone, stars bursting in his line of vision as Curless tumbled backward.

Both men careened to the floor, and Frank put every

last ounce of energy into grabbing that shotgun before Curless could figure out what was happening. Frank got one hand on the butt, then clutched at the stock with the other, and by the time Curless had managed to grab at the weapon, Frank had already yanked it free.

"EVERYBODY BACK!" Frank screamed at the top of his lungs, falling back against the rear doors.

Pope and the others froze.

"NOW!" Frank said, struggling to his feet. He pumped the slide for emphasis, the Ithaca feeling as natural as a girlfriend's hand in Frank's grasp, the product of endless hours on the shooting range, obsessively practicing, exorcising all his neurotic fears.

The Ithaca clanged.

The others stiffened at the sound. Curless glanced toward the cab.

"Keep driving, Briggs!" Frank hollered at the younger marshal.

In front, behind the waffled steel, Briggs was nodding, keeping his hands on the wheel. The tension in the van was like a pressure cooker about to burst, the rain lashing the metal roof, the occasional slash of a streetlight slicing across the dark walls.

Frank jabbed the shotgun at Curless. "Hands where I can see them, guys! Now! Please! Up against the wall! Do it now before somebody gets hurt!"

Curless and Goodwell raised their hands, then slowly backed against the wall opposite Pope. But the psychiatrist wasn't moving. He wasn't budging an inch. He was still kneeling next to the bench where Frank had first pretended to collapse.

"You too, Doc," Frank said. "Over against the wall."

Pope was giving him a sidelong glance. "Aren't you going to introduce yourself?"

"What?" Frank was momentarily baffled.

"I haven't had the pleasure," the psychiatrist said in a steady, measured tone.

"What are you talking about?"

"You're the Sleep Police, I presume."

There was a tense pause as the van splashed through a series of potholes.

All at once it hit Frank just exactly what was going on. "It's not what you think, Doc," Frank said, his eyes welling with emotion, the adrenalin making him tremble furiously, making him sick to his stomach. A flash of tungsten light slid across the dark walls.

"Do you have a name?" the psychiatrist said.

"It's still me, Doc."

"Who's that?"

"It's Frank, it's still Frank, and I am asking you to please go over and stand against that wall."

The psychiatrist licked his lips thoughtfully, rising to his feet, putting his hands in the air. A band of light was angled across his withered face. "Okay, no problem, but I don't believe Frank Janus would ever do anything like this. Do you?"

"Doc, please—"

"I'm just saying, Frank Janus is one of the most decent people I've ever met. Gentle even. I don't think he would ever dream of—"

"MOVE OVER AGAINST THE WALL!" Frank stabbed the Ithaca at Pope's face, hollering at the top of his lungs. "NOW! MOVE! OVER AGAINST THE WALL!"

"Can I speak to Frank—?"

"I SWEAR I WILL PULL THE TRIGGER IF YOU DON'T DO WHAT I SAY RIGHT NOW!"

There was a tense beat of noisy silence, the van rumbling around another curve, splashing through potholes. A carousel of vapor light moved across the walls. Where were they heading now? Panic spurted through Frank's veins. Was Briggs taking them back to Area Six headquarters?

The psychiatrist was reluctantly backing against the wall, facing Frank, hands in the air. "May I ask you a question?" Pope said finally.

"Sorry, Doc, no," Frank said, glancing out the narrow meshed window at the passing nightscape. They were heading down South Michigan Avenue, past the brooding spires of St. Michael's Cathedral, the gray, Gothic towers engulfed in the rain.

"I was just wondering—" the doctor began.

"Excuse me, Doc," Frank interrupted, aiming the gun at the three men. "If you don't mind, I need to ask some questions of my own."

Another tense pause. The swaying movement of the van, the rush of the rain on the roof. Curless and Goodwell eyeing the Ithaca.

"Go ahead," Pope said. "Whoever you are."

Frank took a step closer to Pope, raising the barrel to eye level. "One question, Doc."

"Go ahead."

"How did you know about the 'God's work' reference?"

In the darkness, Pope stared for a moment. "How did I know about what?"

Frank's spinal column was buzzing with nervous energy. "The reference on the video, the videotape, the alter ego saying he was doing God's work. How did you know about that?"

"What are you talking about?"

"I never told you about that part," Frank said.

"Yes, you—"

"No, no! I never told you about that." Frank's knuckles were white around the shotgun. "I never mentioned the God's work part, and I never showed the tape to anyone. Not a soul. Nobody saw that tape."

"Frank—"

"And yet, and *yet*! You knew about the 'God's work' thing. How is that possible?"

Another stretch of silence, the tension pressing down on the dark interior of the van like a gigantic vise. Frank's gaze was fixed on the elderly doctor. The rain was strafing the metal shell of the van, and both Curless and Goodwell were mere seconds away from doing something.

"Frank listen to me," the psychiatrist said. "This is your alter personality talking."

"Shut up!"

"Frank—"

"SHUT—!"

Frank saw the sudden movement out of the corner of his eye, but he had very little time to react as Goodwell went for his midsection, and Curless made a desperate attempt to grab at the shotgun.

The impact drove Frank off his feet, sending all three men sprawling to the floor.

And the shotgun discharged, roaring silver-magnesium sunlight in the dark van.

21

The blast went high, chewing a saucer-sized hole in the ceiling, a puff of metal fragments, vinyl stuffing, and grit filling the darkness.

The van swerved, Briggs reflexively jerking at the gunfire, the g-forces tossing all the passengers against the opposite wall. Frank's shoulder clipped the edge of the bench, and then he went down hard in the corner, but he managed to hold onto the shotgun. Pain exploded in his lower back. The sound of screeching tires pierced the chaos.

Frank managed to sit up, the shotgun still clutched in his sweaty grasp.

The van skidded to a halt.

"STAY DOWN!" Frank howled at them, struggling back to his feet.

The men in the rear were still on the floor. Dazed. Breathing hard. One by one, they showed their hands. Outside, thunder boomed as if answering the pandemonium. Frank could hear the squad car screeching to a halt in front of the van, the sound of the car's engine revving wildly.

"STAY ON THE FLOOR!" Frank bellowed. "HANDS INTERLACED BEHIND YOUR NECKS!" He glanced into the cab, and saw Briggs going for his gun. "DON'T DO IT, BRIGGS! TOSS THE SMITH ON THE FLOOR MAT! NOW! TOSS IT ON THE MAT!"

Briggs did as he was told.

"Hands behind your neck!" Frank hollered at Briggs, his voice hoarse from all the screaming.

There were more noises crackling outside in the thunder and the rain. Radio voices, the sounds of car doors clicking open. Frank tried to focus. Frank tried to put the brakes on his racing thoughts, but his mind was a whirlwind of information streaming into him.

Should Frank go back and recant his confession? Did he have enough evidence to convince anybody? Did he have any evidence at all? Sure, Pope couldn't have possibly known about that "God's work" reference, but what did that prove? That Pope had something to do with the tape? It was still Frank's face on the videotape. Frank's fingerprints at the scene. Frank's shoe prints, Frank's cigarettes, Frank's handwriting. And what about those psychological files at Pope's office? If Frank turned himself in now—with his brain a whirlwind of conflicting emotions—they'd throw him in the booby hatch for sure, no questions asked.

"Don't do this, Frank, don't make it worse," Curless was imploring from across the darkness of the van, lying prone on the floor.

Thunder rumbled outside, lightning flickering.

"That's not Frank anymore," Pope said softly, lying next to Curless.

Frank pumped the Ithaca, the slide clanging loudly. "I'm asking you guys for the last time to be quiet!"

A sudden bolt of dread shot through Frank's brain, so powerful it felt as though he had been electrocuted. It nearly knocked him off his feet. What if Pope were correct? What if Frank had missed some kind of switch being thrown inside him? What if he were actually somebody else right now? He certainly had never behaved this way in his life. At least not consciously. But underlying all this doubt was a raging furnace of conviction that he was innocent. All Frank had to do was start tugging on the loose thread that Pope had accidentally revealed.

But he needed time. He needed time to get his thoughts together, build a case for himself.

"Curless?! Briggs?! You all right?!"

An amplified voice was shaking Frank out of his stupor. It came from the front, and Frank shuffled forward, toward the cab, peering out the waffled metal screen.

Outside, the sheets of rain were billowing down through the blue rhythmic flashes of the squad car. In the distance beyond it, taillights were receding into the mist, the street fairly deserted.

The two uniformed cops were outside their squad car, flanking each side, crouched behind open doors. Evidently, they couldn't see Briggs behind the van's wet, tinted windshield. One of the uniforms was gripping a hand mike, his voice trumpeting through the beat car's PA system.

"Curless? Briggs? Acknowledge! You got a ten-thirty-three in there or what?!"

Frank's sphincter muscle tightened.

From the back, Curless's voice: "They've already called this thing in, Frank. Come on. Where you gonna go?"

"Listen to him, Frank, he's telling you the truth," Pope said.

"Quiet! Please—!"

"Your name's not Frank, is it?"

"Shut up! Shut up—!"

Noises were coming around the sides of the van now, shuffling footsteps in the rain. Thunder tore open a crack in the sky, the lightning turning the van into a flickering nickelodeon. Frank was holding the gun on his hostages with trembling hands. That's what they were now: *hostages.*

"Curless!" From outside, one of the uniforms was hollering over the rain. "Give us a ten-thirteen immediately! Or we're coming in!"

Inside the van, Curless said, "Frank, I gotta tell them something."

"Give them a standby!" Frank ordered.

"Frank—"

"Do it!"

"Johnny!" Curless shouted loudly, loud enough to penetrate the walls. "We got a hostage situation here—"

"God damn it, Curless!" Frank pointed the shotgun at the marshal. "That's not what I asked you to—"

"Stand down, Johnny! You too, Carl!" Curless yelled. "We got a situation."

"Damn it!" Frank hissed, turning away from the back door for a moment. His flesh was crawling. His synapses popping like firecrackers. He couldn't breathe. He couldn't think. He knew his time was running out. Half the CPD and a good chunk of the federal roll call would be outside this van in a matter of minutes.

"Frank?" Pope's voice.

"Shut up! Shut up!" Frank shuffling back toward the front of the van, peering out at the storm like a restless panther in a cage.

"Frank, listen to me—"

"SHUT THE FUCK UP!" Frank shrieked at the psychiatrist, all the fear and rage bursting out of the top of his skull. Outside, thunder pealed. Lightning strobed.

In the flickering light, Frank saw Pope's gray face staring at him from the rear of the van. "You need sleep, Frank," the doctor said.

Cold electricity ran down Frank's spine. Goosebumps crawled down his arms. He flinched suddenly as a fractured image sparked in the back of his mind—

(—his own hand, slick with blood, gently closing the eyelids of a corpse—)

Frank staggered.

Thunder rumbled outside the van, the rain surging against the roof. Lightning flashed again, turning the dark cargo bay into a flicker-film. Frank was struggling to stay focused, keep his mind sharp.

From the back, Pope's soft, gravelly voice: "You need sleep badly, Frank."

Another jolt of electricity, sending fragments of broken images across Frank's mind's eye—

(—*his blood-soaked hand scrawling something on a wall, words and letters written in deep scarlet*—)

Frank flinched again, nearly dropping the shotgun. He shook his head violently as though shaking off toxic water, and he paced along the wall, breathing hard and fast. He could hear a siren in the distance, barely audible above the noise of the rain. He was trapped.

At last, he made a decision.

He whirled toward the front of the cab. "Get down, Briggs! Down in the floor!"

Briggs ducked, and Frank raised the shotgun at the waffled steel screen and pulled the trigger. The blast nearly jerked Frank's shoulder out of its socket, singeing his arm hairs, deafening him. The shot punched a fist-sized hole in the screen, shattering part of the windshield in front of it. Frank's ears were ringing again.

"Stay down, Briggs!" Frank yelled, pumping another shell into the breech, the plastic casing ejecting off across the floor.

From the back: "Frank! Don't do it!—FRANK!"

From outside: *"We're coming in!"*

Frank hollering over the noise: "Stay down—!"

He fired another round into the screen.

Silver light popped inside the darkness, the blast gobbling another huge chunk of screen, dirt and debris and metal frags blossoming in all directions. Another volley of thunder answered the gunfire, blinding flashes of lightning hot on its heels. The air started smelling of cordite.

Frank was completely deaf now, flash-blind and numb. He lurched toward the screen, smashed his shoe through the mangled metal and quickly climbed through the gap. Jagged edges tore at his hospital tunic as he slid down onto the passenger side of the front seat.

Briggs was going for his pistol.

"Don't, Briggs, don't do it!" Frank said, twisting around and shoving the barrel of the Ithaca in Briggs's face. Point blank. Breathing each other's breath. Frank pumped another shell into the Ithaca.

In the rear, the sound of the doors bursting open.

Curless's voice: "He's going out the front!—the front!—THE FRONT!"

Frank scooped up Briggs's .357, opened the passenger door and slipped out.

Rain lashed at him, spit in his face as he staggered across the wet pavement, hurrying around the front of the van, vapor lights in his eye, ears ringing. The night opened up around him like a vast dark throat. In the distance, sirens were singing out of tune. The air smelled of burning chemicals. The cold spray in Frank's face was bracing, and it woke him up, and it made him sharp, and it made him hurry.

He could hear the uniforms coming around the back of the van.

"HOLD IT, FRANK!" One of the uniforms was hollering over the thunder.

One chance. Frank had one chance, and he took it.

"STOP RIGHT THERE!"

A warning shot boomed up into the sky, the echo bouncing off distant tenements.

Frank was rushing around the driver's side of the idling squad car—both doors still gaping. He lunged behind the wheel, head spinning, vision blurred, lungs heaving for air, heart hammering. The uniforms were fifteen feet behind him. Two silhouettes in the van's headlights. Crouching down, both in the tripod position, taking aim.

Frank floored the accelerator.

The squad car shimmied for a moment, engine screaming, rear wheels hydroplaning.

The first shot barked out behind him, a dry-husk pop in the wet air, the blast piercing the rear window, a spray of glass filling the squad car. Frank instinctively ducked, and he saw the chunk in the dash only inches away, over the glove compartment. The bullet had chiseled through to the metal.

Then the wheels found purchase, and the squad car surged into the rain.

More shots rang out in the receding darkness behind him, tiny blossoms of light in the curtains of rain. But none of them landed. The squad car's large-block V-8 engine was gobbling the road, the four hundred horses going berserk, slamming the doors and pinning Frank against the seat.

For years Frank had commandeered one of these patrol boats, and in a lightning flash, it was all coming back to him. He reached the next light in a heartbeat and turned west on Eleventh, glancing up at his rearview for any signs of pursuit. He expected to see the van coming around the corner any second now.

But nothing appeared in the mirror.

By the time he reached South State, he was thinking clearly enough to put on his emergency lights. From there, he turned south and drove deeper into the Loop, catching his breath and organizing his thoughts. If he could only block out those images lingering like flashbulb spots burned onto his retinas. Images of his own hand, covered with blood, finger-painting words on a wall. Writing in blood.

He was a hunted man now, and there was much to do. He would have to be careful if he was going to prove his innocence. In fact, he would have to be more than careful; he would have to be lucky.

He would have to survive impossible odds.

By the time he reached Eighteenth Street, he was already making plans.

22

Frankie is eleven years old and bundled in his Bradley Braves sweatshirt, his snowsuit, his insulated boots, and ski mask. It's a brutally cold, starry winter's night, and Frankie sits on the passenger side of his Aunt Nikki's 1970 Pontiac Tempest station wagon, staring out the ragged holes of his mask at the desolate, snow-encrusted farms of Central Illinois. They are heading north on Highway 55 toward Bloomington. The moon is high and thin in the ink-black sky, a cold diamond shining down on the barren fields, and Aunt Nikki is singing a Chris Montez song over the whir of the defroster while she drives.

"The more I see you, the more I want you," she warbles in her cracked falsetto. She glances over at Frankie, "Come on, honey, sing with your Aunt Nikki."

Frankie refuses to sing, and he refuses to take his ski mask off. There's something comforting and protective about the mask, even though it's making Frankie sweat, and it smells like wet dog fur against his nose. It's a small price to pay to be invisible. Which is exactly what Frankie wants to be at the moment. In fact it is exactly what he has wanted to be ever since his mother was sent away to the funny farm.

"Somehow this feeee-linnnng," Aunt Nikki goes on crooning, "Just grows and groooooows."

Frankie slumps down lower into the back seat, pretending to be asleep. He doesn't want to hurt Aunt Nikki's feelings. Aunt Nikki is not a bad woman. There's even something sad about her—that round face always squinched by the nylon scarf, and that hairy mole right on the end of her nose, and the smell of day-old talc always hovering around her. And besides, Frankie is not a confrontational boy. He doesn't even like to argue with his brother Kyle. He just wants to stay to himself and read his Homer Price mystery books and pretend he's somebody other than a skinny little Greek kid with a nutcase for a mother.

"Almost there!" *Aunt Nikki announces when they pass a green mileage sign.*

They're on their way to see Bradley University play at Illinois State. Frankie loves basketball, and since Nikki works part-time in the Bradley cafeteria, she has two free tickets. A few minutes ago, they dropped Kyle off at a neighboring farm while Uncle Andreas stayed home to rest. On paper, the whole trip seemed like a good idea, but now that Frankie was alone with his thoughts and the desolate passing landscape—not to mention Aunt Nikki's singing—it's turning out to be not so good an idea after all.

Another sign looms in the headlights.

"Your Aunt Nikki has to pee-pee," *says Aunt Nikki, noticing the Stuckey's Truck Stop billboard, turning her blinker on.* "We'll take a quick pit stop."

They zoom down the icy ramp, and make their way into the crowded parking lot.

"You want to come in, honey?" *Aunt Nikki asks after pulling into a parking place.*

Frankie peers up at her through ragged holes in his ski mask. "Um . . . I don't know."

"Do you have to tinkle?"

Frankie shakes his head.

"Okay . . . you wait here, I'll just be a second. I'll leave the car running."

She gets out and waddles across the brittle layer of dirty ice and into the truck stop.

Frankie waits.

And waits.

And waits.

And after a while, he gets bored, leans over the front seat and turns on the radio. And he waits some more. And he starts to wonder what happened to Aunt Nikki. Did she fall in? That's what his mother used to say when Frankie would take too long in the bathroom. Did you fall in, Frankie? Right then, Frankie pictures his Aunt Nikki in a comical mishap, falling headfirst into the toilet, her legs sprouting out the top, scissoring back and forth.

"Jeez Louise," Frankie mutters under his breath, finally opening his door.

The frigid wind curls around his head as he climbs out into the night. The sweat-damp ski mask freezes instantly, and his boots crunch through the ice as he trundles across the parking lot toward the truck stop entrance.

He goes inside.

It smells like a party in there—cigarette smoke, spilled beer, and frying grease. Boisterous laughter, the cha-ching of a cash register. Frankie immediately feels uncomfortable. All the noise and smells and strangers. He walks along the counter, past all the butt cracks and shopworn cowboy boots and grizzled old truckers nursing brown bottles. Nobody notice him. Nobody gives a whit.

The arcade is even more crowded. Loud country rock music playing, the cacophony of video games all going at once, and big fat men with Caterpillar Tractor caps, hunched over pinball machines, jerking and twitching furiously. Frankie looks for the bathrooms.

He sees a sign in the far corner, an arrow pointing the way to the rest rooms. Frankie elbows his way through the throngs, then makes his way down a narrow corridor to the ladies room door. He waits.

A black woman comes out.

"Excuse me?" Frankie says, working up the nerve.

"Yeah, sweetie?"

"You see another lady in there with a scarf on her head?"

The black woman shrugs. *"Sorry, sweetie. Nobody in there but me and a little old stool."*

The black woman walks away.

Frankie stands there for a second, puzzled. Aunt Nikki must have gone back out to the car. Frankie must have missed her coming the other way through the crowded arcade. Frankie turns and walks out.

By the time he gets back outside, he's shivering. He trudges down the third row of cars, boots crunching, and he gets all the way to the end of the lot without seeing the Pontiac. He turns around and backtracks, and he scans the other rows. There are plenty of pickups, old sedans, and semis. But no idling Pontiac Tempest station wagon.

Panic pumps through his veins.

He starts jogging up and down the aisles, frantically searching for the Pontiac, his breath pluming through the hole in his ski mask. He searches and searches and searches, and he refuses to believe that his Aunt Nikki would leave him there. She would never do that. There has to be a logical explanation. There has to be.

Now his side is aching from all the running, his lungs sore from the frozen air rushing in and out. He sits down on the curb by the entrance, breathing hard, terrified, jittery as a hen in a fox hole.

Sudden noises behind him.

Three gigantic leather-clad people are coming out the Stuckey's exit, weaving drunk, their breaths showing in noxious puffs of smoke and liquor. A bulky fat man with a long, straggly beard, a bosomy woman with peroxide-blond hair, and a lean, weathered man with a scarred face and a bandanna around his head. Their boots jangle as they crackle through the ice, their tight leather pants making whispery noises.

"Motherfucker can eat shit and die," the buxom woman is saying.

"*I'll fucking show him what pain is,*" the weathered man says.

All at once their milky gazes find Frankie sitting alone on the curb. "*Aaawwwwwww,*" the woman purrs drunkenly. "*Look at the widdle boy, ain't he darlin'.*"

Horrified, Frankie springs to his feet and rushes off across the parking lot.

There's a vast concrete staging area adjacent to the Stuckey's, drenched in sodium-vapor light, crowded with countless semitrailers lined up for either refueling or servicing or rest breaks. Frankie sprints along the rows of Kenilworths and Diamond Reos, and eventually crosses the property line into the darkness of the neighboring farm.

He uses the highway as a guide, and he runs southward for quite a while.

The sound along the edge of the field is frozen stiff, his boots slipping and sliding awkwardly on the hard-pack, but he keeps going. His lungs ache. His eyes sting. Even inside his mittens, his hands are numb. But he keeps going at a steady jog, refusing to stop.

He knows this much: Aunt Nikki's farm is just outside of Funks Grove, Illinois, which is a straight shot down Highway 55. Maybe ten miles or so. If Frankie stays on course, following the highway, he will run right into it.

By the time he reaches the first billboard, his side is aching so severely he has to slow down to a walk. Very few cars have passed. He limps down a gentle slope, then follows a frozen creek. He is alone now. More alone than he has ever been in his life.

And that's when the first trickle of cold dread runs through his guts.

Somebody is following him.

For a while, he figures the sounds are mere echoes of his own boots crunching over the icy ground. Like the feeling he gets when he comes up the basement stairs at his aunt and uncle's old farmhouse, when he hears his own footsteps, and then hears something else behind them,

like a second set of footsteps, and there's that little mo-
mentary tickle of fear in his heart. But right now, that
tickle is becoming a virtual flood of terror coursing
through him.

There truly seem to be footsteps behind him, and he
barely has the courage to look back over his shoulder to
see who it is. He is filled with a primal sort of infantile
terror, the same kind of fear that first gripped him when
he was five, and Helen Janus took him to see One Hundred and One Dalmatians, *and Cruella DeVille had first*
slunk onto the screen. The same kind that had flowed
down his spine when he was eight and had gotten lost at
the K-Mart while his mom dickered with a clerk in the
garden center. The same kind that had paralyzed him
when he was ten and was nearly bitten by the mutant
snake at the Heart of Illinois Fair freak show.

He manages to pause next to a skeletal oak tree, catch-
ing his breath, throwing a furtive glance back the way he
had come. In the moonlit shadows, he sees nothing. No
menacing figures in black leather. No maniacs on the
loose. Nothing but a rickety, windblown fence, a few scat-
tered bare trees and acres of snow-covered farm land. The
hills in the distance are a luminous blue.

The highway is a silent river of black ice winding all
the way back to the horizon-glow of Bloomington.

Frankie lets out a pained sigh of relief and continues
on his way.

A moment later, the footsteps return. Louder than ever.
And Frankie stiffens with adrenalin and fear. He turns
and runs headlong across the icy fields, his heart galloping
in his chest, his eyes tearing from the wind and the cold.
He sees a barn in the middle distance. A yellow light is
burning in one of the ground-floor windows.

Frankie runs toward it.

He reaches the barn, a mammoth conglomerate of old
worm-eaten siding, and he goes around to the double
doors at one end. Something is moving inside it. There's
a low rumble like an engine or a transformer, maybe a

heater. The doors are open a crack, and there's a fire burning somewhere inside. The orange flame flickers and shifts in the gap, sending a slash of warmth across the indigo night.

Frankie opens the doors.

The blood is everywhere, spattered across the barn's rough-hewn walls, pooled on the dirt floor, smeared on the bales of hay that are strewn haphazardly across the length of the place. It looks like a tornado has recently touched down. A fire has started near an overturned oil lamp, and there's that low buzzing noise like a huge electrical transformer. Then Frankie's gaze falls upon the first body.

It's lying in a heap under a long wooden table, its legs curled inward against its ravaged belly, its oval head limp against the floor. Its big brown eyes are open and glassy and staring up at the ceiling beams. The calf looks as though it's been eviscerated by a chain saw, its entrails spilling out in a bloody knot.

Other carcasses are splayed across the inside of the barn, some of them on the floor, some of them on the table, some of them wedged up in the throats of support beams. Mangled chickens, a couple more calves, even a few hogs. The air is thick with the soupy smell of death, and there's a delicate veil of steam coming off some of the remains.

Frankie realizes his feet are moving, slowly, reflexively, backing away from the massacre. And that's when he sees the source of the low, droning noise.

A wild dog is huddled just inside the doors, hunched in a threatening posture, its feral eyes shimmering a phosphorous amber in the firelight. The thing is growling at Frankie. The dog's coat is the color of moldy, wet ash, and it's huge, some kind of German shepherd-wolf mix. Its black lips are curling away from prehistoric-looking fangs.

Frankie lunges through the open doors.

A gigantic man in a down coat and cowboy hat is waiting for Frankie outside the doors. The man raises a shot-

gun and either grimaces or grins—it's hard to tell—his
face a shadow beneath his hat, his yellow teeth glimmer-
ing. He utters something like, "Whoever so lies with the
beasts in the field shall be unclean, sayeth the Lord!"

Frankie turns and runs away.

He runs for all he is worth, and he gets maybe a hundred yards away when the first blast rings out—a sonic
boom that shatters the icy night air and makes Frankie
jump midstride, nearly tumbling into the snow. Somehow
Frankie manages to keep sprinting toward the tree line. He
reaches a dark copse of elms and vanishes in the shadows.

Now he's truly lost in a whirlwind of darkness and
terror. He swims through the thicket, the bony arms of
tree branches and undergrowth clawing at him, and he
finally makes it to the other side.

A road looms ahead of him.

He starts down it, and he runs along the ice-varnished
shoulder until his lungs are about to burst. He hears gravel
crunching behind him. A beam of light slicing through
the darkness. Frankie whirls, and his legs tangle, and he
careens to the ground.

Now he can barely see. His head is a block of ice.
Maybe even racked by a concussion. He gazes back at
the road behind him through bleary eyes.

They're coming for him: three, maybe four, maybe as
many as a half-dozen enormous men in uniform, walking
in lockstep on the icy macadam like giant black monoliths,
their boots making rhythmic cracking noises. Their shoulders are impossibly broad, and they have no faces—only
shimmering black pools of nothingness under the bills of
their hats. They're coming for Frankie, coming to take
him to jail.

The Sleep Police.

Frankie opens his mouth to scream.

A giant gloved hand swoops down and covers his
mouth, cutting off his voice.

The darkness devours him.

He wakes up some time later: it's hard to know how

long. Maybe a day. Maybe a week. Eyes fluttering open, he manages to focus on the faded buttercup wallpaper, the pine dresser with its yellowed doily, and the bentwood rocker in the corner. He's in Aunt Nikki's room, and rays of winter sunlight filter through the ruffled country curtains. He feels hot, feverish, his hands and feet bandaged.

There are four other people in the room, hovering over the bed: Aunt Nikki, Uncle Andreas, little Doctor Moser with his Coke-bottle glasses, and Sheriff Simms in his gray county uniform. Frankie manages to speak, and he tells the whole story, and the others listen intently, Aunt Nikki is devastated that she lost Frankie in the crowded Stuckey's, and Uncle Andreas is trying to hide his tears, and Doc Moser is inspecting Frankie's frostbitten hands.

But Sheriff Simms is quietly standing back with his arms folded, a weary smile on his face. He's the one who found Frankie wandering the snow fields, frost-bitten and delirious. He's the one who saved Frankie's life. The sheriff is a hero.

Or is he?

In the weeks that follow, Frankie gets better. The frostbite heals, and the nightmares fade, and Frankie goes back to normal activities. But little does he know, a seed has been planted in his subconscious.

The following summer, he goes to camp, and the following school year he enters the eighth grade and gets straight A's. He even kindles an interest in girls. But deep beneath the surface, his obsession is growing.

Upon entering high school, he becomes extremely popular with the young ladies: he's darkly handsome, quiet, thoughtful, gentle, sensitive, and polite—all the things for which the rest of the beer-swilling, hormone-wired boys are ill equipped. But very few girls know about Frankie's obsession. Starting with the trauma of his mother's murderous breakdown—and sealed with that fateful winter's night along a lonely highway—young Frankie becomes fixated on violence.

He loathes violence. He detests it. Violence ruined his

life. *Violence destroyed his mother, and violence obliterated his family. But for Frankie Janus, violence is more than an isolated experience. It is more than just something that happened to him. Violence is woven into every fiber of his being, like a genetic defect, like autism or spina bifida. And the only way he knows how to live with it is to encapsulate it, and study it, and understand it.*

He decides that he wants to be the one who catalogues the misery, labels the bloodstains, photographs the murder scenes, and bags the evidence. And as he wends his way through his higher education, he becomes a ravenous reader of everything criminal—criminal psychology, the criminal codes, forensic science, even dime-store crime novels—everything from Dashiell Hammett to Dostoyevsky.

Eventually Frank Janus becomes one of the very few people walking the streets with a badge and a gun who is literally destined to do that very thing.

He becomes Fate itself, heading toward some inexorable finale of blood and tears, the very same violent end he always feared and detested . . .

. . . and it all starts tonight . . .

. . . right here . . .

. . . right now.

23

BOOM! the fanfare rang out, an atonal symphony flooding the dark orchestra pit: cymbals erupting, timpani drums exploding in a cacophony of pain and terror and noise, a pinwheel of garish Day-Glo colors—*crash!-crash!-CRASH!*

Frank jerked awake in the darkness, his heart about to burst, the small of his back pressed against a moist stone wall. He sat up, blinking away the fog, trying desperately to see. He reached out reflexively for something to hold onto, something to steady him, but he found nothing.

His hands clutched at the air.

The muffled sound of thunder rattled the floor suddenly, the storm raging nearby. But where? Where was he? He was shivering furiously, but it wasn't from fear. He was actually cold. In fact, he was freezing. He had been dreaming of a boyhood trauma on a wintry night. Was that why he was so cold? He felt along the damp stone beneath him. He couldn't see a thing. His hands were wet, and they were trembling convulsively.

Eyes adjusting to the darkness, he saw that he was in a empty room piled with rubble. Scarred brick walls, no windows, the door missing. The walls were shiny with something, but it was too dark to identify it. Pain jolted up the tendons of his arms, throbbed in the back of his neck. He was so cold. His hospital togs were soaked through to the bone.

Lightning flickered suddenly—

—and in the sudden burst of illumination, Frank saw the blood. It was all over him, splattered across the front of his tunic, soaking the arms, deep scarlet-black stains. It was on the walls, too.

Frank slammed backward against the back wall, gasping, panic seizing him. The lightning faded. Frank tried to stand up, but he was shivering so violently now that he could hardly coordinate his movements. His arms ached. He felt as if he was in a giant walk-in freezer. His hands were oily with blood, and he tried to wipe them on his pants, but he was shaking like a man with cerebral palsy.

Lightning flashed again—

—and the words scrawled in his own blood yammered at him. They were written across the moldering brick in huge, looping cursive letters: *I'm a bad boy! I killed Jane Doe! I want to go to sleep! I'm a bad boy! I want to go to sleep! I need to go to sleep forever!*

More lightning.

And that's when Frank saw the wounds on his wrists— deep, ragged, diagonal slash marks—and the glint of a broken bottle on the floor next to him, and all at once the gravity of the situation was becoming clear to him. He struggled to stand up. His legs were weak and frozen stiff, and his wrists were throbbing unmercifully, but the adrenalin was juicing through him now as well.

He managed to stumble over to the doorway and gaze out across the darkness of the main room—a deserted, rat-infested hovel of trash, cinders, and narrow shafts of dirty sodium light coming through the cracked walls and boarded windows. Frank recognized the place immediately, the memory piercing the haze of his pain and terror.

"My God," he uttered in a broken voice, pressing his wounded wrists against his chest to staunch the bleeding.

It was the abandoned Jewel warehouse where they had found the second Jane Doe.

Sudden pain stabbed up his arms, his wrists stinging. How much blood had he lost? How long had he been unconscious this time? Had the pain awakened him? Frank remembered trying to make it up to Chloe's place on the north side, and then getting dizzy. He remembered pulling the squad car between two buildings off Western Avenue, but then everything went pitch-black.

The squad car.

Frank staggered across the filth, cradling his bloody wrists, searching for the exit, the lightning fizzing and popping and flickering outside. For a moment the dark warehouse turned silver like a photo negative, and a wave of nausea curled through Frank's belly. He had to find the squad car quickly if he was going to survive.

He was already going into shock.

In the far corner of the warehouse, a sheet of black plastic was flapping in the wind. Frank pushed his way through it and stumbled into the rain. The storm had picked up. It was coming down in biblical proportions now, a steady, billowing typhoon of water. Thunder rattled the heavens, bolts of lightning fracturing across the sky.

The squad car was sitting in the darkness about fifty feet away, where Frank had left it, its front end canted against the edge of a garbage Dumpster. It was dark and silent. Frank hurried over to it, the rain washing the blood from his arms.

He got inside it and found the wireless cellular clipped to a hook under the dash.

He punched in a number with blood-slick fingers.

"Chloe?" Frank said after hearing a click, and a familiar voice on the other end.

"Frank?" Her voice was as taut as a banjo string.

"Yeah, listen—"

"Frank, what is going on? There's a thing on the news, the phone has been ringing—"

"Chloe, listen, I'm sorry, I'll explain everything when I see you, but I'm bleeding pretty badly right now, and I think I'm gonna need to go to the emergency room as soon as possible—"

"Frank, my God. I can't—I mean—what is it that you want me to do?"

"I need you to meet me outside the St. Francis ER as soon as you can—"

"That's right down the street—"

"Please just listen! I might only have a couple minutes until I go into shock."

"Jesus."

"I'll be in a black-and-white pulled over to the side on Oakton. Do you understand?"

"Yeah, okay."

"I need you to bring a few things: something I can wear, jeans, a T-shirt, anything. And your insurance card, and your IDs with your maiden name on them."

"Okay—um—"

"Go there now, Chloe! Now!"

Hypovolemic shock is a tricky thing. The state of physical collapse caused by a person losing more than one fifth of their total blood volume, it manifests itself first as clammy skin, a feeble pulse, and too-rapid heart beat. But these symptoms are subtle, and are complicated by similar symptoms brought on by panic reactions in the midst of profuse bleeding. A person who is going into hypovolemic shock may not know it until it is too late. The body will simply shut down. In other words, it simply bleeds out.

Frank was flirting with the edges of hypovolemic shock when his ex-wife arrived with the duffel bag. Her whippet-thin body bundled in a yellow rain slicker, her streaked blond hair looking like a wet rat, Chloe Driscoll took one look at Frank through the car window and went as white as skim milk. He had pieces of his bloody shirt-tail wound around his wrists, and his breathing was labored. He assured her that he would explain everything once they had stopped the bleeding and gotten him back on track. He told her exactly what he needed her to do. Chloe listened intently while she worked him out of the bloody togs and into a waterproof windbreaker, T-shirt, and khakis that she had brought from her attic.

Then she quickly ushered him through the rain and into the ER pedestrian entrance.

A third-year resident happened to be walking past reception when Frank came shuffling in. The doctor quickly called for a triage nurse and rolled Frank into the first available trauma room.

The fluorescent light shrieked down at Frank while they worked on him. The doctor cleaned and examined Frank's wrists, then put pressure bandages on the wounds while the nurse started an IV push. They took his vitals, and they did a type and cross-match. The noise was like a metallic carnival in Frank's head. His blood pressure was borderline, and his heart was speeding along at 140 bpm. The doctor decided to transfuse a few units of whole blood into Frank just to be safe, and keep his vitals monitored until he was out of the woods. Frank fought to stay alert while they sewed him up with dissolving ligatures. The final tally was forty-six stitches—eighteen on one wrist, twenty-eight on the other.

While all this was going on, Chloe was out in reception, feeding a bunch of lies into the system. She told them Frank's name was David Driscoll, and she gave them a bunch of bogus background on him, and she put everything on her own insurance card.

It was a lucky break that it was such a slow night in the ER: the whole process took less than a half an hour.

"I'm scared shitless, Frank," Chloe whispered at him in the recovery area after the nurse had pulled a privacy curtain around Frank's gurney.

"Keep your voice down, please," Frank said. He was sitting up against the inclined back rest, his wrists thickly bandaged. An IV drip was still connected to him, the soft pulse of the cardio monitor next to the bed. His vision smeared and unfocused, his head full of cotton, Frank was so woozy now he felt almost buoyant.

"They're sending a shrink down here to talk to you," Chloe whispered. "From the psych ward."

Frank looked down at the IV puncture above the knuckles of his right hand. He had never removed one from his own body before, but he had seen the EMTs do it many times. "I'll be long-gone before he gets here," he murmured.

Chloe grabbed his arm. "Are you gonna tell me what's going on, or do I have to read about it tomorrow in the papers?"

"Calm down, Chloe."

"Calm down? Calm down? Are you serious?"

Frank gave her a hard look. "I'm in trouble, Chloe. I'm being framed. That's all I can tell you. I didn't kill my brother."

Chloe put her hand to her mouth, looking away, her eyes wet all of a sudden. "I heard about Kyle."

Frank swallowed a twinge of agony. "I'm gonna find out who did it."

"Who's framing you, Frank?"

"I think Henry Pope has something to do with it."

Chloe looked at him. "Who?"

"Pope, the shrink at Area Six."

"The stress-management guy?"

Frank nodded. "I need time to figure it out."

"Why would he frame you?"

"Maybe he's protecting somebody. I don't know. I'm going to find out."

"But why you?"

"Because—I don't know—because I'm frameable."

She sighed nervously, glancing at the edge of the curtain. "You're frameable because of what? Your problems?" She looked back at him, a weird shimmer of emotion in her eyes. "Because of your history?"

Frank felt a tug of regret. "Chloe, I never meant to—"

"Don't," she said suddenly. "I don't want to go back down that road. Not right now."

"I was a nightmare to live with; I realize that."

"Frank, please—"

"All I'm saying is, I'm sorry I made it so difficult for you." His eyes were welling up. There was a lump in his throat. "You tried to make it work."

Chloe was looking away, saying nothing.

"I really am sorry, Chloe," Frank added softly before his voice broke.

She leaned closer, reaching out and touching his hair. "I know, Frank."

He touched her hand. "It was never you."

"Frank—"

"No, I'm serious." He looked at his bandaged wrists. "I wasn't ready to be married."

She shrugged. "Who knows why things fall apart."

Frank looked at her, a tear rolling down his cheek. "I really blew it, Chloe." He closed his eyes and let the grief shudder through him. "My brother's gone," he uttered in a strangled whisper.

Chloe leaned down and put her arms around him. "I'm so sorry, Frank."

Frank sobbed in her arms for a moment, the pain seeping out of every pore.

A few moments passed. Outside the curtain: amplified voices, crepe-soled shoes squeaking on the tiles.

Finally Chloe glanced down at his bandages. "Why would you do something like that, Frank?" She gently ran a slender fingertip along his self-inflicted wounds. "Why would you do that?"

He looked down at his bandages. "Funny thing is, I didn't do it."

She wiped her eyes, then gave him a quizzical look. "What do you mean?"

"It happened while I was in a blackout." He wiped

his face with the back of his hand. "I would never try to kill myself. Not consciously, at least."

"Jesus, Frank."

"I know," he sighed, lying back on the gurney, closing his eyes.

"You're exhausted."

"Tell me about it."

"You need some sleep," she said.

Frank shivered suddenly, a cold finger running down his spine.

Something sparked in his midbrain like a snippet of static electricity, a single frame of a motion picture running too fast through a projector, flashing shards of images across Frank's mind-screen: *the bloody blade of a carving knife.*

Frank sat up and looked at her. "What did you say?"

"What?" Chloe looked puzzled.

"Just now. What did you just say?"

She shrugged. "I said—um—what?—you look like you need some sleep?"

Frank froze for a moment, the vague sensation of biting too hard on an ice cube throbbing at his temples. Something was sizzling in the back of his brain like an electrical terminal arcing, and all at once, a series of synapses were firing inside him, and he was stricken with a realization. He tried to speak, but the words wouldn't come.

"Frank, you're scaring me—what's the matter?" Chloe was staring at him.

" 'You need some sleep,' " Frank murmured, hardly aware that he had spoken.

"What?!" Chloe said.

Frank didn't reply. He was rigid against the back-rest, caught in the grip of a revelation, a surreal revelation. It was like stepping back from an enormous, abstract mural done in the pointillist style, which at first appears as a wash of tiny, meaningless colored dots, but begins to take shape the farther away one goes. Soon Frank saw the whole puzzle stitched together in his mind. " 'You need some sleep,' " he repeated under his breath.

Suddenly, in one terrible flood of recognition, it all struck him at once.

"My God," he uttered in a voice barely above a whisper. "My God, my God, my God—"

24

"What? What is it, Frank?" Chloe's eyes were big and filled with dread.

The revelation slammed down on Frank like a hatchet cleaving through his skull. Pain erupted in his head, throbbing in his wrists, shooting down his spine. He was like a computer overloading. He saw stars, and his guts clenched up, and he had to hold onto the guardrail just to steady himself. "That's what Pope said," he uttered breathlessly.

"Who?"

"Pope—Pope!—the shrink, the police shrink! That's what he said to me—"

"I don't understand what you're—"

"He said it to me in the van, and he said it at the hospital! He said it over the phone!"

"So?"

"He said I could use some sleep, and I thought I was just hallucinating!" Frank reached over and lowered the railing, then sat up on the edge of the bed. "I gotta get outta here, I gotta get outta here right now."

"What's going on, Frank? I don't get it."

"That's how he's been doing it!" Frank said, grabbing her arm, his IV stand jiggling. "It's goddamn Pope, it's him, it's Pope! I know how he's been doing it!"

"Doing what?"

"Making all the—"

Frank abruptly froze up, his words catching in his throat. A noise was echoing down the hallway, raising the hackles on the back of his neck. Heavy footsteps were coming, slowly, deliberately toward his cubicle.

"Frank, what are you doing?! Frank?!" Chloe was backing away.

Frank was detaching his IV drip, unscrewing the tube from the needle puncture, leaving the collar taped to his arm. "I need you to do one more thing for me," he whispered, climbing out of the gurney.

He dropped to the floor, lowering into a crouch, the tiles cool on the soles of his bare feet. His head spun wildly, his vision blurring, his balance compromised from the blood loss.

"You're leaving?" Chloe said.

"I have to get outta here, Chloe," Frank said, searching for his shoes.

"What do I tell the shrink?"

"Tell him whatever—tell him you went to the bathroom, came back and I was gone," Frank said, finding his shoes, slipping his feet into them, then buckling his pants, and staring at the thin cotton chiffon of the privacy curtain. "I need you to find that small anvil trunk in the attic for me, okay? Can you do that for me?"

Chloe chewed on her lip, glancing over her shoulder.

"Chloe, come on, come on!" Frank was getting frantic, his flesh crawling. He pulled on his windbreaker.

The ponderous footsteps were approaching, but these were no ordinary footsteps. These were huge wooden pilings being driven into the floor, the footsteps of a giant, vibrating the very foundation, shaking IV bottles and instrument trays. They were about fifteen or twenty feet away now, and they were coming down the aisle with such casual purpose, such indifference, they seemed like a force of nature.

Frank recognized these footsteps as a dog recognizes an ultrasonic whistle.

"Small trunk? The one with all the tax stuff in it?" Chloe was saying.

"No, no, no—the small black one—the hard one—the one with the metal corners."

"Why in God's name—?"

"Chloe, just do it!" Frank hissed, squeezing her arm. A shadow was climbing up the curtain. A familiar figure silhouetted by the fluorescent light.

"Okay, okay, the black trunk," Chloe was whispering, "what do you want me to do with it?"

"I want you to drop it off for me," Frank said, then hurried around the gurney to the opposite side of the curtain.

He glanced through a narrow gap in the curtain and saw the back corridor bathed in jaundiced light, crowded with idle equipment. The recovery room looked fairly deserted: a half a dozen other empty cubicles, a row of gurneys lined up against the wall like a used car lot.

"Where, Frank? Where?"

He turned and saw the shadow rising up as big as the Golem against the thin curtain. "Corner of Kedzie and Foster," he whispered furiously, "near North Park, there's a footbridge across the river. Put it under the south entrance. Okay? You got that? The Foster side, under the bridge. Okay?"

Chloe nodded.

The curtain shivered—

—and Frank whirled around and slipped out the rear of the cubicle.

The voice came from long ago and far away—yet sounded as clear and articulate as someone whispering into Frank's ear, directly into his auditory canal, straight down into his nervous system. The voice was deep and rich and authoritative in its stentorian baritone, a booming, modulated clarion that cast out at Frank like a gigantic bell: FRANK JANUS!—HALT!

Startled by the voice, Frank slipped on a wet tile and tumbled to the floor.

He landed on his side, a fist of pain hitting the bridge of his nose, sending stars across his line of vision. He slammed into an equipment cart, sending a portable EEG, three IV stands, and several coils of cable careening to the floor. A specimen bottle shattered.

He struggled back to his feet immediately, hurling himself toward the exit.

Ahead of him the corridor seemed to stretch like taffy, the dirty tile flowing under him, the green light forming a tunnel around him. His legs were moving in slow motion. He could hear the whisking sound of iron slipping out of a leather holster behind him, the telltale metallic *CLICK!* of a hammer being pulled back on a service revolver.

He didn't want to look back over his shoulder but he couldn't stop himself.

They were emerging from the gap in the curtain like huge, dark blue sharks breaking the surface of the ocean, throwing a wake of thin fabric on either side, their broad shoulders the size of steamer trunks, their uniforms gleaming in the sick green light. They came toward him, marching in lockstep, their faces obscured in the shadows beneath the brims of their hats.

Frank turned and raced toward the end of the corridor, terror shrieking in his brain.

He could see the exit ahead of him, about ten feet away, an illusion of sorts, so close, yet so far out of his grasp. It was a huge gray door marked EMERGENCY EXIT in red letters, and it had a metal bar across it, the words ALARM WILL SOUND, stamped in the metal.

If Frank could only make it through this door without being captured by the monsters in blue.

"HALT, FRANK!" one of them cried, drawing a gigantic service revolver, his voice like a battering ram. The other one pulled a huge black baton.

Frank lunged at the door, head lowered, forearms, up like a football lineman.

He smashed into the metal release bar, and the door sprung open with loud iron clang.

Frank hurtled across a small landing, then fell head-long down a short flight of stairs. A loud warning buzzer erupted in the still air, filling the stairwell with a sharp, keening tone as Frank hit the bottom step, then slid across another landing, crashing hard into the wall.

Pain blasted through Frank's pelvis and lower back, several of his stitches ripping open, but he was driven by terror now, an engine chugging toward one inexorable purpose, and he managed to climb back to his feet.

He crabbed down the remaining steps toward the outer emergency door.

Behind him, the Sleep Police were coming down the stairs. Broad shoulders churning, boots crashing down the steps, both of them were running now. Their shadowy faces were either grimacing or grinning—it was hard to see anything in the darkness under their hat-brims other than a couple of crescents of sharp white teeth.

At the bottom of the staircase, Frank shoved the doors open and stumbled out into the dark alley behind the hospital, the door slamming shut behind him.

The sky seemed to bellow at him as he staggered through the rain. Thunder laughed uproariously in his face, the lightning giggling at him. He raced toward the mouth of the alley, his brain blazing.

Within moments, he had escaped into the night.

"My husband's going through a difficult time," Chloe was saying, standing outside the curtained cubicle. The emergency alarm had just mercifully shut off. Chloe was trying to control her shaking by keeping her skinny arms folded across her chest, but she had a feeling she wasn't fooling anyone. She was dying for a cigarette.

"We'll have to fill out a report," the little shrink in the crew-neck sweater was saying. He was an officious little twit, and Chloe loathed him immediately. "And we'll have to file a copy with the police," he added.

"I don't know why he took off like that," Chloe said, her nervous gaze drifting over her shoulder toward the overturned equipment cart.

"Does your husband have a history of this kind of behavior?" the twit doctor was asking, writing something on his metal clipboard.

"Do we have to bring the police into this?" Chloe said suddenly.

"I'm afraid so, Ms. Driscoll."

"My husband's a law-abiding citizen," Chloe said, marveling at the spontaneous bullshit coming out of her mouth. She had no idea what she was supposed to say. She wondered if the shrink could see her trembling.

The shrink started to say something else when the sound of sneakers squeaking on the tile floor cut him off.

A pair of orderlies were returning from the stairwell at the end of the corridor. They were stepping over the fallen medical gear and broken glass, shaking their heads in dismay. The one on the left was a middle-aged, balding black man dressed in hospital greens with a tuft of gray hair around his skull like a cottony halo. The one on the right was a younger man with terrible acne, also dressed in drab green togs. They both wore chagrined expressions.

"We lost him in the alley," the black orderly told the shrink as he approached, wiping the moisture from his head.

"Guy was pretty much psychotic," the acne-scarred orderly added.

"I'll do the diagnoses around here, thank you very much," the twit shrink retorted. "Did he say anything?"

The black orderly just wiped his mouth with the back of his hand, then sighed wearily before answering. "Didn't say a thing, just looked at the two of us like we were a couple of one-eyed monsters."

25

The storm lashed the elevated platform on Howard Street, the hard rain slanting down through cones of sodium light and striking the weathered boardwalk like tacks from a nail gun. The wind was a bullwhip, shaking the stalls, rattling the fiberglass canopies, the wind and thunder making primordial moaning sounds. In the distance, the skyline shimmered like a mirage.

Frank stood alone at the end of the platform, huddled next to the deserted rail shack in a solitary pool of hazy yellow light. He was gripping the pay phone receiver so tightly it was making his knuckles white and threatening to pop the stitches in his wrist.

"This is Deets," said a voice on the other end after the fifth ring.

"D, thank God," Frank said into the phone. He was shivering in his rain-slick windbreaker. His instinct told him that he should be indoors, wandering through innocuous public places, hiding in plain sight and all that. But a deeper knowledge of the streets told him that was wrong. He had chased enough skels to know that a person is harder to catch on the street. There are too many avenues of escape.

"Who is this?"

Frank wiped moisture from his face. "Jesus, I can't believe I remembered your cell number, I can't believe I remembered it."

After a millisecond of tense silence: "You got to be kidding me."

"Where are you, D?"

"Where am I?—Jesus, Frank, it's three in the morning—where do you think I am?"

Frank took a breath. "I'm sorry for all the shit I've been putting you through, and I might as well tell you before we go much further, I'm at a pay phone right now, and I'm going to be long gone before you run a trace."

"Frank, don't do this to me."

"D, you're the last guy I would want to jack around—"

"Turn yourself in, Frank. You're not right in the head. It's not a sin."

"I can't turn myself in yet, D, not yet. If you could just hear me out, just do me this one solid."

"They got a freakin' bulletin out for your ass."

"D—"

"You're number one on the hit parade, Frank. They'll find you."

"D, listen, please. I'm just asking you to do me this one favor, and listen to what I have to say."

Another shot of taut silence, as the rain lashed the platform around Frank. The noise was tremendous. Frank nervously threaded sore fingers through his curly, wet hair. He had stopped at a Walgreens pharmacy a few minutes ago and picked up some more Benzedrine diet pills with a few dollars that Chloe had stuffed in the khakis, and now he was wired on a double dose. Every raindrop sounded like a stick of dynamite, every volley of thunder like a cannon shot inside his skull. Even the throbbing in his wrists had a sound to it, a hollow thumping noise like a tattoo in a funeral march.

"They could take my badge for this, Bambi," the voice finally said.

Frank swallowed hard. "Not after I clear myself. Do you understand what I'm saying?"

"Clear yourself? Chrissake, Frank, you're in a hole so

deep now you're halfway to Hong Kong. You ain't digging yourself outta this one."

"Reopen the case, Sully."

"What do you mean, reopen the case?"

"The thumb sucker file," Frank said. "I'm close to breaking it up into a million pieces."

"The thumb sucker case is a wash, Frank, it's over. It already went downtown with Krimm."

"Shit," Frank hissed, clutching the receiver even tighter. If the files had already gone down to the Daily Plaza with Krimm, it meant there was probably already a full-blown IAB investigation under way. That would make it next to impossible for Deets to work under the radar. "Did you make copies?" Frank asked after a tense moment.

"Frank, you gotta turn yourself in—"

"Did you make copies, D?"

After a pause: "Yeah, actually, I got a whole file still in the drawer, but it doesn't matter. I've been over it six ways from Sunday."

"I'd like you to go over it again, D—I mean—I'm asking you as a friend."

Another pause.

Lightning flickered across the heavens, illuminating the platform, making the raindrops seem to hang in midair in suspended animation. Frank squeezed the receiver tighter, the plastic as cold as a frozen bone in his grip. His shoes were soaked.

The voice finally replied; "I'm sorry, Frank. I can't help you."

"D, please—"

"You need sleep, Frank, that's what you really need."

Something fizzed in the back of Frank's brain, buzzing in the base of his neck.

"What did you say, D?"

"I said, you need sleep."

The receiver moved suddenly in Frank's hand.

Frank glanced down and saw that the receiver had become a snake.

He jerked away from the phone, dropping the receiver. The handset had metamorphosed into a scaly, glistening reptile in the darkness. It hung there, undulating wildly in midair, connected by its tail to the pay phone.

Frank was paralyzed. The snake's slimy arrow-shaped head was cleft down the middle, ending in two separate snouts, each flicking a separate little pink tongue at the rain. Fear boiled in Frank's midbrain. It was the same mutant black mamba that had horrified him as a boy at the Heart of Illinois Fair freak show.

Lightning flashed—

—and the receiver was hanging there by its frayed cable, twisting in the wind. Frank stared. It had reconstituted just like that. He picked it up carefully, looked at it, felt it. It was no longer a snake.

Heart thudding in his chest, Frank brought the receiver to his lips. "D?"

On the other end of the line: "What's the matter, Frank? What happened?"

"Who told you to say that?"

"What?"

"The part about me needing sleep. It was Pope. Right? Pope told you to say that?"

After a beat: "Yeah, as a matter of fact he did, but what difference does it—"

"Listen to me, D," Frank said in a measured tone. "I'd like you to—"

Thunder roared suddenly, reverberating down through the ancient wooden trestles of the "El" station and shutting off Frank's voice. A pinpoint of white light was coming from the north, coming down the center track. A train was approaching the station.

Lightning crashed, and in the flickering light Frank saw figures on the edges of his vision. *Dark, hulking figures.* They were lurking in shadows along the edges of the platform, huddling behind concrete ramparts and light poles. Were they hallucinations? Were they real? Were they following him?

A sudden current of panic shot through Frank's nervous system.

"I have to get outta here, D," he said into the phone, wiping the rain from his eyes.

The platform was starting to vibrate softly, the oncoming train getting closer, maybe a hundred yards and closing fast. The headlamp bloomed in the rain, a cornea of magnesium white. The metal wheels were shrieking, blue sparks shooting out into the mist.

From the phone: "Turn yourself in, Frank. You're not well."

"Look at Pope," Frank said, throwing a fearful glance over his shoulder. The figures were creeping closer, moving from shadow to shadow. "Did you hear what I said, D?"

"Pope?"

"Look at Henry Pope," Frank repeated. "That's all I want you to do."

"Frank, stay on the line—"

"Look at Pope, D."

"Frank—?"

Frank hung up the phone, then scurried across the platform toward the staircase.

A moment later, the train arrived in a cyclone of noise and light.

Nobody on board noticed the fugitive slipping through the turnstile and heading down the stairs.

Down in the Loyola student ghetto, just off Pratt Avenue, on a narrow side road paved with aging brick and long shadows thrown by old gas lamps, there was a little all-night diner that had been retrofitted for the twenty-first century by some enterprising computer geek. It was called The Cathode Cafe, and it featured a narrow room with burlap on the ceiling and school desks along each wall. At each desk was a computer—Macs on one side,

PCs on the other—and for a nominal fee customers could sip latte while they surfed on the Internet.

Frank was in the back, shivering at a terminal, frantically pecking at the keyboard. He was on his second large espresso, trying to stay focused on the screen, his hands trembling uncontrollably now from all the amphetamines and fear and adrenaline sluicing through him. His bandages were soaked from the rain. Every now and then, muffled thunder would boom outside, shaking the ceiling and making Frank jump.

He was peeling away the veil of privacy around Henry Pope, the blocks of data and graphics wiping on and off the twelve-inch screen: Text from the American Psychiatric Association's Website on Pope's curriculum vitae, various Pope family Web pages and genealogical data, crime reports on assorted cold cases from the VICAP site.

"Come on, come on, come on," Frank was uttering compulsively under his breath.

The answer was right in front of his nose, but he still couldn't see it. It was like a partially formed sculpture in his head, made up of jagged fragments of information and clues, something profound buried in the phosphorous dots glowing on the screen: *A year and a half as a patrol officer in a tough district in California. Decorated for saving three children from a tenement fire. Medical school at the University of Chicago. Spent residency as a pediatric psychiatrist at Cook County Hospital. Deacon at the Apostolic Faith Church. Divorced from first wife on grounds of irreconcilable differences—*

Thunder rattled the cafe suddenly, drawing Frank's attention toward the front.

The cashier was standing behind the counter, eyeing Frank suspiciously. A skinny kid in a silk bowling shirt and goatee, he was sucking on a toothpick and glancing out at the rain, then back at Frank, then back out at the storm. Did he know something? Was there a TV somewhere broadcasting Frank's face? Frank was the only customer in the shop. Were the bandages on his wrists making the kid nervous? Frank had worked off the IV puncture, but he still looked like a refugee from the funny farm.

Frank glanced back at the computer. "Come on, come on, come on, where is it?" he was muttering. "Where's the linkage?"

He scrolled down more fragments of Pope's life, searching for a hook: *APA membership terminated ten years ago. Served on several Pentecostal missionary trips to the Sudan. Married for eleven years to his second wife. Grandfather of eight. Moderate republican, diabetic, gun control advocate, little league coach for fifteen years, pro life—*

Lightning flashed outside the front window.

Frank looked up for a moment and let out a tense sigh, then looked back down at the computer screen.

The screen had changed into a woman's belly, a scalpel embedded in its soft, doughy flesh. A phantom shriek filled Frank's head, and blood burbled from the incision, oozing down in rivulets of scarlet-black claret.

Frank screamed, jerking away from the apparition, blinking, and the blank computer screen stared back at him. No blood, no scalpel, no flesh.

Just a computer screen.

"Oh Jesus," Frank moaned, running fingers through his hair.

"What's the matter?"

Frank looked up and saw the cashier standing a few feet away, clearing a nearby table. "Nothing," Frank said. "I was just . . . nothing."

"Your time's almost up," the cashier informed him.

"My time?"

"You paid for an hour."

"Right," Frank said, wiping his mouth with the back of his hand, urgency burning in his gut like a smoldering ember. He had to get out of there.

But something wasn't right.

Frank looked at the clock on the opposite wall.

"Wait a minute," Frank murmured. "That's impossible, right? Tell me that's impossible. . . ."

The cashier just stared at him like he was from another planet.

The clock said 4:25, but it seemed that Frank had been in The Cathode Cafe for hours. How could it only be 4:25? Frank licked his cracked lips thoughtfully, then turned to the cashier and said, "I'm sorry, but what I'm really wondering is, is that clock right?"

The cashier looked at the clock. "Yeah, I guess. It's about four-thirty."

Frank shook his head. "That doesn't make sense."

The cashier shrugged. "It could be wrong—I don't know."

Frank sat there for a moment, running back over the events of the night.

Uneasiness started seeping into him like cold water through a busted hull in a boat. How could it possibly only be 4:25? The prison van had left Cook County at midnight, and he had been running for hours. It should have been morning by now.

Hell, it should have been the middle of the day.

But the night just seemed to press in on him from all sides, endless and limitless, eternally dark.

26

"You okay?" the cashier's voice tweaked at Frank.

Thunder cracked outside.

Frank glanced up.

Through the grimy front window he saw a squad car splashing through puddles, its taillights coming on. It rolled to a stop a few doors past the cafe, then backed up and stopped in front of the cafe. Frank's heart jittered in his chest, his scalp tingling suddenly.

The car doors sprang open, and a pair of patrol officers emerged, each dressed in identical navy blue rain slickers with identical plastic hat covers. One of them was smoking, and tossed his cigarette into the gutter as he hurried toward the cafe door.

Frank sprang to his feet, pulled on his windbreaker. "Is there a back way outta here?"

"Um—" The cashier was shifting his nervous gaze from Frank to the door.

"Please! Is there a back way out?!" Frank was slowly shuffling toward the rear.

"Past the bathroom," the cashier said finally, pointing at the rear.

Frank turned and hastened down a narrow corridor, past the men's room to an unmarked door. He turned the knob, and the door opened, and he slipped out.

The storm engulfed him.

He hurried across a small cinder lot, sidestepping puddles, moving toward Pratt Street, squinting to see through the sheets of rain billowing in his face. The noise of the storm drowned out his footsteps, drowned out his thoughts. He ducked under a line of trees and strode west, staying on the sidewalk, moving through lattices of vapor light and swaying shadows. Every time a car passed him, his gut tightened. But nobody seemed interested at the moment.

By the time he reached McCormick, he was completely drenched. His jacket was adhering to his back, and his shoes were soaked. He found a garbage Dumpster behind a darkened Foto-Mat, and he searched through it for a discarded umbrella or anything else he could use to keep the rain off, but he found nothing. Of course, he half expected the garbage to metamorphose into mutant snakes or Cruella DeVille's dead puppies, but nothing of the sort happened.

He continued on toward North Park.

Plodding along through the storm, Frank lost all concept of time. He was trapped in his own nightmare, the questions plaguing him. Was he doomed to wander this endless night? A ghost in a dead city? His mind a broken Rubik's cube, shifting and reshifting the fragments of Pope's backstory?

There was something important in the shards of Pope's history, something critical that Frank had missed. Why had the American Psychiatric Association terminated the doctor's membership? Around that same time—according to a small item in one of the Pope family Websites— Henry Pope had participated in a right-to-life protest march for Operation Rescue. But how did that link up with anything else?

Frank ruminated on this as he headed west, trudging through the rain . . .

. . . trying to ignore the moving shadows all around him.

North Park College and Theological Seminary lies north-west of the city, in the throat of the Chicago River, scattered over thirty-five acres of flat, scabrous grassland. Made up of blocky, utilitarian redbrick buildings, interspersed with the occasional Gothic spire and turret, the campus is a brooding affair. At night, it looks like a haunted necropolis, the floodlights throwing harsh beams on the buildings, the lightning sparking off the towers.

Frank approached from the east, padding along the wrought-iron fence that ran parallel to the river.

He found the footbridge near the east gates. A crumbling gray monstrosity that spanned the black waters, it was covered with dead ivy and deep shadows, and every time the lightning flared, it looked as though it were swaying in the winds. A chain cordoned off the Kedzie Street side.

On the other side of the footbridge, a giant, tarnished bronze sculpture of the Roman god Mercury stood on a huge cement pedestal, rising up against the night sky. It was part of the school's longtime delusion of grandeur, as though the place were some celebrated edifice out of Henry James, instead of the jerkwater little parochial college it would always be. The statue was covered with bird shit, which had turned to a pale, wormy paste in the storm.

Frank made sure nobody was watching and stepped over the chain.

He crossed the footbridge and paused at the far gate, gazing down at the riverbank fifteen feet below. In the rain and the darkness, it was hard to tell what kind of footing he would find down there. But he could see a darker object down in the shadows, buried in the weeds.

God bless you, Chloe.

Frank levered himself up and over the side of the footbridge, clutching the slick iron guardrail and cringing at the stabbing pains in his wrists. He lowered himself down the bank. His shoes sank into spongy mud. The rain blurred his vision, and sharp pain wrenched his spine as he searched the undergrowth and the cattails for the trunk.

It was waiting for him at water's edge.

He crouched down in the weeds, rubbing the beads of rain off the top of the trunk. It was about the size of a small microwave oven, covered in ratty imitation leather, reinforced with rusty metal corners. It was a remnant of Frank's sad past, and it seemed all the more pathetic in the weeds and the rain and the dark. It looked like something Willie Loman might have tossed off.

Frank got his arms around it and lifted it off the ground. It was surprisingly light, considering all the worthless, old memorabilia stashed within it. Frank took a deep breath, turned, and hauled it up the side of the riverbank to the footbridge.

A beam of light erupted in Frank's eyes.

"Oh shit, oh shit," Frank uttered, standing there motionless in the rain, holding the trunk like a looter.

Three more beams of light struck Frank in the face—FLASH!-FLASH!-FLASH!—each light coming from a different direction: one behind the trees to the north, one from the Foster Street side to the south, and one from the edge of the deserted parking lot, and in that frozen moment Frank recognized the sources of the lights, the motes of rain canting down through the beams, the glare streaking in his bleary vision. Panic bolted through Frank's heart.

"DETECTIVE?"

The amplified voice pierced the storm and sent gooseflesh rippling under Frank's wet clothing: the telltale sound of a portable PA from one of the unmarked Tactical vehicles, its trademark feedback squealing. Frank willed himself to move, forced his frozen body to lurch to his left, then toward the shadows to the east.

"DON'T MAKE IT HARD ON YOURSELF!"

Frank raced toward a grove of massive elm trees on the south edge of the campus, running full speed like a lunatic, the trunk rattling in his arms. He could barely hear the car engines revving behind him, the radio voices crackling, the storm swallowing the noises. He was running as fast as he could—considering that he was hefting a thirty-pound trunk in the driving rain, sprinting over mushy, wet turf, almost completely night-blinded by the lights.

A single thought was chiming in Frank's brain as he hurtled through the mist: They must have followed Chloe. They must have gotten a tap on her. They must have picked her up when she returned home for the trunk, and they must have followed her here.

"FRANK, COME ON!"

He was halfway to the trees when he slipped on a wet patch of grass.

The trunk flew out of his hands, and he went down in a frenzy of pinwheeling arms and legs, hitting the ground hard and sliding several feet in the mud. The trunk flopped end over end across the grass.

It landed twenty feet away, its latch snapping, the contents spilling out across the sodden ground.

"THERE'S NO WAY OUT!"

Frank saw the dull gleam of the .38 caliber Colt Diamondback lying in the grass, and all at once he made a series of instant decisions, a little like a parachutist finally deciding to jump out of the plane, culminating with the singular conclusion that he would not let them take him before he had cleared himself. He would not. He would not let that happen.

"STAY DOWN AND PUT YOUR HANDS ON YOUR HEAD!"

Frank rolled across ten feet of ground and scooped up the Diamondback.

In that terrible instant, a flood of thoughts streamed through Frank's mind—a frantic strategy, a way out of this ambush—and for the first time in his life, all his post-academy firearm training, and all the neurotic insistence on learning Israeli tactical shooting, and all the paranoid safety measures that had drawn such ridicule and laughter from his fellow detectives—all of it—was now finally paying off.

The gun felt as natural as a sixth finger as he spun toward the shadowy figures approaching from behind him. There were a half a dozen Tac guys dressed in black Kevlar vests and nightvision goggles, fanned out in assault formation, hustling toward him through the rain, and Frank simultaneously thumbed the hammer back and aimed, filling the chamber with a 158-grain wadcutter and pointing at the nearest inanimate object above the oncoming SWAT guys—

—because tactical shooting relies on human instinct to strike its target, which means a shooter moves his gun to his eyes to shoot, just as he moves his finger to his eyes to point, which means the gun becomes an extension of his arm, and his hand, and even his pointing finger.

Frank fired off six rounds.

The sound was a wild animal roaring above the rain, the six discrete muzzle flashes like bright silver teeth, chewing through the air, striking the high-tension wires above the SWAT guys. Six plumes of sparks looped out of the transformer, a sudden spurt of flames rising up into the mist, an unexpected fireworks display igniting the sky.

The black-clad cops all ducked reflexively like a school of fish in the darkness.

Frank moved quickly, taking advantage of the chaos, whirling toward the trees, scooping up a speed-loader and the rest of the contents of his trunk which were now strewn across the lot. He stuffed the clothes back into the trunk as he stumbled toward the elms.

"LAST CHANCE, DETECTIVE!"

A shot rang out.

He dove to the ground as a rubber dum-dum whizzed past his ear.

Frank slid across the muddy grass, ears ringing, bright dots in his eyes.

He clutched at the trunk, his knees slipping on the wet

grass. He started dragging the trunk toward a long shadow thrown by a streetlight on the edge of the woods. His mind was pulsing with white-hot panic. He made it to the woods just in time: Three more shots barked in the night.

The crowd-control bullets popped through the foliage, puffing hot breath across the top of his head.

Frank hit the ground, and banged against a tree. He saw stars and tasted old pennies in his mouth. Working in the dark, hands trembling, the muscle memory of a top-flight shooter, he flicked the release, thumbed down the cylinder, slammed the speed loader in, ejected the rounds, clicked it back home, and thumbed the hammer.

In one violent yank, he wrenched around and aimed at the statue of Mercury.

He got off six shots, the blinding white light arcing out of the Diamondback, blazing through the darkness, all the shadowy figures hitting the deck again like a choreographed routine. The wadcutters struck the bronze effigy fifty yards away like a string of blasting caps popping against the ancient metal—*PING!-PING!-PING!-PING!-PING!-PING!*—and the golden sparks glittered and spewed into the mist.

The statue doubled over suddenly.

Frank froze in the darkness of the woods, gaping wide-eyed at the miracle, the Diamondback still raised in his trembling hand. He couldn't believe what he was seeing, he just couldn't accept it. His traumatized mind would have nothing to do with it. His body was encased in ice.

Through the curtains of rain, the bronze sculpture had fallen to his knees. Blood the color of India ink spurted from its tarnished metal flesh, and a hellish moan swirled out of its chasm of a mouth.

Frank stared with burning eyes.

The statue of Mercury had collapsed, turning the color of eggwhites, its body softening, elongating. It was a woman suddenly, and she was choking on her own blood, naked and choking, a shroud of flies billowing off her. She was a prostitute, a woman named Sandra Louise Dreighton, a skinny girl with needle tracks on her arms and plastic surgery scars on her artificial breasts.

It was the Jane Doe from Little Pakistan.

"No, no, no, no, no, no, no, no, no," Frank was gibbering softly now as he dragged the trunk toward the deeper woods. He managed to get back on his feet, and he turned and staggered away.

In the darkness behind him, the Tactical team was fanning out on either flank.

Frank got lucky. Stumbling through the tall weeds and twisted branches, ankle-deep in the mire, he ran into a cloud bank of human stench. The smell was so thick it was like an invisible netting.

"JANUS!—GOD DAMN IT!—YOU CAN'T GET AWAY!!"

Frank saw the concrete apron to his right, buried in leaves and detritus, partially obscured in the deeper shadows. It had a rusty iron manhole cover embedded in it, the stink of sewage seeping out its pores.

"JANUS!"

He took a chance, rushed over to the manhole cover, and quickly tried to claw it open. His knees sank into the cold, sodden ground while he struggled. His icy fingers were too sore and clumsy to get under the iron, but the Colt's six-inch barrel was a decent crowbar. The wind howled through the trees, and rainwater filtered down on him while he worked frantically at the manhole cover.

Behind him: twigs snapping, footsteps, the unmistakable clank of a Winchester scattergun.

Frank got the manhole cover open, found a series of iron steps and lowered himself down into the pitch black, the trunk under his arm.

He landed in a fast-moving stream of black water, the stink choking the breath out of him, the noise like an echoing jet engine. He couldn't see a thing—the lid above him had fallen back into place, blocking out all the remaining sodium light. He stumbled, and his hand brushed across a slimy stone wall. He felt the other side: the same thing; moist, moldering stone oozing slug trails.

Above him, footsteps were thumping.

He willed himself to move, forward, wading through the moving water, moving through the fetid darkness, through the invisible curtain of stench. The water was running so fast, he could barely keep his footing, but the adrenalin was keeping him going. He heard the ground above him vibrating. Had they missed the manhole cover?

Another few feet, and he paused and listened.

Either the footsteps had dwindled away, and the Tactical guys had missed the sewer, or the rushing noise of the water was drowning out all the other sounds. Frank glanced over his shoulder: nothing but darkness.

Wouldn't the cops bring a flashlight down here? Were the night-vision goggles powerful enough to work in this shithole? Frank continued on, lugging the trunk through the sewer, trying to see through the gloom.

In time, his eyes adjusted somewhat to the darkness, and he began to make out certain features on the walls, certain landmarks in the moldy stone. He saw the silhouette of a rusty old valve, and a few minutes later, he saw a crumbling, oxidized cage-light which some streets-and-sanitation worker had left on. His legs were almost numb, and his skull was throbbing, but he kept on.

He had no choice.

Another few feet, and he noticed a huge brown cable running along the wall. His heart flip-flopped for a moment, expecting the cable to turn into a monstrous boa constrictor, but nothing of the sort happened. He figured it was a telephone or TV cable, and he was closing in on another junction, perhaps another manhole.

He kept his gaze riveted to the darkness ahead of him, his vision blurred with white spots.

Some time later—who knew how long?—he noticed the faintest blush of light ahead of him.

A thin beam of dull light from above.

A way out.

27

Henry Pope was in one of his favorite places when he heard the noise.

It was in the wee hours of the morning, and the house was mostly silent except for the steady whir of rain outside, and the occasional clap of thunder. The doctor was sitting in the big bentwood rocker next to the fireplace, doing one of his favorite things: holding one of his eight grandchildren.

Dressed in his cotton pajamas and terrycloth robe, with his half-glasses propped on the end of his nose, Pope had been gently rocking little Mary Elizabeth, softly singing "Waltzing Matilda," when he heard the noise, barely audible above the storm, coming from somewhere outside. Mary Elizabeth belonged to Pope's youngest daughter, Sarah. A little cherub with tulip lips, fat cheeks, and peach-fuzz hair, the baby had just turned four months old and was sleeping almost straight through the night.

Almost.

A few minutes ago, the baby had awakened the whole household with a round of ululating sobs, and Pope had gotten up and told Sarah—who was visiting from Boston—that he would be happy to sit with the child until she went back to sleep. An exhausted Sarah had been more than happy to take advantage of her father's offer. She had just flown into Midway earlier that night with her husband Michael, and it had been a nightmare flight through heavy weather. Besides, the doctor was still awake, having been at work until the wee hours trying to sort out the Frank Janus debacle.

So . . . for the last ten minutes or so, Pope had been sitting in the living room, singing old college drinking songs to the little duffer, marveling at every twitch of her little fingers, every flutter of her delicate lashes, every flare of her tiny pink nostrils. Holding her miniature hands in his huge, withered, leathery fingers, Pope had silently thanked God for such miracles.

To say the doctor was crazy about babies was a monumental understatement.

Henry Pope probably should have been a pediatrician, or perhaps an OB/GYN. He adored the purity of the little creatures, the innocence, the absolute honesty in their every move. A baby didn't know how to lie or hate or cheat or manipulate or obsess or worry or dig any of the other holes that human beings dig for themselves and each other. A baby was truth personified, a noble little nerve ending that only asked for the most essential necessities of life.

Of course, that didn't prohibit Henry Pope from giving his beloved grandchildren every luxury available to the modern toddler. He loved to spoil his grandchildren with surprise trips to the amusement park, shopping sprees at F.A.O. Schwartz and Toys "R" Us, and elaborate miniature golf excursions. Last summer he built an entire backyard recreation center for his three eldest grand kids, Tommy, Skyler, and Jeremy. And the previous winter, he had gotten Schwinn bicycles for all eight kids. He even started playing Santa Claus at the Pope family Christmas gathering every Christmas Eve.

Which was why the doctor had been reveling in his quiet time with his darling little Mary Elizabeth when the noise had suddenly disrupted the pristine calm. It was a muffled thump out in the back yard somewhere, just beneath the sound of the rain, maybe near the back porch. Like something big and heavy striking the cement stoop.

Pope glanced up at the Seth Thomas clock perched on the mantel. It said it was 5:20 A.M. Too early for the paper boy. Besides, one of the officers assigned to watch his place would have surely intercepted the paper. At the present moment, there were three cars assigned to the Pope house, two squads and one unmarked cruiser—a total of seven men. One of the squads was parked out in front, the two uniforms inside it playing cards. Another black-and-white was in the driveway. And the third car—a service-issue Taurus—was down the street at the corner of Isabella and Fee Roads, keeping tabs on every car that entered or exited the Kenilworth gated community.

After coming home, Pope had insisted on sleeping in his own bed, despite the Frank Janus crisis. And even his wife, Mary Ann, had been in favor of continuing on with life as usual—which included having family visiting from out of town. After eleven years of marriage, Mary Ann Pope had grown accustomed to these kinds of crisis with emotionally unstable cops, and no matter how gravely the FBI warned them, the Popes refused to be intruded upon. Lieutenant Krimm had been the one to strike a compromise: He would station police around the Pope property until such time that Frank Janus could be apprehended. This had been fine with Mary Ann, just so they didn't trample her impatiens and daffodils like that lummox Sully Deets.

Pope carefully craned himself out of his rocker, wincing at his arthritic joints, paying special attention to the slumbering child in his arms. The baby had fallen fast asleep on the second chorus of "The Tables Down at Morrie's," and Pope didn't want to disturb her. Cradling the blanket around her, he felt her warmth against his chest like a perfumed ember.

He padded across the living room to the kitchen.

The light was off, and the kitchen was awash in shadows. The dull gleam of chrome appliances, a Sub-Zero freezer, and Viking range. Mary Ann's expansive pot rack, laden with hanging copper and wrought iron. A watery shadowplay of raindrops streaming down a window, throwing patterns across the immaculate linoleum floor.

Pope heard something dripping nearby like a leaky faucet, but the sink was dry. The doctor shivered. There was a draft coming from somewhere. A gust of cold, wet wind, and the smell of earthworms permeating the kitchen.

"Don't move."

The voice came from across the kitchen—in the shadows of the mud room where the back door was a few inches ajar—and it sent a jolt of panic up Henry Pope's spine. The voice was eerily familiar.

"I'm not moving," Pope said, his spine stiffening, the baby oblivious in his arms.

"Don't signal anybody, and don't wake the baby."

"I'm not about to signal anybody, Frank, and don't worry, the baby's sound asleep."

Frank Janus emerged from the shadows, dressed in a patrol uniform.

He stood there for a moment, holding the revolver on Pope, the rain dripping off the brim of his hat and plunking to the linoleum. He was soaked, and he was trembling slightly, but his eyes told another story. His eyes were glittering with determination, fixed on Pope.

"Frank, all I ask is that you don't hurt the child," Pope said softly.

"Why in God's name would I hurt a child?"

"I didn't mean anything by it, Frank. All I'm saying is, this is my granddaughter."

"I won't hurt the child, Doc."

A beat of incredibly awkward silence.

"What do you want me to do, Frank?" Pope asked.

Frank Janus stared at the doctor for a long moment, and in that horrible pause, it seemed that Frank had no idea what to do next.

* * *

Frank felt as though a fist were turning inside him as he stared at the kindly old psychiatrist, the baby cradled gently in the old man's arms, those hound dog eyes peering over tortoiseshell reading glasses. Could this possibly be the man who set Frank up? Could this be the man responsible for Kyle's murder? Frank swallowed his anguish, holding the gun as steadily as possibly, wiping his face with his free hand. "We're going to go put the baby back in its crib," Frank heard himself say.

"We're going upstairs?" Pope said, the alarm bright and shimmery in his eyes.

"Nobody needs to get hurt," Frank reiterated.

"My wife's a light sleeper."

"Nobody else needs to get involved," Frank said. "I just want to make sure the baby is safe."

The doctor looked at him for a moment. "Okay, Frank, fine, let's do that."

"Go ahead, Doc."

The child stirred suddenly in the doctor's arms, its tiny lips pursing and suckling. Pope gazed down at the baby and said very softly, "If the child comes awake, Frank, her mother will be up in a second."

"I give you my word I won't hurt anybody."

Pope looked up at Frank and nodded sheepishly. "Fair enough, Frank."

"I'm going to need you to get moving, Doc," Frank said, allowing just a trace of urgency to seep into his voice. He could sense his time ticking away with every low rattle of thunder outside.

What a shame it would be to blow it now, here in Pope's house, especially after all bullets—both symbolic and literal—that Frank had dodged over the last forty-five minutes. Especially after making it through the netherworld of the sewer system, and then managing to get all the way over to Kyle's faculty office at Loyola without getting nailed, and then managing to get into the office without setting off any alarms. And even then, it was a miracle that Frank's old uniform had fit him so well, right down to the old radio mike he used to carry clipped to his shoulder. The trunk had been full of old threadbare memories, but thank God the moths had not yet gotten to his old patrol uniform.

"Okay, Frank, I'm going," the doctor said finally, and started across the kitchen.

They made their way across the living room, and past Mary Ann Pope's elaborate dining table. Candlesticks and Waterford crystal gleamed in the darkness. The air smelled of potpourri and lemon wax.

Frank kept the gun at waist level, holding it as discreetly as possible on the doctor in case one of the other uniforms surveilling the place happened to look in a window. They reached the staircase.

"The baby's in the guest room at the top of the stairs," Pope whispered.

"After you, Doc."

They started up the carpeted steps.

Lightning flickered through the front drapes, hitting a chandelier at the top of the stairs, reflecting tiny spangles of light on the walls. Frank blinked away the fatigue, wiping his eyes with his free hand. He felt sick, yet energized by the tension. The tension was good. The tension was working in his favor.

"How are you feeling, Frank?" Pope asked in a low, gentle voice as he ascended the steps. Frank could see the back of the doctor's head, the dim light accentuating the downy tufts of gray fuzz around his ears.

"Doc, if you could just stay quiet for next few minutes," Frank whispered, "I'd really appreciate it."

They reached the top of the stairs.

The second floor hallway was tastefully decorated, and also shrouded in shadows. The door to the baby's room was closed, and Pope paused outside it. Frank shot a hand up, silencing him. Then Frank indicated that he would open the door. Thunder boomed outside, and Frank cringed. Every single creak, every footstep, every squeaking floorboard was lessening his odds of getting out of here without a fire fight.

Reaching down and very carefully turning the door-knob, Frank opened the door and nodded at Pope.

Pope carried the child into the darkness of the room, over to a corner crib, and gently laid her down. It was one of those foldup travel cribs with the plastic padding and metal frame. The baby settled into a corner with her thumb in her mouth. Pope sighed.

Out in the hallway, Frank heard a noise.

"What's going on?"

The voice was like an icicle stabbed between Frank's shoulder blades.

Frank whirled and saw the middle-aged woman in a silk robe standing outside her bedroom door, about ten feet away, wringing her hands. Her eyes were taking everything in all at once, and they glinted with anger. "I thought you people were going to stay outside," Mary Ann Pope said.

Frank let the gun fall to his side, out of the woman's line of vision. "Yes ma'am," he muttered, scrambling for words, searching for the appropriate response.

Henry Pope materialized in the guest room doorway, his crooked finger pressed against his lips. "Ssshhhh—honey, please," he whispered. "I just got the baby to sleep."

"What the hell is going on?" the matriarch demanded.

"Mrs. Pope—" Frank started.

"Honey," the doctor jumped in. "This fine young man just needs to go over some things, security stuff."

"At 5:30 in the morning?"

Pope nodded, and told her it was safer that way.

"Oh, stop it," Mary Ann Pope said, waving the notion off like a bad smell.

"Honey, please," the doctor pleaded.

"No, dammit, I've had it up to here with this disruptive nonsense. It's one thing to post guards in front of the house, but this is ridiculous."

Pope let out a nervous sigh.

Frank's heart was racing. His hands were tingling. An idea was worming its way into his consciousness. "Actually, ma'am, what we're going to need to do is borrow your husband for a few minutes."

"*Borrow* him?"

"That's correct, ma'am." Frank gave her a terse smile. "No big deal, just another briefing down at the Twenty-fourth on this Frank Janus situation."

Frank was edging closer to Pope, pushing the .38 against the old man's leg, pressing the tiny metal sighting notch against Pope's thigh just to drive home the point.

"Honey, look," Pope said softly, looking the woman square in the eyes, "I realize I'm putting you through the wringer here, but this guy Janus was one of mine. And this is a bad one. The worst ever."

An intense pause. Mary Ann Pope's lined face in the dim light:' world-weary eyes staring at her husband, turning things over in her mind.

"It won't take long at all," Pope added. "I'll be back before anybody's up."

Another anguished pause.

Thunder rolled outside, and finally Mary Ann Pope pulled her robe tighter. "You're telling me this nonsense is absolutely necessary?"

"I'm afraid it is, ma'am," Frank told her. "In fact, I'm going to need your help."

"My *help*?"

Frank could feel Pope's urgent stare on the side of his face. The corridor felt narrower. The tension was squeezing Frank's chest. "If it's not too much trouble," he said, "I'm going to need one of your raincoats, maybe a scarf or a hat, for the doctor to wear."

The woman stared incredulously. "You want one of my rain coats for Henry?" The lines around her mouth deepened for a moment, her dishwater eyes narrowing. This was a woman who had suffered every kind of fool-ishness known to man.

Frank started to say, "The idea is to—"

"Is something wrong?"

Another voice came from across the hall, to Frank's immediate left, and Frank whirled toward it. Another woman was standing in the dim light of another bedroom doorway. Thirtyish, long brown hair, oversized Chicago Bears T-shirt, she was probably the mother of the baby.

"It's nothing, sweetheart," Pope was saying, carefully closing the guest room door. "Mary Elizabeth is fine, sawing logs like a good little squirt."

"I heard voices," the woman said, giving Frank a suspicious glance.

"Everything's fine, ma'am," Frank said, managing his officious smile. Inside he was seething with panic, his pulse thumping in his ears. He had to get the doctor out of there soon, before the whole house of cards came tumbling down. The only thing Frank had going for him was unpredictability. He knew the doctor didn't want to involve his family in the machinations of a crazy man.

"They're taking your father away again," Mary Ann Pope informed her.

"They're what?"

"It's just a routine trip down to headquarters," Frank said, then looked at Mary Ann Pope. "The only thing is, we need to sneak him out the back way in case there's any danger."

"What do you mean by danger?" she asked.

"Well—" Frank began.

"Darling, *please*!"

The doctor's voice woke everybody up, the sudden display of nerves like a cold shower. Frank wondered if Pope was losing his composure.

Pope glowered at his wife. "Find something I can wear, and let's get this thing over with!"

Mary Ann Pope stared at her husband for a moment, then turned in a huff and swished back into her bedroom.

Pope turned to his daughter. "You go back to sleep, Sarah, go on."

"But, Daddy—"

"Mary Elizabeth's fine, sweetheart."

The woman in the T-shirt let out a strained sigh, then retreated to her room. The door closed behind her with a resounding click.

Anguished silence returned to the hallway.

Pope said under his breath, "I don't suppose you're going to tell me where you're taking me."

"Somewhere quiet, where we can talk."

"How are you possibly going to get past the black-and-whites downstairs?"

"Don't worry about that, Doc."

"I'm not worrying, I'm just saying—"

"Just keep playing along, and we'll be outta here before you know it."

"Why are you doing this, Frank?"

Frank looked at Pope's gray face. "That's exactly what I'm going to find out."

Pope started to say something else when the matriarch suddenly emerged from the bedroom with her arms full of navy blue nylon and pink chiffon.

"I guess you can go ahead and rip these to shreds," she said, offering the fabric to Frank.

Frank didn't even have to look at them. "Excellent, thank you."

Frank looked at the doctor, something unspoken passing between the two men.

Inside Frank, a clock was ticking.

PART IV

The Classroom of Broken Glass

"Strange, is it not? That of the myriads who
Before us passed the door of darkness through,
Not one returns to tell us of the road,
Which to discover we must travel too."
                              —OMAR KHAYYÁM, *Rubaiyat*

28

At precisely 5:37 A.M., a uniformed officer and a stooped figure in a woman's navy blue raincoat emerged from the basement door of the Victorian two-story on Isabella Street.

The officer had his arm around the figure, and they climbed the mortar steps toward ground level with a brisk sort of purpose. The officer was careful to keep low, yanking his hostage along a row of large hemlocks bordering the side yard, avoiding the sight lines of the other cops in front.

The cop and the figure made their way across the slick grass and through the neighbor's gate. From this point, they proceeded along the neighbor's back fence and out the other side, shielding their faces from the rain.

They reached Fee Street, and caught the attention of the unmarked squad sitting under a streetlamp at the corner.

The two detectives inside the unmarked Ford simultaneously glanced up from their card game. One of them rhetorically asked what the fuck was going on, and then wiped the condensation from the windshield, squinting to see through the predawn squalls. The other detective flipped on a searchlight, which was mounted near the side mirror, and swept the beam through the storm.

The light landed on the retreating uniform and the figure in the raincoat.

Frank Janus never broke his stride. He just waved at
the unmarked squad with the kind of studied noncha-
lance that most cops acquire over many years on the job
and then he pointed at the doctor and made a quick
gesture with his hand—

—*because there's a gesture known only among street
cops, a sort of circular "winding" movement of the hand,
with the index finger pointed upward. It's the same sort of
gesture that television floor-directors give their on-camera
talent when something is running too long, meaning "wind
it up," but to cops, it means something quite different.
Cops have many such gestures, but this one is a classic.
It means, "I got this character under control, so don't
worry, I'm going to take care of it."*

The two detectives recognized the signal immediately
and flashed their headlamps twice.

Frank threw a nod over his shoulder as he ushered the
psychiatrist across Fee Street and down the sidewalk. It
took about a minute and a half in the rain. Frank hurried
the doctor through the gates of Riverlook Estates, then
into the forest preserve that ran along the border of
Sheridan Road and the lakefront.

The plan had worked.

It took the two detectives several minutes to realize
something was off the beam, and several more minutes
to radio back to one of the squads in front of the Pope
place. The problem was, the other uniforms were all inside the house by that point, getting their asses chewed
off by a livid Mary Ann Pope. And when the detectives
finally learned what was going on, all hell had broken
loose.

The two detectives made a valiant effort to save the
day, hastily following Frank's trail into the forest preserve, but it was too late.

By the time the detectives reached the tree line, Frank
and Dr. Pope had already reached the Linden Avenue
"El" stop and were boarding the last train of the graveyard shift.

*   *   *

"After you, Doc—come on—down the steps."

Frank was standing in the rain near a kiosk of graffiti-stained cement where an iron staircase descended into deeper shadows. His Colt was partially obscured under the hem of his uniform, and his heart was pounding. Pope was pausing on the first step, reluctant to go any farther, still in his wife's raincoat. The psychiatrist was soaked through to the skin, his gray hair pasted to his skull under his scarf, his pouchy eyes red from the wind.

"What is this place, Frank?"

"I'm surprised you don't know," Frank said, wiping his face with his free hand. "You know everything else about me."

Thunder droned in the distance like a tired old man clearing his throat. The sky was the color of nicotine. The dawn had barely made a dent in the night, and the light was now a filthy shade of gray.

"I'm too old and too wet for games, Frank," the doctor said.

"Come on, Doc—down the steps," Frank said, then nudged Pope in the kidney.

The older man turned and trundled slowly down the iron stairs.

At the bottom of the staircase was a litter-strewn landing of cracked concrete. The smell of urine was strong, and there was a flattened carcass of something mashed into one corner—a pigeon or a rat. There was an unmarked door on the building side, padlocked and reinforced with burglar mesh.

"Are you going to tell me where we are?" Pope said, wiping the rain from his beard.

"An old haunt," Frank said, digging a set of keys out of his belt. They were old keys from his patrol days. Very few of their corresponding locks still existed. But a couple of them—like the door in front of him—were still around.

"You wouldn't say a word on the train, Frank, I think you owe me an explanation."

"Stand over there, please, Doc." Frank motioned the psychiatrist away from the door.

Pope obliged. "Don't you think this has gone far enough?"

Frank found an old brass skeleton key and worked it into the rusty padlock. "Let's get out of the rain, and then we can have our little talk."

The padlock snapped. Frank pulled the lock apart, then pushed the door open.

They entered a vestibule that stank of pigeon droppings and pasty filth. It was too dark to see anything yet, but Frank remembered the place vividly. The odors and textures were pouring through him, evoking childhood memories. He was lightheaded. His groin throbbed as he urged the doctor through the shadows, their footsteps crackling on cinders. Frank kept the gun trained on Pope's midsection.

"My brother and I used to come here as kids," Frank told the psychiatrist as they approached a ragged velvet curtain. Filmed in dust, stiff as board from age, the curtain hung in the corner across a doorway into the main room.

"Frank—"

"Years later," Frank went on, "when I was walking a beat in the Twentieth, I ended up checking this place every night."

Frank ushered the doctor through the curtain and into the past.

The Bijou was breathtaking, even in the darkness, even in its dilapidated condition. The size of an airplane hangar, with two tiers of box seats, and sweeping balconies, the place was crumbling like a ruined Greek temple. Frank heard his own voice echoing off the gilded walls: "At one point in our lives, this place was a sanctuary for me and my brother. You remember my brother, don't you, Doc?"

"Frank, I never—"

"SHUT UP!" Frank boomed, his voice reverberating like a ghost trying to get out of the theater.

A flurry of whispers trailed after the sound, the voice of Frank's Other, his murderous dark half. Then the whispers faded away.

Frank swallowed his emotions for a moment, gazing around the old movie palace. Thin shafts of daylight shone down from holes in the high ceiling. Half the seats were missing, like rotted-out teeth. The once-golden walls were chipped and peeling, and a huge, tattered screen rose up in front, riddled with gouges and water marks. Frank and Kyle used to come here and watch Christopher Lee and Peter Cushing battle each other in *The Curse of Frankenstein* and *The Mummy* and *Dr. Terror's House of Horrors,* and reality would be swallowed up on a wave of Juju-Bees and Dots and Good & Plentys.

Frank glanced over at the real Dr. Terror, standing there, dripping on the sticky floor, his long, pallid face framed by the soggy scarf, looking like some demented old charwoman from some lost Dickens story. Frank kept the gun raised and aimed at the psychiatrist.

"May I take the coat off now?" Pope asked.

Frank's eyes were adjusting to dark. He could see Pope's face clearly now. "Be my guest, Doc."

The older man shrugged off the raincoat and peeled the scarf off his head. He carefully draped them across the back of a padded seat. "I assume there's a point to taking me here? Some sort of symbolism?"

"What did you do to me?" Frank asked very softly.

There was a pause as the doctor very calmly fixed his gaze on Frank. "I didn't do anything to you, Frank. I don't know what you're referring to."

"Who killed my brother?"

"You did."

"That's a lie."

"Whatever you say, Frank," the doctor said. "Whatever you say."

Frank raised the Colt higher, aiming it at Pope's face. A little more serious now. "I could no more easily kill my brother than kill myself."

"If you shoot me, Frank, that's exactly what you'd be doing—killing yourself."

"Why? Are you me?"

"No."

"You never answered my question about the videotape."

"What about it?"

Frank burned his gaze into those hound dog eyes. "You knew about the reference to God's work."

"Yes, and I told you—"

"You *knew* about it because you *saw* it, you saw the tape before I did."

"Whatever you say, Frank."

"Or maybe you saw me make it. Maybe you were there when I made the tape."

"Now you're really grasping—"

"What did you do to me, Doc?"

"Not a thing, Frank. I didn't do a thing to you. Everything that's happening to you, you're doing to yourself. Or should I say, your brain chemistry is doing it to you."

Frank thumbed the hammer back with a loud *CLICK*! "Did you kill my brother?"

Pope stared calmly, unblinkingly down the barrel of the Diamondback. "Listen to me, Frank. You're having a psychotic episode. And I can help you—"

Frank lunged at him, pressing the barrel against the bridge of his nose. "DID YOU KILL MY BROTHER?!"

A sudden noise from above: a rush of feathery, screechy sounds.

Frank glanced up at a flock of pigeons, roused out of their nest by the commotion. The birds poured out of a chandelier, flapping and fluttering up into a column of sickly daylight, then shot out a gaping maw in the ceiling as puffs of ancient plaster sifted down through the shaft of light.

When Frank looked back at Pope, the psychiatrist was smiling. "You need some sleep, Frank," he said with his yellow grin, his droopy eyes glinting.

Frank looked at him. *"What?!"*

Pope repeated the words, the litany: "You need some sleep, Frank."

An echo of whispers gusting through the empty theater like an ill wind—*I warned you, I warned you. I warned you. I warned you, I warned you.*

"What are you doing?!—those phrases!" Frank demanded, squeezing the grip tighter.

"Look at the time," the doctor went on, a weird light in his eyes.

Whispers swirled through Frank's brain, and he winced, and he struggled against the tide. He looked at the doctor, pressing the gun barrel harder against the old man's skull. "You keep repeating those phrases!—like mantras or memory devices!—what are they?!"

"You should be in bed, Frank," Pope said with a grin, locking gazes with Frank.

Frank felt the first tremor travel up his spine as though a nerve ending had been strummed. His hand felt cold on the grip of the gun, and his arm felt heavy, and the tremors shot across his shoulderblade and down his arm. A wave of whispers crashed inside his brain.

"What are you doing?!" he said, his voice sticking in his throat, his esophagus seizing up. "I'll—I'll blow the back of your head off!—I'll—!"

The doctor grinned calmly at him. "It's way past your bedtime."

The next wave of current shuddered through Frank like a fist, and his jaw violently snapped shut, and his back arched—his eyes welling up so badly he could hardly see—and all this happened in the space of an instant. Frank struggled to keep the gun aimed at Pope, but Frank's right hand had the palsy now, and the gun was trembling.

The theater was dimming as though some horrible show was about to begin. Near the front: a single pigeon tossed and flapped against the projection screen, confused by the noise and movement.

"You know what happens to little boys when they stay up past their bedtime?" the doctor asked.

The gun slipped out of Frank's hand and clattered to the floor.

Electricity blazed through Frank's body, and he stood there for a moment, completely paralyzed now, shivering convulsively, his jaw frozen shut like a puppet being shaken by a petulant child.

Then he fell to his knees, his body engulfed in sub-zero cold.

"The Sleep Police find you," Pope said, enunciating his words as though they were poison darts. "And they take you away forever and ever."

Frank flopped to the floor like a fish on a hook, the cold current flooding through him, making his nerve endings shriek, encasing his body in ice. He couldn't even scream. It was as though his jaw was wired shut all of a sudden, and all he could do was lie there in a jumble of tics and chills, staring up at the psychiatrist.

Pope sighed, glancing around the deserted theater, then glancing down at Frank. "For a long time I wondered about you, Frank," Pope said. "I wondered how long it would take you to put it all together."

Terror howled in Frank's brain.

Pope was towering over him, the doctor's stooped form silhouetted in the gloom. His face was haloed by a nimbus of light. "You're a good cop, Frank. You deserve an explanation."

29

It all starts with a complex tapestry of events, like all of God's work.

On that fateful day fifteen summers ago, he awakens early—before the sun. He's been waking early for months. The lithium does little to ease his pain anymore. The practitioners call it manic-depression. Bipolar. But he knows it is merely training for his larger purposes. Like the Benedictine monks of the seventeenth century. His brain is his cloister.

That morning, he prepares for the march carefully. He wears modest clothing—Sansabelt slacks, golf shirt. He has a light breakfast. He has prepared placards, pro-life slogans on cardboard signs, and he stacks them carefully in the rear of the Suburban van.

He takes the highway downtown, listening to hymns. His experience as a policeman helps him function in the urban ghetto, his skills as a therapist help him deal with people on the edge. The clinic is on the southwest side, on the border of an industrial district. It is a shell-shocked place, ravaged with crime and poverty. He parks several blocks north of the clinic, then walks the rest of the way over broken glass and urine, like Job walking into the whirlwind.

By the time he arrives at the clinic, there are other marchers already picketing the cursed place. He joins *them, comrades in arm, allies in the holy war against the heretics who would kill babies. It is a blazing hot day, and he sweats profusely as he marches, his anti-abortion sign raised high. Within hours, he is exhausted. Drenched in sweat, voice hoarse from shouting righteous chants.*

And that's when he encounters his destiny.

She is coming out of the clinic with a backpack: a young girl—couldn't be more than twenty, young enough to be his daughter—with a sheepish expression on her face. And all at once, he knows. He knows what she has done— even in the midst of the protest. She has murdered her own child. Drawn and quartered its tiny limbs. Sucked it into a toilet.

And yet. And yet.

This young mother who is hurrying down the sidewalk, trying to avoid the shouts and feverish gazes of the protest- ers, seems so innocent, so young, so impressionable. The sun is dappling her blond hair with a soft, luminous halo, and he takes this as a sign.

This woman is his destiny.

"Sister!" he cries out in his most charitable, benevolent voice. "God forgives you!"

She is approaching him, an intense, pinched expression on her face. He gets a closer look at her. Her midriff is bare, her top stretched across loose-hanging breasts. Her hair is bottle-blond, and she has tattoos on her upper arms, and her face has a certain hardness to it. "Why don't you leave me alone?" she says as she passes.

"I can help you," he says to her.

She pauses, chewing gum, her eyes caked with dark makeup. It's becoming clear that this girl is no college student. She's a working girl, maybe a prostitute. "How the hell are you going to help me?" she says, her eyes flaring with contempt.

"I can help you understand what you've done," he says, and he means it with all sincerity. He can show her the studies, the biological reality. The fully formed nervous

system of a fetus. The horrors of abortion. And he can ease her guilt by helping her find God, helping her find a truer path down which to lead her life.

"What?!—what did you say?!" she hisses at him with a glowering look.

"What you've done," he says. "You should know how it feels. To an innocent, unborn child."

She stares at him for a moment, aghast, like a soldier stumbling upon an atrocity of war. Then the rage and the self-loathing take over, and her expression tightens into a mask of hate.

She takes a step closer and spits at him.

The glob of mucous and saliva hits him in the eye, and the sheer surprise of it jerks him back with a start. His foot catches the edge of the curb, and he tumbles backward to the pavement. He lands hard on his posterior, and the pain shoots up his spine. A few gasps rise up from the other protesters, a smattering of nervous laughter.

The girl is still standing there, staring at him. "Fuck you," she says.

Then she walks away.

He watches her, the center of his chest like a block of ice. The others help him to his feet, and he keeps watching her as she vanishes around the edge of the building.

He wipes the spittle off his face. The cold is spreading through him, down his arms, into his fingertips. He feels like an ice sculpture.

Something deep inside him clicks suddenly like a switch being thrown.

"Henry? Are you all right?"

The voice is a fellow protester standing next to him, sounding as though it were underwater, coming from a great distance. His mind is rearranging itself, his molecules realigning. The cold is turning to heat. The heat turning to energy. The energy turning to purpose. The revelation galvanizing him.

"Henry?"

He turns away from the picket line and starts across the

*street. There is much to do. He has been asleep all these
years. The harlot has opened his eyes. The girl is indeed
his destiny.*

There is so much to do.

*He will demonstrate to these women—these wretched
whores—what it's like to be an innocent child of God and
be snuffed out by a metal probe, or be torn apart by
forceps, or be flushed by suction. He will show them what
it's like to be an unborn child and have your life ripped
out, without anaesthesia, without warning, without reason.*

He will make them feel what it's like.

*He will make them know the consequences of their
actions.*

Starting tonight.

The psychiatrist paused.

His story had taken less than ten minutes, but it had
pierced Frank like a grappling hook through his brain.
In the gloom of the empty theater, lying on the sticky
floor, his pulse pounding, his body stiff and inert,
Frank had absorbed each word as though it were a
bullet.

"And that brings me to you, Frank," Henry Pope said
then, pacing through the shaft of jaundiced light beaming
down from the ruined ceiling.

The doctor's voice had a dull echo to it, as though it
were rattling around in Frank's head, and every subsequent echo sank deeper into Frank's subconscious, re-
minding him just how close a homicide detective can be
to the truth of a case, and never connect the pieces.
Motive and opportunity.

Of course, of course.

Frank had seen patterns in Pope's background, but
hadn't recognized the link. The connection to children
through pediatrics, the right-wing politics, the troubled
history with women. Henry Pope had turned his medical
training, and his skills as a policeman and a social

worker, into a horrifying modus operandi of Old Testament vengeance. The signature of an angry God.

The thumb suckers had nothing to do with sleep.

The victims were posed as babies, molded in the image of the unborn children they had aborted. Frank knew the truth now, the fragmented memories of coroner reports and victim histories streaming through his mind. The victims all shared a history of multiple abortions. They were the ideal examples upon which Pope could fulfill his spiritual mission: surgical eviscerations emulating abortions, and the horrible tranquility of those cold, dead thumbs inserted between livid, blue lips.

For one brief instant, Frank's mind conjured terrifying Technicolor glimpses of the doctor hunting down candidates late at night from the comfort of his Lincoln Town Car, consulting medical records from welfare clinics on strippers and high-priced escorts, moving through the shadowy world of sex clubs under the guise of a social worker ministering to the unwashed. And the ultimate surgical precision of each murder, the use of pentobarbital, the subtle misdirection of the strangulation wounds, not to mention the elaborate process of planting evidence.

Pope was the thumb sucker killer, and he had found his perfect patsy in Frank Janus.

"I must say," the doctor mused aloud, his voice echoing across empty shadows. "I was always a little taken aback that you never figured out the fetal position. Something a good detective would tap into immediately."

Frank managed to sit up, leaning back against a broken theater seat. His body was limp. His nerve endings felt as though they had been scoured. He took a shallow breath and managed to say, "How did you do it? Hypnosis?"

Pope was on a roll, pacing along the ramshackle rows of chairs, pontificating in the darkness. Pigeons rustled somewhere off in the shadows of the theater. "All those poor, sweet, innocent babies," he said, gesturing expansively. "It's the invisible holocaust, Frank. Can't you see the need for atonement?"

Frank saw his .38 lying under a chair less than ten feet away. "What did you do to me?" he asked softly.

"Frank, I know it's painful, losing your brother like that, but if you had any idea what kind of pain these innocent children go through."

The gun lay within Frank's grasp, if he could just make the lunge across the aisle. "I asked you a question," he said, wiping his eyes.

"There were others, Frank." The doctor paused then, looking down at Frank slumped on the floor. "Other Jane Does in other districts. I was able to do my work for quite a while, and watch the blotters chalk them up as cold cases that would never be solved. Forgotten women, Frank. Society's invisible cast-offs. Then there was the one from the Nineteenth District, the stripper, the one I left under Wacker Drive. That was one of your first cases, Frank, and you blew it. You came to see me, and you were spooked, and I filed that away."

"Are you going to answer my question?" Frank said, glancing at the gun under the chair, summoning all his strength. If he could just get to it before Pope did any more hocus-pocus.

"I'm getting to that, Frank," the doctor said. "Believe me. It all goes back to that first case. You wouldn't quit digging. And then it hit me. You could be my insurance policy. With that horrendous childhood, all that emotional baggage, all those delusions and phobias, all that stuff tied up in knots inside you. I started working on you. Just in case. I started slipping things in when you weren't looking."

"I'm not going to ask you again," Frank said in a measured voice, his body coiled like a spring, ready to explode.

The gun was lying there, waiting for him.

Across the theater, a flock of pigeons were flapping against the screen.

"You've heard of Punch and Judy, Frank?" the psychiatrist said.

Frank sprang to his feet suddenly and went for the gun.

And time seemed to freeze.

30

The Diamondback is a single-action revolver commonly carried in Condition Two, which means the chamber is full, but the hammer is depressed, so the best position for a shooter under pressure is the "tripod" posture, which means legs are slightly bent, and elbows are locked, and the left hand is steadying the bottom of the grip, and the right hand is around the grip with the index finger on the trigger and the thumb on the hammer so that the hammer can be cocked in one, easy, reflexive movement—

—and that's exactly what Frank did as he lurched across the aisle suddenly, snatching the gun out from under the seat and slamming into an adjacent chair, sending dust and moths into the air.

Somehow he managed to get both hands around the Colt, and he scrambled back to his feet, the fundamental lessons he had learned in the academy spinning through his brain. He managed to face the doctor, aiming the gun as best he could with his blurred vision, trembling hands, and wobbly knees.

"WHAT DID YOU DO TO ME?!" he thundered one last time, his voice sending the pigeons into a frenzy, bouncing off the walls, dive-bombing the screen.

The doctor just stared calmly at the gun. "Ask the Sleep Police, Frank."

Frank pulled the trigger—

—except his finger would not depress the tiny rubber-coated lever. It would not fire the gun. It would not budge. It was as if the gun had jammed, but the gun had not jammed, the gun was fine, the gun was well oiled and in fine working order, and Frank knew instantly that it was not his gun, but his *finger* that had jammed—

—or, more precisely, it was his brain that had seized up, refusing to send the proper signal to his finger.

"It was easy, Frank," Pope was saying, strolling slowly toward the gun, whose barrel was still aimed right at the doctor. Pope paused, peered down the muzzle, then shook his head in a "tsk-tsk-tisk" manner. "And you were right about the hypnosis. But it was much more than mere posthypnotic suggestion. I got inside your head, Frank, and I rearranged the furniture."

Frank focused his concentration on pulling the trigger, but his hand just hung in midair like a brick. A cold sweat had popped on his forehead, and his whole body was trembling with furious effort. Frank heard his teeth cracking in his skull as he squeezed.

Dr. Pope was circling him like a man visiting a museum, looking at an exhibit. "Remember the medication for the insomnia? Did you ever wonder why your HMO always refused to cover it? Didn't that seem strange?"

Tears oozed from Frank's eyes as he stood there in the darkness with the gun hanging before his face, his arm starting to bend under the weight of it. Somewhere, outside, far in the distance, thunder rumbled.

"It's called Lixotheopental," the doctor announced almost gleefully, circling, circling. "It's a new psychotropic drug that puts you in a hypnotic state every time you go to sleep. It's like having a remote control to a person's behavior, Frank. It's incredible."

Frank was having trouble standing up. The gun felt as though it weighed a thousand pounds in his hand. His arm was drooping. He cringed and said, "You better kill me now, Doc."

"I would never do that, Frank. Good Lord." The doctor continued nonchalantly circling him. "It was so easy, though. Such a wonderful subject. It was so easy. All that baggage, all those fears to work with. At first I tried to simply drive you away from the investigation, planting little suggestions. Like training a dog to stay off the couch."

Frank collapsed, fell to his knees, his hand still clutching the Colt.

He was silently sobbing now. The gun was so heavy in his hand it tipped him forward, then lay on the floor in his grip like a dead weight.

"You're too professional—too good of a cop, I suppose—to walk away," the doctor went on. "That was when I realized you were the perfect candidate to crack into separate personalities. All that latent anger, separation anxiety. Such a polite young man. All those demons."

Frank was on his hands and knees now, weeping, gaping down at the gun frozen in his grasp, weighing him down. The gun weighed a million pounds now.

"We did a lot of therapeutic hypnosis the first time," Pope was saying. "It was so easy, Frank. Planting all those posthypnotic suggestions. Creating an entirely separate personality to take the fall. It was so systematic. Getting you to make the videos."

Frank tried to speak, tried to answer the doctor, but the emotions were choking him, crushing him. To lose the battle like this—like a sick animal—was almost beyond comprehension for Frank.

"You know the irony of all this?" the doctor asked, somewhat rhetorically. "It turns out you were the perfect profile for the murderer. All those buttons. I just had to press them." He paused then, his monstrous, elongated shadow falling across the aisle. He took off his bifocals and rubbed his eyes and said, "Like the number *eleven* for instance."

The gun shivered suddenly in Frank's hand, like a small animal convulsing. Frank stopped crying and looked down at the revolver.

"I respect you, Frank," the doctor said, standing over him, putting his glasses back on. "As a detective. As a man. I really do. That's why I built some safety features into the programming. Key words. Behavioral cues drawing on childhood terrors. Hypnotic triggers. Like the number *eleven*."

Frank stared at the gun. It was vibrating softly, pulsing in his hand as though it were alive.

"You were so forthcoming in our sessions, Frank." The doctor looked at him almost sadly. "Always willing to share your fears, your deepest emotional scars. Very useful. Which brings me to the number *eleven*."

Terror trumpeted in Frank's brain as the vague connection was made between the number eleven and a foggy, partially formed memory from his childhood—

—*sitting alone in a strange room at his Aunt Treva's, a week after his mother was sent away, the notion first strikes little Frankie: a way out of this mess, an answer, a solution to all his problems, and he realizes it comes to him at eleven o'clock on the eleventh day of the eleventh month—*

Heat was flowing through Frank's arm now, his tendons spasming. The gun was twitching. Frank stared at it. Something terrible was happening.

"I hate to see it end like this, Frank," Pope said, his voice heavy with regret. "You were an incredible subject. But you can imagine the kind of toll all these killings must take on a person after a while. The guilt must be tremendous. Which again brings us to the number *eleven*."

The Colt was rising off the floor on its own power.

Frank fought it. He rose to his knees, and squeezed and grunted, sweating profusely, teeth clenching, but he was powerless to stop his rebellious arm from lifting the gun. And he knew what was happening, as surely as he knew the significance of the number eleven—

—*for an eleven-year-old boy contemplating suicide for*

the first time in his life, as the clock strikes eleven on the eleventh day of the eleventh month.

"Please," Frank mewled breathlessly, watching his arm raise the gun.

"I'm sorry, Frank," the doctor said, watching the process unfold. "There's nothing I can do. The work is too important. It's a modern holocaust."

Frank watched in horror as his puppet arm slowly turned the gun toward his face.

"All those innocent souls," Pope was saying. "Dying hideous deaths because of a few selfish, soulless whores. Something has to be done."

Frank tried desperately to grab the Diamondback with his free hand, shove it away, avert it. It was as though an enormous magnet were pulling it toward his chin.

Pope turned away, not caring to watch the gruesome outcome. "Goodbye, Frank."

"Nuh—n-nn—no," Frank uttered through gnashing, clenched teeth. He was soaked in perspiration. He didn't want to kill himself.

Almost tenderly the barrel touched the sensitive skin under his jaw.

"P-please," Frank pleaded, frantically digging down into the pit of his psyche for a way out.

Behind him, a pigeon rustled furiously against the torn fabric of a movie screen.

Frank's trigger finger tingled, a pearl of sweat tracking into his eye.

Outside, in the far distance: the low growl of thunder.

Frank's eyes slammed shut.

He pulled the trigger.

31

He's outdoors. He's moving. The thick, green landscape is a blur on either side of him. He's fourteen years old, stewing in hormones and adolescent angst, and he's footracing his brother down a remote, rutted dirt road in the deep woods north of Uncle Andreas's farm.

There's a huge, hollowed-out tree at the end of the road, sheltered by a thick screen of foliage. This is their sanctuary, their respite from the trials and tribulations of puberty. They come here to chill out, to commiserate, to smoke cigarettes and vent their frustrations and philosophize. There's a stash of skunk weed that Frankie got from a senior at Funks Grove High School hidden inside the tree under a dead root. It's in a little lacquer box that Aunt Nikki brought back from Greece. The pot is harsh and makes Frankie dizzy, but it's the best way to escape reality.

They reach the tree, each boy panting like crazy, giggling. They lean against the tree for a moment trying to catch their breaths. Kyle jokes that he's going to puke. Frankie playfully kicks him in the ass.

After a moment, they go inside.

They settle down on the moldy rug that they brought out from the landfill near McLean, and they dig out their stash box. There are a couple of packs of Camels, a single Baggie of stale marijuana, a book of Zig-zags, a rusty Swiss army knife, some naked-lady playing cards and a *plastic-wrapped condom. Frankie proceeds to roll a joint, while Kyle comments on the new math teacher at Wilburn Middle School.*

After a few minutes, Kyle is first to hear the noise: an intermittent hissing sound, like an aerosol spray, coming from somewhere behind Frankie. Kyle comments on it, and Frankie glances over his shoulder.

A pair of beady black eyes are glaring back at him, a pointed snout flashing pearl-white fangs, hissing fiercely.

Both boys reflexively jerk away. Kyle tumbles on a root and falls outside the tree. But Frankie cannot move. He is paralyzed with terror, crouched in the dank shadows, staring nose-to-nose with a large, mangy, irritable raccoon.

Maybe it's the shock of being so close to the thing— not to mention seeing its impressive incisors—that has something to do with the fact that Frankie cannot move. Maybe it's just instinct, maybe some kind of primal muscle-memory that's keeping Frankie glued to that ground.

It's more likely, however, that it's the memory of a cold winter night, and a wild dog hunched in the shadows of a bloody barn, its feral eyes shimmering in the firelight, that has Frankie all jacked up.

"Frankie!" Kyle whispers frantically from outside the tree. "Don't show fear."

"What?!—what?!" Frankie says, keeping his gaze fixed on the animal. The raccoon is arching its back, hissing, clenching its claws.

"They're mean, Frankie, they can take a full-grown dog."

"Kyle, please shut up!"

"You can't show it you're afraid!"

"What are you talking about?!"

"Do the opposite!" Kyle whispered.

"What?"

"Do the opposite of what it expects—do the opposite— it expects you to run—do the opposite—show it you're meaner than it is!"

"What the—?" Frankie starts to say, then stops. All at once he gets it. In a single millisecond of clarity, he gets it. He gets what his brother is trying to tell him. In his adolescent way of understanding things, Frankie realizes that you've got to absorb the danger. You've got to turn the danger back on itself. You've got to turn the tables, and become the attacker yourself.

You've got to find the feral side of yourself and become more dangerous than the danger.

"Fine!" Frankie barks all of sudden, lurching toward the raccoon.

The raccoon hisses, rearing back.

"Let's do it!" Frankie growls at it, showing his teeth, and for one instant, Frankie becomes a rabid raccoon himself. And for one terrible moment, all the rage comes boiling out of him.

"Motherfucker!" he thunders at the animal, striking out at it. His hand catches a corner of the raccoon's snout, ripping a gouge of flesh. Blood spatters, and the animal yelps, then jerks away, cowering.

"Go ahead!—go ahead!!" Frankie shrieks at it. "Attack me!—attack me!—you motherfucker!"

Frankie lunges at the raccoon, grabbing it by the throat. The animal howls, twisting in Frankie's arms. It's a horrifying sound. Primordial. Like a cat being skinned. Frankie slams the raccoon against the wall of the massive trunk, again, and again, and again.

The sound of delicate little bones snapping is unlike any other sound.

Outside the tree, Kyle is watching in wide-eyed horror, mouth gaping, mortified, as the raccoon finally manages to wriggle out of Frankie's grasp—its bloody limbs flailing— fleeing out a hole in the opposite side of the trunk.

Frankie cannot shut off the motor inside him. He slams a fist into the tree, again and again and again, until his hand is throbbing. The raccoon is long gone, but Frankie's rage is still flaring into the air like static electricity.

A pause, as Frankie stands there, breathing hard, holding his hand.

Kyle is standing in the opening, staring.

A long pause as the two brothers gaze at each other, each learning something about the other.

Something very unexpected and disturbing, something beyond words . . .

. . . and now, in the great dream factory, the place where the two brothers had once come to see evil personified, to see the shifting, flickering shadows moving across the screen, to see the monsters rule in garish, Day-Glo, celluloid colors, all that muscle memory was returning to Frank.

Lying in the forgotten darkness, the sound of a single gun blast ringing in his ears, Frank was waiting for death to come and absorb him into the screen forever. He waited, and he waited, and he wasn't afraid. He wanted death to come take him away. He wasn't afraid anymore. He was fighting that rabid raccoon again, and he was ready to do . . .

. . . and that's when he realized the extraordinary thing that was happening.

He was not dying.

He was still alive, and he was still breathing, and his brain was still working.

Lying on his back in the darkness, completely deafened by the blast of the .38, Frank was blinded by a pinpoint of dirty daylight shining down through the cordite smoke swirling above him from the gunfire. He blinked, and he squinted against the corona of light flaring in his eyes, and he could barely see a pigeon up there in the cobwebs, flapping and convulsing against the timeworn patina of the theater's ceiling. What happened? Where was the gun?

A new voice spoke aloud in his mind: *Time to get moving, Frank, time to take care of business!*

Frank sat up with a start, a ripple of dizziness moving

through him. His scalp was stinging, and something wet oozed behind his right ear. He felt his head, and looked down at his bloody fingers. It was a contact wound, a minor one at that, the side of his face prickling from the powder burn, his ears still ringing fiercely. How was that possible? He had the barrel of the Colt pressed under his chin as he pulled the trigger. Was it the raccoon syndrome? Was it something that he done at the last minute to throw the programming off?

He frantically scanned the shadows around him and saw that he was still on the sticky floor of the Bijou Theater, the Diamondback lying next to him, gleaming in the low light. And all at once a whirlwind of information swirled through his brain, making him realize what had happened.

The voice. The angry voice in his head. Somehow it must have possessed him at the very last minute, filling him with enough inertia to break the hypnotic bond. It must have nudged the barrel of the gun a few centimeters to the right, just enough to save his life, sending the wadcutter off into the wall of the theater.

The voice in his mind, clamoring through a loud-speaker in his head: *The son of a bitch is still in the theater, Frank—he's right there, across the aisle! He doesn't believe his eyes, he's stunned, he can't move—take advantage of it!—nail the bastard, Frank!—nail him!!*

Frank scooped up the gun, then spun toward the shadows near the broken EXIT sign.

A tall, stooped figure stood near the curtained doorway, his hands at his side, his fists clenching and un-clenching rhythmically. He was coiled and tense like a wild animal that had been surprised very suddenly.

"You're not leaving yet, are you?!" Frank called out at the figure, rising up on two feet, aiming the Diamond-back. "Just when the feature presentation's about to begin?!"

The doctor took a step forward, his withered face illuminated by a shaft of daylight. "Very impressive, Frank," he said.

"Wrong," Frank said, the sound of his own voice a little odd in his blast-deafened ears. He aimed the gun at the doctor. Eight, maybe ten feet away. At this range, the bullet would remove Henry Pope's face.

"Excuse me?" the doctor said.

"I'm not Frank anymore," Frank heard himself tell the psychiatrist, for lack of a better explanation. It wasn't precisely true, but at this point it was the simplest way to describe what had happened.

"Is that right?"

Frank yanked the hammer back, the metallic snapping noise echoing in the dark theater. "That's right, Doc. I'm the new kid on the block."

"That's very interesting," the older man said, glancing around the theater, stalling, looking for something. "What shall we call you? Video-Frank?"

"Wrong again."

The psychiatrist frowned. "You're not Frank's alter ego?"

"Let's put it this way, Doc: I'm the new Frank. New and improved."

"You're not the Sleep Police?"

"Not exactly."

"Then who are you? What should I call you?"

Frank squeezed off a shot.

The gun roared, a silver flame leaping out of the muzzle, the blast gobbling a plaster divot six inches above the psychiatrist's shoulder, sending a puff of dust down on him. Pope ducked instinctively, covering his head with his hands, shuddering at the shock.

"How abut *Mister* Janus?" Frank heard himself say, his adrenaline spiking, his skin tingling.

"Easy, Frank," Pope said, raising his hands. His eyes were glittering, his wheels turning now. The doctor was a tough old buzzard.

"I'm very easy, Doc, I'm extremely easy."

"That's two shots you've fired now," Pope said.

"And I've got four left."

"They'll be sending a car out here, maybe several cars, any minute now."

"We'll be done by then," Frank said.

"What do you mean?"

Frank smiled mirthlessly. "Our business will be concluded."

"What business is that, Frank?"

"Call it justice."

Pope showed his yellow teeth. "The only one who deals in that business is God, Frank."

Frank took a step closer—maybe six feet away now—and aimed the gun at the bridge of the doctor's nose. Frank was like a substance that had been denatured. He was anger on two legs. And for the first time in his life, he was free of doubt, of self-loathing, of regret. He was a machine, and he was calibrated for a single purpose: destroying Pope. "Let there be light," Frank said very softly.

"Frank—"

"On your knees, Doc."

"Frank, I'm not—"

"ON YOUR KNEES!"

"I will not!" the old man said, shaking his head like a petulant child.

Frank aimed at the old man's shoulder, then pulled the trigger—

—and right at the same moment, Pope cried out at the top of his lungs one word: "SLEEP!"

The unexpected shock wave slammed into Frank's brain, throwing off his aim, and the blast went wide, the concussion erupting magnesium-bright in the darkness, chewing through the curtain and part of the plaster door frame behind Pope, sending fragments and debris flying.

A firebomb exploded in Frank's brain.

He doubled over, cringing in agony, the pain shooting

up his spine like a Roman candle. A rushing sound ignited above him, behind him, all around him like a giant turbine fan sparking to life. Shadows were coalescing in the darkened theater, something awakening. Or was it all in his brain? It was impossible to tell anymore.

Frank blinked away the pain, straightening up and glimpsing the apparitions.

They were emerging from the screen like wax figures in a vacu-form, congealing magically, absolutely *immense*. First their mammoth arms, then their torsos, then their legs. Gigantic monolithic policemen with huge, broad shoulders, birthing themselves from the amniotic fluid of the tattered movie screen, the womb of dark dreams. One by one, they lurched into Frank's three-dimensional space.

"NOT REAL!" Frank bellowed at the ghosts coming at him.

They shook the floor as they approached, their massive boots marching in unison down the aisles. There were dozens of them. Their heads rose up thirty feet high, enormous blocky shadows under the bills of their hats. They had no souls, no hearts, no humanity.

They were coming to put Frankie Janus down for an endless nap.

"NOT REAL!"

Frank fired at the phantoms, his gun roaring hellfire in the darkness.

The bullets chewed through the nothing, pinging and banging and flickering off the far gilded columns. The theater awakened in showers of sparks. Frank's scream was drowned by the noise.

All at once an alarm shrieked in Frank's brain: *Pope!*

Frank wheeled around toward the door and saw that the doctor was gone.

Frank fired at the doorway.

Sparks bloomed in the darkness, the blast gobbling the curtain, ripping another ragged hole in the fabric, and Frank kept on pulling the trigger, again and again and again—*click!-click!-click!-click!-click!*—firing at the empty doorway. "You old fuck, I told you!" he howled in a cracked voice, struggling to his feet. "It won't work anymore! POPE?! DO YOU HEAR ME?!"

Frank started lumbering toward the doorway, still firing the empty pistol: *Click!-click!-click!-click!* "I'm overriding the program!" he hollered at the darkness.

He pushed the curtain open, and the light assaulted his eyes, the smell of wet winds permeating the room. Heart chugging, adrenaline pumping, he quickly scanned the vestibule, the breeze tossing litter across the wasted cement. The meshed door on the opposite wall was partially ajar, rapping against the jamb in the wind.

Pope must have just slipped out.

Frank hurried across the vestibule and dipped outside.

32

Yellow daylight stabbed at Frank's eyes, blurring his vision as he emerged from the building. The wind whipped at his uniform and sirens keened in the distance. He bounded up the steps and hurried across the kiosk, madly searching the street, looking for the old man.

The rain had settled into a dirty mist, and the warehouse district was fairly slow today, a few delivery trucks parked along the rows of loading docks, a handful of teamsters and stevedores unloading crates up and down Franklin. They must have heard the shots but their faces remained stoic under the hoods of their raincoats.

Frank heard sudden noises—metal rattling, footsteps splashing through a puddle.

He raced across the street, then peered down the alley between two warehouses. He saw a stooped gray figure at the end of the alley, dressed in jeans, slippers, and a pajama top, striding along in a kind of half-hobble, half-gallop. The figure was moving pretty swiftly for an old man.

Don't let that fucking monster get away, Frankie. You know what you have to do.

Frank started down the alley in a dead run, clawing at his belt for the second speedloader—he had three cylinders altogether, a total of eighteen rounds. He would use every last one of them if he had to, but he would have to be judicious now that he was on the street. He would have to make every round count. Thankfully, he was still dressed in his patrol uniform, so most bystanders would get out of the way and figure he was simply chasing a bad guy.

In the distance, the psychiatrist had already vanished around a corner.

Frank reached the end of the alley and punched the speedloader into the Diamondback. He was breathing hard, and he was trying to get the bullets into his gun and see through the haze at the same time. To the south, the street terminated at a sprawling train switchyard full of abandoned freight cars and rusty, weed-clogged storage tanks. To the north, the street intersected with a busy commercial avenue.

Pope was approaching this intersection, trying to flag down a passing truck.

"HOLD IT!" Frank called out over the wind, struggling with the gun. He finally got the rounds into the Colt, tossed the empty loader over his shoulder, and ran as fast as he could toward the intersection.

Pope was fifty yards ahead of him, limping out into the path of an oncoming truck, waving his arms wildly. The truck's air breaks hissed. Its horn yammered.

"HALT! CHICAGO POLICE!" Frank cried, approaching at a full sprint.

The truck swerved, barely missing Pope. The doctor slipped on a puddle and went sprawling to the pavement. Another car lurched around him, its horn blaring. Pope struggled to his feet. Frank was thirty yards away now and closing, gun raised, sights set on a graffiti-stained newspaper dispenser only inches away from the doctor.

Frank fired at the dispenser.

The gun barked, and the slug slammed through the back of the dispenser twenty-five yards away, shattering the Plexiglas front. Pope ducked into a panicky crouch. Frank approached at a dead run. Twenty yards, fifteen, ten . . .

Pope turned and faced Frank, a strange sort of calm

on the old man's grizzled face. Frank approached with
gun ready. The doctor pointed an accusatory finger at
Frank like a school teacher about the discipline a child,
then hollered at the top of his voice, *"HOT!"*

Orange flame spurted from the psychiatrist's fingertips
like luminous ribbons—the same flame that had sputtered off an old oil lamp that had overturned in a blood-
spattered barn, the same flame that had flickered and
reflected off the marbled eyes of a rabid dog—and it
happened so abruptly that Frank had no time to duck or
get out of the way or even slow down. He ran directly
into the nonexistent fire, gasping at the sudden heat raging in his face.

The shock made him stumble, and he careened to the
ground, hitting the cracked sidewalk hard, knocking the
air out of his traumatized lungs. He managed to hold
onto his gun as he caught his breath, shaking off the
feeling of being scorched in napalm. He looked down at
his hands. They felt burned to a crisp but looked normal.
He swallowed. His throat was as sore as if he had inhaled
pure flame.

In one terrible instant Frank knew exactly what had
happened: All the secretive imprinting on his psyche in
Pope's office—all the verbal implants, all the posthypnotic suggestions that had been buried in his subconscious—it was all being used against him now like an
arsenal. There was a minefield in his head, and Pope
knew how to detonate each and every bomb. And even
though Frank knew intellectually that he wasn't burned,
his body told him otherwise. His brain cells—his neuro-
peptides, the place where the pain lives—were as good
as toast.

He scrambled back to his feet.

Pope was already halfway down the street, waving and
calling out for help.

Frank hurried after the old man.

By this point, dock workers and secretaries were coming out of their offices, peering through open windows

and around the edges of doorways at the commotion. Frank was convinced that as long as the citizenry saw a cop chasing a suspicious man in pajamas—and nobody recognized Frank—there shouldn't be any interference. But if another squad car or emergency vehicle came upon them, Frank was dead.

There were sirens approaching in the distance, probably responding to the gunshots at the Bijou. Of course, Frank had more immediate problems to deal with—such as the posthypnotic booby traps that Pope was throwing in Frank's path.

A half a city block ahead of Frank, through the veils of mist, Frank could see Pope trundling toward a subway kiosk. The weathered gray sign over the kiosk said CHICAGO TRANSIT AUTHORITY—RED, BROWN, AND PURPLE LINES. Frank picked up the pace. He didn't want to lose the doctor in the dark labyrinth of the subway where it was dark and full of nooks and corners in which an old man could hide.

Ahead of Frank, the psychiatrist shot a glance over his shoulder, then turned toward the subway entrance.

"DON'T DO IT, POPE!" Frank called out, racing across the street directly in front of a truck. Air horns blasted in his ears. Frank ignored it. He sped straight for that filthy Plexiglas entrance.

Pope was already inside the kiosk, already descending the greasy subway steps. In the shadows, his pasty face seemed to float there for a moment as he glanced back at Frank, who was approaching fast.

Frank reached the kiosk just as the sound of Pope's mucousy voice bellowed over the winds: *"COLD!"*

It was too late.

Frank just had time to glance down at the imaginary black ice coating the steps—which was the same black ice that had covered a lonely Central Illinois highway on a winter's night years ago, the same black ice over which ghostly footsteps had pursued a frightened young Frankie Janus through the dark—and all at once Frank's feet slipped out from under him, and he went careening down the stairs.

He landed on the edge of an icebound subway platform, sliding several feet, then smacking into a row of turnstiles. Goosebumps crawled over him as his lungs heaved for air in the sudden deepfreeze. The smell of ammonia was sharp in his nostrils, and the sound of cracking glass resonated through his skull. He shivered violently as he struggled to sit up, to see around him, to find Pope through the arctic vapors.

The underground station had transformed into a glacial hallucination. The tunnel was a black, crystalline mine shaft carved through an iceberg, and the deserted platform was a shelf of ice. A clear, hard shellac rimed all the benches. Overhead, frozen cobwebs clung to the exposed plumbing like spun glass as the flickering fluorescent light shone down through stalactites of icicles.

Frank scooped up the .38 and buoyed himself to his feet on the unsteady floor. His fingers were stiff, maybe even frostbitten, and he had trouble just holding onto the gun. He shivered convulsively as he swept his gaze across the station, hunting for Pope.

At the far end of the platform, a hunched figure was squeezing through a narrow passage into the shadows beyond the station.

"POPE!"

Frank's voice was strained to the breaking point as he started toward the far shadows, his breath showing in thin, white curls of smoke. He thumbed the hammer back on the Colt. His body was barely working now, his brain sending lies to all his senses: He heard the crunch of his boots as he trudged over a nonexistent crust of ice; he smelled the odors of dirty snow and salt; he felt the bitter cold on his face like a razor; he tasted the bite of a bitter frost on his tongue—

—and he saw Dr. Henry Pope fifty feet away, climbing down a quickfrozen ladder.

Don't let that sick motherfucker get away, Frank. You've got to finish it.

Frank hurried toward the end of the platform, breathing hard and quick, the Diamondback locked on its target. He could see the psychiatrist descending the ladder.

"POPE! IT'S OVER!"

Frank's cry echoed through the deepfreeze, bouncing off distant ice floes.

The psychiatrist had vanished.

At the end of the platform, just beyond a frosted sign that said CAUTION: CTA PERSONNEL ONLY BEYOND THIS POINT, Frank came upon the narrow iron ladder leading down into the tunnel. A single cage-light hung in the near distance. Frank could see Pope's shadow slithering away into the darkness like a tide going back out to sea.

As Frank hurried down the ladder, the hallucination began to decay around him like a faulty television signal. The cold sputtered away. The crackling sounds faded, and the ice glittered for a moment, then melded into billions of tiny bendai dots like a digital dream decomposing before Frank's eyes. The sound of hissing steam rose up around him.

His foot touched the floor of the tunnel, and he was immersed suddenly in the dank warmth of the subway. He blinked. A noxious hot wind slammed into him, ripe with urine, hot iron, and ancient mold. Frank wavered for a moment, gripping the bottom rung of the ladder.

The tunnel stretched before him, a narrow channel of filthy darkness broken only by the occasional green and red directional lights dangling over the track.

In the murky distance, a stone's throw away, Frank could see the psychiatrist scuttling furiously into the depths of the tunnel. Frank aimed the Diamondback, and he lined up Pope in his sights, and he considered firing for a moment, then thought better of it. The doctor was too far out of range. Frank needed to get closer, and he had to do it quickly, before a train came and squashed both of them.

Frank plunged headlong into the tunnel.

He ran down the center of the rails, boots splashing through stagnant pools of brackish water, his heart like a kettledrum in his chest.

And even in the throes of the chase, the mixture of fear and rage a potent cocktail in Frank's veins, he knew he was probably making a big mistake.

He knew he was probably stumbling directly into another trap.

33

Pope was hurting, hurting badly.

The last time he had run this hard, he was in his forties and working with the kids down at the Catholic Charities, putting them through their paces on the police academy obstacle course. Back then Henry had run the entire gauntlet right alongside those kids, hardly breaking a sweat. But that was back when he had been working out on a daily basis at the Y, and had been watching his diet.

Now he was an old geezer with high triglycerides, fallen arches, and early-stage arthritis, running through a dark subway tunnel in a life-and-death battle with a man twenty years his junior. But it didn't matter. It didn't matter to Henry Pope because he was engaged in a holy war. If Frank Janus had to be a victim of the war, then so be it. Henry Pope would not allow the detective to interfere with God's work.

Faint vibrations were rising off the rails beneath his feet as Pope scuttled along through the dark subway, making sure to avoid the electrified third rail. Was there a train coming? The doctor's slippers were soaked through, and they felt as though they were lead weights on the end of his spindly legs. His lungs ached, and his joints were full of ground glass. The detective was gaining on him. Pope could hear the younger man's footsteps echoing behind him, drawing closer. But now all the doctor could think about was completing the process that he had initiated ten years ago . . .

(. . . in that little cinderblock cubicle down at Area Six, back when they didn't even have a permanent Stress Management department, and that young detective from District Nineteen comes in after a nervous collapse at a crime scene.

Doctor and patient hit it off immediately, and they meet regularly in that little room, Frank on the settee by the window, reclining with a cold rag on his forehead, Pope in his swivel chair nearby, speaking so very softly, as the electronic metronome clicks rhythmically on the desk behind them.

"When I reach the count of one, and I snap my fingers, you will awaken with absolutely no knowledge of what we've discussed."

"I understand."

"Let me hear you say it."

"I will awaken with absolutely no knowledge of what we've discussed."

"And you will dream every night."

"I will dream every night."

"And what kind of dreams will you have?"

"Dreams that teach me things."

"That's good, Frank . . . that's very good—")

—and now there were waves of vibrations intensifying with each passing moment.

Pope could feel them through the soles of his shoes, a rushing noise in the distance, a metal-on-metal sound like a knife being sharpened on a whetstone wheel. A train was coming. He was sure of it.

The detective was less than a city block behind him and gaining every second. Pope realized he would have to do something evasive very soon, or he would be crushed like a bug on the track. But right now he had to keep moving, and keep out of range of the detective's gun.

It was astonishing to Pope that Frank Janus was still

standing, let alone still pursuing the doctor. Perhaps something had gone wrong with the hypnotic programming. Pope was frantically searching his memory for a clue—

(—*the detective lying on the divan, speaking very slowly, very deliberately, his eyes tightly shut, his arm raised and floating in midair. "I will carry out my duties as a detective without incident," he says.*

The doctor's voice: "What if you get too close to solving the thumb sucker?"

"If I get too close to solving the thumb sucker. I will start to fail."

"And what else?'

"I will have dreams of the other me."

"And who is that?"

"The man who lives inside me, that man who doesn't want the crime to be solved.

"And what will this other Frank Janus do in order to stop the crime from being solved?"

"He'll convince me it shouldn't be solved."

"How?"

"He'll leave me notes."

"And what else?"

"If that doesn't work, he'll try to sabotage the investigation.")

—and now something was happening.

In the gloom ahead of Pope, there was a bend in the tunnel, a dull gleam of light on the moldering stone wall. The train was approaching. The whetstone noises were rising to incredible levels, like metal tearing apart, reverberating through the darkness.

Pope kept hobbling along, planning his next move. On either side of him, along the edge of the rails, was a narrow ledge of about eighteen inches. Caked with grime and rat droppings, it was designed as a catwalk for CTA maintenance people. Every few feet, it widened to accommodate an electrical junction box. If necessary, the doctor could climb up on that ledge to avoid getting clobbered. But what about Frank Janus? The detective was less than twenty-five yards away now, and he might fire at any moment.

His mind churning with options, the noise rising all around him, Pope flashed back on the brainwashing—

(—*the detective lying in deep hypnotic trance, listening with his subconscious.*

The doctor's voice piercing his mind: "Frank, who is this other you?"

"It is the part of me that's guilty."

"Guilty of what?"

"Killing those women."

"That's right, Frank, and do you remember the words and phrases from your past that I programmed into you?"

"Yes."

"What will happen when you hear these words?"

"I will be afraid."

"Why?"

"Because these words scare me."

"And what happens when you hear them?"

"The words take me back to those bad times when I was a kid, and I'll be back in those times."

"What happens then?"

"I lost control."

"That's good, Frank."

"Yes, that's good."

"What about the other you? Will he be afraid?"

"I don't understand."

"Will the other you be afraid?"

A long pause. "No."

"Why not?"

"Because he's a killer—")

—a supernova of noise and light erupted suddenly in the subway tunnel.

Pope scrambled up the side of the ledge just as the train arrived.

The train sped by Pope in a cacophony of rancid wind and flickering light. Pope was stricken for a moment, his back pressed against the wall, his heart racing, his eyes tearing. The noise was monumental. It was like being swallowed by a jet engine.

The car passed so quickly it was impossible to see any of the passengers. Pope tried to cry out but his voice was nonexistent in the crushing wave of sound. The light inside the car strobed and flashed like an old-fashioned peep show for a moment.

Then it was gone.

And the last car hurled into the darkness, sucking all the noise and wind with it. Debris and pieces of litter swirled after it.

"Hey, Doc!"

Pope glanced up and saw the apparition perched on the ledge across the tunnel. The detective was breathing hard, having run a great distance, and was either grimacing or smirking, it was hard to tell in that horrorstricken instant before the attack. His gun was holstered. Pope tried to say something, but he couldn't get the words out in time.

The detective leapt across the gap—

—and it was as though a battering ram had slammed into the doctor, driving him against the stone.

The two men bounced off the rock, then careened over the ledge and onto the rails.

Pope landed with a thud on the small of his back, a bolt of agony shooting up his spine. The detective landed on top of the doctor, an audible grunt puffing out of the younger man. Pope tried to shove the detective off, but the detective was already going for Pope's throat.

Pope managed to call out another trigger-word, one of the last ones he remembered: *"NUMB!"*

The detective shuddered suddenly, his hands going soft and flaccid on the doctor's throat.

Pope took advantage of the momentary lapse and wriggled out of the detective's grasp, struggling across the cinders and filth, gasping for air in the dank darkness. The doctor labored himself up to his feet, then managed to back away a few paces from the detective, who was now on his knees, straining to clench his hands into fists.

For a brief instant, Pope watched the detective, teeth clenching, veins popping in his neck, willing his numbed extremities to move, to make fists, to rip through the neurological bondage. The doctor had never seen a man override posthypnotic programming through sheer brute force. This was a new phenomenon.

And that was when the realization struck Pope like an icicle through his forebrain: This was no longer Frank Janus, the mild-mannered, traumatized detective with tons of emotional baggage and crippling insomnia. Nor was it the Other Frank Janus, the wicked, scheming, amoral serial killer. This was a third personality. A wholly separate, discrete personality born out of a cauldron of terror and rage.

The was the new Frank Janus, a relentless, pig-iron stubborn manhunter.

The doctor turned and fled.

But it was too late.

Frank lunged across the third rail, boiling with adrenalin, his arms cold and prickling. He managed to get a handful of the doctor's pajama top, then yanked the old man backward.

The doctor tripped on his feet and fell into a stagnant, oily puddle.

Frank stood there for a moment, catching his breath, gazing down at the old man. Fever burned in Frank's head, his eyesight tunneled. There was an engine inside him, revving. Maybe it was a third personality. Maybe it was some repressed well of anger that had always been there. But whatever it was, it needed to strike out.

It needed to hurt the psychiatrist.

"Look at me," Frank said to the old man, his breathless invocation echoing in dead-silence.

Pope gazed upward, out of breath, fixing his milky

gaze on Frank. "What are you gonna do, Frank? Kill me?"

"Nope," Frank said, reaching down and clutching the doctor by the collar. He yanked the old man to his feet. "I'm going to arrest you for the murder of Kyle Janus."

Frank's fist came up hard under the doctor's jaw.

The blow made a snapping noise, like old cordwood breaking, and Pope's head jerked back. A string of saliva looped off the old man and across the darkness, as he staggered backward for a moment.

Frank threw a second punch into Pope's stomach just as Pope yelped, *"SHOCK!"*

High-voltage current surged suddenly in Frank's hands, sending him staggering. The electricity jolted up the tendons of Frank's arms, and he slammed backward against the ledge, letting out a startled grunt, his body stiffening, starbursts dotting his vision.

Pope got his legs back under him and lurched across the rails at Frank, driving a blow into Frank's solar plexus.

Frank doubled over for a moment, gasping for air, and Pope tried to drive a bony knee up into Frank's face, but Frank got a hold of the older man's legs and threw Pope off his feet. The psychiatrist landed on the outer rail with a *hrrrrmph,* and his feet nearly brushed the live center rail. The ground was starting to tremble again.

In the distance, the knife-sharpening sounds were returning, as Pope levered himself off the ground.

Frank pounced.

The two men collided on the outer rail and tumbled several feet, grappling wildly, Pope gasping for air. The rage was working inside Frank like a nuclear reactor, and he was no longer a cop, and he was no longer a fugitive from justice. He was a predator now, and he was unleashing his wrath in a barrage of jabs to the older man's midsection, culminating in a massive blow to Pope's kidney.

Pope exclaimed in agony, flopping backward on the rail, clutching at his back.

The metallic shrieking noise had risen to unbearable levels now, and the glare of xenon light tore a hole in the darkness, but Frank was far beyond caring. He climbed on top of the big-boned old man and grasped Pope's turkey neck and squeezed and squeezed, and as the light grew, Pope's ashen face became luminous, his blood-veined eyes growing wider and wider, gleaming like big cat's-eye marbles, and Frank strangled him with every last shred of strength—squeezing so hard his stitches were popping beneath his sleeves.

Another train was coming, roaring metallic dragon-breath in the dark tunnel, the metal wheels shrieking. Pope managed to hiss a choked scream over the noise: *"SHARP!"*

Fiery pain sliced up the undersides of Frank's arms, invisible razors gouging his flesh, but he refused to let go, refused to give into the neurological tricks. The train was bearing down on them, maybe sixty, maybe fifty yards away. The ground was shaking.

Pope uttered another strangled cry: *"BURN!"*

Frank's skin rippled with liquid agony, second- and third-degree burns sweeping over him like a brush fire, but he kept squeezing, he kept strangling, as Pope's face turned livid in the rising noise and light from the approaching train. The rails were singing.

The train was twenty-five yards away.

"DIE!" Pope croaked through his contracting windpipe over the incredible noise.

Frank glanced over his shoulder just as several things happened at once: His heart stuttered inside him, stealing his breath away; the train appeared in their faces in a nebula of pure-white light and sound; Pope managed to slither out of Frank's grasp, rolling out of the train's path, choking and gasping all the way; and somehow, through some self-preservative instinct, at the very last possible moment, Frank managed to dive toward the opposite side of the tunnel himself; and it all happened in one sudden paroxysm of violent movement.

Frank landed on the opposite ledge just as the train thundered past him.

The rotten wind engulfed him for a moment, the furious clacking noises drowning out everything else, shoving him against the stone. Light strobed and flickered maniacally in Frank's face, and Frank clutched at his chest, gasping for breath. A band of numbness was tightening around his left arm, and his vision blurred. He felt as though he were having a heart attack.

Was it the trigger word *DIE?*

Frank gazed through the veil of glaring white light, and saw in his mind's eye the windows of the train rushing past him, transforming into the sad, wan faces of mourners looking down at Frank's casket. Was he dying? Was it possible to just keel over from a posthypnotic suggestion? Frank could hear the voice of his little brother from many years ago—

(—*you die in your sleep, Frankie, you die for real in real life*—)

Frank opened his mouth and howled into the tidal wave of noise, "NO!"

The tail-car suddenly clamored past him, leaving behind a tiny whirlwind of red light and litter in its wake.

Frank doubled over for a moment, stunned by the sudden, dark calm.

He looked up.

Twenty feet away, a few paces down the ledge, Pope's gangly legs were visible dangling out the bottom of a service hatch, scuttling up an emergency ladder. He had evidently discovered the emergency porthole only a moment ago, and now he was getting away. *God damn it, he was getting away!*

Frank vaulted over the center rail, then hurtled toward the ladder.

Pope was already at the top of the steps, pushing the leprous emergency hatch open.

A column of washed-out daylight slashed down through the darkness.

Frank followed the psychiatrist into the light.

And one last deadly dance.

34

The sky had darkened significantly over the last few hours, as though the relentless rainstorms of the last couple of days had wounded it somehow, bruised it beyond recognition. And now the air was laden and musty, and the streets were slimy, and Frank had no idea what time it was as he emerged from the manhole and saw the dead city rising around him, all the tired old high-rises like phantoms in the gray, featureless mist.

Frank could see Pope in the distance, about a half a block away, limping hastily toward a vacant lot at the corner of Canal and Fulton. It was a run-down industrial neighborhood, and the few passersby were stepping back away from the commotion, huddling in doorways, watching with weary unease. Over by the bus benches, a homeless man was crouching behind a grocery cart full of castoffs, watching the world as though he were a refugee in some war-torn city.

Frank started after the doctor.

It wasn't easy. Frank's side was bound up in pain, and his lungs were sore, and his nerve endings were fried. How long had he been operating on negligible sleep? His body was starting to shut down.

Ahead of him, the psychiatrist was struggling over a low cyclone fence, then lumbering across a weedy, litter-strewn vacant lot. It looked as though the old man was in worse shape than Frank. He was limping furiously over the scabrous ground, holding his side, already so winded he could barely hold his gray head up. Frank had done some damage in the subway, but the old man was still kicking, and as long as he was functional enough to call out trigger-words, he was still dangerous.

Frank reached the chain-link fence, vaulted over it, then raced across the lot.

Up ahead, Pope vanished around a corner. He was heading south now, down a side street, and Frank found himself wondering if the doctor had any idea where he was going. It was clear the older man could not keep evading Frank forever, no matter how fatigue and bleary-minded Frank happened to be at the moment. But what if Pope had a destination in mind? What if Pope were leading Frank into another trap?

Frank approached the corner of the lot and careened around the end of a broken hurricane fence.

He spotted the doctor instantly, hobbling furiously along a row of boarded store fronts in a burned-out neighborhood. The sky seemed lower now, as though the tar-stained clouds were pressing down on the skyline. Dusk was coming. Frank could smell it on the wet winds as he raced after Pope.

"Hey!"

The voice pierced Frank's awareness. It came from behind him, off to his left, and it sent a jolt of electricity down Frank's spine. Without breaking stride, he shot a glance over his shoulder.

A plump black woman in a blue uniform—probably a meter maid—had stepped out from behind an abandoned pickup truck parked against the curb, and now she was watching the chase. "You okay?" she hollered.

Frank gave her hasty wave, trying to find his voice. "Got it covered!" he yelled back in a hoarse growl.

The meter maid called back, "You want me to call it in?!"

"No—that's okay—I got it!"

"You sure you don't need no backup?"

"Nope, no thanks!"

Frank turned back to the chase.

The psychiatrist had vanished around another corner, and Frank followed close behind.

It was becoming more and more obvious that Pope was leading Frank somewhere, and in that single instant of doubt, Frank wondered if he truly *was* making a fatal error in pursuing the doctor. But the thing inside Frank didn't care. The thing that had awakened inside Detective Frank Janus would not stop until Henry Pope was destroyed.

Forty yards ahead of Frank, an abandoned building loomed. Wooden construction fencing wrapped the foundation, and yellow CONDEMNED placards were posted every few feet. Inside the fence, a Gothic monstrosity rose up against the brooding, late-afternoon sky. The midsection was a decaying pile of stone and broken arched windows, the single belfry tower still vaulting upward into the clouds, the rusted cross rising off the uppermost finial like a stubborn avatar.

Frank didn't recognize the church. In his frenzied approach, his pulse quickening, he saw the building as merely one more casualty of a dying inner city, a failing infrastructure that left the dinosaurs of old mosques, temples, and churches to rot like fossilized carcasses. In fact, at the moment, the only thing about this church that concerned Frank Janus was the locked gate hidden behind a forgotten Dumpster at the southeast corner: The psychiatrist was fiddling with the lock.

A moment later, Pope had slipped through the gate and inside the lot.

Frank reached the gate a split second later and slammed his boot into the door. The rusted hinges jettisoned, and the door broke free, sliding across the muddy turf inside the opening. Frank lurched through the doorway.

The church grounds were a wasted battlefield of litter, discarded building materials, and bare earth. The oncesplendorous gardens had been reduced to cracked concrete troughs and crumbling ruins of featureless marble. The once-grand front steps were whiskered with weeds and crab grass.

A noise drew Frank's attention to the entrance—*the musty crack of a rotten plank.*

Pope!

The doctor was squeezing through a gap in the planking, then vanishing inside the church.

Frank hurried across the muck, his boots making suction noises, his heart slamming in his chest. He felt the size and the weight of the church pressing down on him as he approached, like the petrified remains of a mythic god. He found the loose plank through which Pope had slipped. He paused, taking in a few shallow, nerve-wracked breaths.

What are you waiting for, Frank? You got the son of bitch cold!

Frank slipped inside the church.

The shadows mocked him.

He pulled the .38 out of its holster, thumbing back the hammer as a stream of sensory information poured into him: This was bad, this was a bad place, from the rancid odors of ancient wax, and sweat, and moldering wood, to the frenzied sounds of footsteps receding down some inner sacristy, to the sickly light filtering down through broken stained glass mullions rising over the deserted foyer, he felt the overwhelming feeling that he should not be here.

Pull yourself together, Frank, and close this fucking case!

At last, he willed himself to move, across the vestibule of rotting tile and empty coatrooms and into the church.

The main cathedral was a haunted place drowning in a sea of shadows. Great pillars rose up at every corner, chipped and cracked from neglect. Cobwebs and filth choked the ceiling beams and gallery windows, and milky shafts of light crisscrossed the upper decks. Some of the pews were gone, like limbs amputated from a corpse.

Frank hurried toward the altar, toward the broken-down circular staircase to the left of the choir loft.

Footsteps were vibrating up there somewhere on the iron steps as the doctor ascended, sending echoes reverberating down through the darkness. Frank rushed toward the staircase with his gun raised and cocked and ready, and his heart racing wildly, his mind swimming with contrary emotions.

Go! Now! Finish it!

Frank started up the stairs. The iron banister trembled under his weight, and the steps squeaked as he ascended, and he realized in a terrifying moment of clarity that he was heading upward toward the belfry, and the mere thought of confronting this warped, Old Testament monster in the spire of a church was making Frank buzz with terror. He reached the top of the staircase and found another set of narrow, rotted, wooden steps leading up into the shadows.

What are you waiting for?!

He scaled the narrow steps, his weight making the ancient risers creak. By now he was at least four or five stories above ground and still climbing. At the top of the stairs he came upon an unmarked plywood door.

Do it! Come on!

Aiming the gun with a white-knuckle grip, teeth clenched, Frank yelled, "CHICAGO HOMICIDE! POPE! BACK AWAY FROM THE DOOR! AND PUT YOUR HANDS ON YOUR HEAD!"

He kicked the door open.

Shafts of blood-red light assaulted his eyes, and he took a tentative step inside the crow's nest with the gun gripped in both hands—tripod posture—his muscles coiled and ready for anything.

He was in an airless chamber at the top of the belfry tower, the south wall slashed down the middle with a jagged crescent of broken stained glass. The place probably once served as a choir loft, with padlocked double doors on the inner wall opening out over the congregation. But now it was transformed into some sort of demented sanctum sanctorum.

Frank swept the gun barrel across the walls. They were plastered with photographs, placards, and snapshots of medical procedures, and in a single, frenzied moment, Frank realized what he was looking at: *photographs of abortions*. Closeups of mangled fetuses on laboratory paper. Propaganda posters with slogans like "Stop the Silent Holocaust" and "Abortion Equals Murder." Even tiny wallet photos of babies and small children, arranged in feverish mosaics across water-warped posterboard.

Standing there, breathless, gripping the .38 in trembling hands, Frank felt his heart turn to ice. Dizziness slammed into him.

In the shadows across the room, something moved.

Frank tensed, pointing the Diamondback at it, calling out, "On the floor, Pope! It's over!"

The thing in the shadows writhed for a moment, then made a feeble, muffled sound. Frank took a tentative step closer. His gun was raised and cocked and ready to roll at any second, and he squinted to see through the shadows as he approached. Pupils dilating, adjusting to the darkness. The shape coming into focus. It was a figure.

A woman was tied to an armchair in the shadows. Mouth duct-taped. Head bound by the neck with thick cable. Eyes sleepy. Woozy. Probably drugged.

Approaching slowly, gun raised, the barrel jerking from shadow to shadow, Frank's brain was still piecing the forensic puzzle together. Frank was still a cop after all, and he could not stop making the case: The pentobarbital in the victims' bloodstreams was in order to keep them cooperative while Pope brought them here, and the unexplained lesions across the platysma muscles of the their necks were from the cable, which was designed to keep their heads in place so they would pay attention.

The realization just now seeping into Frank's mind: *This was a classroom.*

Then Frank glanced down at the woman, and all at once the terror blared in his brain like a broken horn because he recognized the women. He recognized her bony shoulders, her streaked blond hair and frightened hazel eyes.

"Chloe—?!"

Frank was starting toward her, reaching out for her, when he heard another sound.

It came from behind him, and before he even had a chance to whirl around he saw two things that told him it was already too late: Chloe's eyes widening suddenly, expanding to the size of half dollars, and a long, stooped shadow slithering up behind him, emerging from behind the door.

Frank spun around just in time to see a blur of wood coming at him.

The two-by-four struck him so hard across the bridge of his nose that it made his skull ring like a broken bell.

35

The doctor stood there for a moment in the scarlet light and the sound of Chloe's muffled screaming, watching the detective stagger on watery knees.

Pope struck the detective a second time—a hard, dry slap against the side of Frank's head—and that was enough. The detective folded up and toppled to the floor, dropping his gun and landing flat on his back.

Pope was trembling with fatigue and adrenalin now as he stood over the detective, gazing down at the young man with a strange mixture of repulsion and admiration. Pope tossed the two-by-four across the room, the board making a loud clatter as it landed in the corner.

The woman in the chair kept screaming underneath the duct tape.

The doctor took some deep breaths, smoothing down his matted gray hair with trembling, arthritic fingers. He was shivering under his damp pajama top. He was exhausted, too, and his chest was tight, and he was having trouble getting a full breath into his lungs. He had allowed things to get out of control, and now he would have to clean up his mess. Such a pity, too. After all he had been through. Especially last night. Staying late at the precinct house after Frank's escape, then slipping out the back, then finding the ex-wife's two-flat, then waiting for her to come home from her rendezvous with the detective, and finally snatching her from her bedroom.

Across the room, the woman named Chloe ran out of breath, her scream deteriorating into muffled sobs.

What a perfect student she had turned out to be—considering her history—and what a coincidence that Frank Janus had been involved with such a woman. Pope had only discovered the facts a few days ago. Thumbing through Frank's old files, he had stumbled upon the psychiatric history of Chloe Driscoll. She had been treated for bouts of reactive depression twice in her adult life, and when Pope tracked down her insurance claim history, he saw the sources of her anguish. Two—count them!—two separate dilatation and curettage procedures. A pair of abortions—ordered as casually as root canals.

A sudden, garbled groan came out of the detective, and Pope glanced down at Frank Janus.

The younger man was still conscious—albeit barely—which was precisely how Pope wanted him at this point. Pope knelt down on sore knees, bending down close to Frank, close enough for Frank to hear him. "It's a shame, Frank," the doctor purred. "That it has to end like this."

The detective's eyes were barely open.

"A young man in the prime of life," Pope went on, tugging on the neck of his pajamas, reaching down into his shirt. He pulled out a gold crucifix that was hanging on a chain around his neck—the same crucifix that the doctor had tried to give to Frank in the transport van.

"Tortured by the fact that his own ex-wife murdered two babies while they were married." The doctor dangled the gold cross in front of Frank's heavy lidded eyes. "He does the only thing makes sense to him."

Frank tried to speak, but only a watery gurgle came out.

"He kills her," the doctor said softly.

Pope reached down with palsied fingers and carefully pried open the gold cross. It was hinged, and when it clicked open, it began to play "That Old Rugged Cross" in tiny, delicate notes—a miniature music box.

"And then he kills himself," the doctor whispered, the chain dangling in front of the detective.

All of a sudden the music hit a glitch. A tiny skip in the clockwork of the music box. And the hymn got stuck—a single note repeating endlessly.

And the crucifix continued dangling, swinging gently back and forth, the single dissonant note chiming with the steadiness and monotony of a metronome.

And the doctor started speaking in a soft, rhythmic voice, the perfect cadence to initiate the induction phase of a rapid hypnosis session.

36

Frank tried to look away, tried to yank his mind away from the crucifix, but that single note—that tiny piece of metal clicking inside the mechanism of the cross, chiming ever so softly under the sound of Chloe's muffled moans—was irresistible, and the pain was like a vise grip on Frank's skull, holding him in place on the floor, and all he could do was stare at that radiant golden cross floating in front of his face, swaying ever so gently in the darkness.

"It'll all be over soon," Pope was softly informing him. "Because you're back on that beach, Frank, the one that takes all the pain away."

The cross . . . swaying.

"I'm going to count backwards from ten again, and by the time I reach one, you will be completely under. Ready? Here comes the first wave—ten!"

Chime!

Frank tried to concentrate on his brother. Yes. Kyle. That would counteract the trance. Memories of Kyle. But something was wrong. It wasn't working. The more Frank tried to remember his brother and block out the sound of Pope's voice and resist the images being conjured in his mind's eye, the more he saw that beach from his imagination. The one with the pristine white sand like sifted flour. Frank was lying there, and the opal-colored sea water was lapping over him in great rhythmic waves, and he was sinking through the floor of the belfry tower.

"Here comes another wave, Frank—nine!" Pope was murmuring, dangling the locket, the single chime striking. "It gently washes over your feet, as warm as a mother's womb, and here comes another one—eight!"

Chime!

Frank's body was getting heavy now, and there wasn't a thing he could do about it. The pain was throbbing in his skull, and his vision was all smeared and gauzy, and all he could see was the dull glimmer of that crucifix swaying before his eyes, and all he could hear was Pope's coarse, honey-sweet voice.

"Here comes another one, Frank—seven!—washing over your feet and legs. It's the most relaxing sensation you've ever felt, and it's putting you into a deeper trance—six!"

Chime!

The floor of the belfry tower was turning soft like taffy, and Frank could feel himself sinking deeper and deeper, and he could hear the angry voice in his head—*Fight it, God damn it, think of Kyle, think of something, but don't let this son of a bitch put you under!*—but the voice was fading, and the crimson light was gleaming off the gold cross, and Frank was sinking into a deep hypnotic sleep.

Pope murmuring softly: "The warm salt water is washing over your feet now—five!"

Chime!

"And it's washing over your legs and your midsection now, relaxing every muscle, sending you into a deeper level of sleep—four!"

Chime!

Frank was covered in warmth now, and Pope's voice was as soft as a lullaby: "Another wave, another surge of warmth flowing over your feet and your legs and your midsection, over your chest and your arms—three!—and you're almost completely under, and you can still hear me."

Chime!

Frank could barely see anything, his body completely submerged now. Only his face rose above the soupy, warm quicksand of the floor. And all he could see was the faintest glimmer of a scarlet-hued crucifix swaying gently before his eyes.

"Here comes one final wave—two!—and the warm water finally covers your face."

Chime!

Pope snapped his fingers. "One!"

37

Darkness engulfed Frank. Deep, black and eternal. Not at all like the darkness of a country night, or an unlighted room, or even deep space. This was darkness that suggested a tomb. This was the darkness of the grave. Dead, empty, closed-in darkness.

And the silence was broken only by the sound of a soft, gravelly voice.

"That's good, Frank, that's very good. Can you still hear me?"

Frank heard the reply—a voice very much like his own, but disengaged and out of sync with his lips, saying, "Yes, I can hear you."

"We've come a long way, Frank."

"Yes."

"We've made some amazing discoveries."

"Yes."

"There's another personality inside you, isn't there?"

After a pause: "I think so."

"This isn't you, and it isn't the thumb sucker killer that we created, is it?"

"No, I guess it's not."

"Who is it?"

No answer.

"Frank, please answer me."

Something flickered suddenly in the darkness, and Frank caught a glimpse of it. It was a blur of white slashing across the blackness, and it seemed to stain the back of Frank's retinas, too indistinct to identify.

"Frank?"

"I don't know," he heard himself any.

"Is it the angry version of you?"

"I don't know."

"Is it where all the anger lives?"

"I don't—I don't really know."

"There's something else I want you to do, Frank, okay?"

"Okay."

"It's the last thing that you'll have to do, and then we'll be all done."

"All right."

"I want you to kill that other Frank."

Something flashed again across the blackness, and Frank recognized it this time: the gleam of tiny ivory fangs ripping through the dark, the pointed snout of a rabid raccoon. The creature was there one moment, and gone the next, but it seemed to slash out at Frank, waking him up, waking up his rage, peeling away the darkness.

"Frank? Did you hear what I said?"

"Yes."

"Will you do that for me?"

"Okay."

"Do you know how I want you to do it?"

"No."

"I want you to write a suicide note, and then I want you to jump out the window. Okay?"

"All right."

"And it'll all be over, and there won't be any more pain. Okay, Frank?"

"Okay."

"Good, very good." The sound of dry, papery rustling, and shadowy objects moving around the room. "I want you to give me your hand, Frank," Pope's voice was coming from somewhere nearby. The darkness was peeling away, and the floor of the belfry tower was coming into focus. "Here," Pope said. "Right down here, your hand."

Frank's eyelids fluttered, and he saw the floor, the side of his face pressed against the filthy tile, little puffs of dust with every breath. He looked to his right and saw he was holding a Magic Marker, and Pope was steering his hand over a piece of brown butcher paper.

"I . . . Am . . . Sorry . . ." Pope was reciting, pressing Frank's hand against the paper. Frank watched his hand begin to write the words.

"For . . . All . . . The . . . Pain . . . I . . . Have . . . Caused . . ."

A low, buzzing sound was building in the back of Frank's brain, the same feral noise that had once come out of the raccoon so many years ago.

". . . To . . . My . . . Fellow . . . Policemen . . ."

Frank saw something gleaming on the tile about five feet away, and he fixed his sights on it like a predator preparing to pounce.

". . . And . . . To . . . My . . . Family . . ."

The growling vibrations were spreading down Frank's spine, and through his marrow, as though his body was a superconductor.

". . . I . . . Now . . . Leave . . . This . . . World . . ."

Inside Frank a spring was coiling, tensing, preparing to strike. He could see the .38 lying just out of reach across the room.

". . . May . . . God . . . Forgive . . . Me."

Frank suddenly sprang to his feet—

—as the doctor toppled backward in shock, careening to the floor—

—just as the tape burst free of Chloe's mouth, her scream filling the air like shrapnel.

38

It all happened with the surreal undercranked motion of
a dream or a very bad car accident where violent actions
and reactions spin off each other in seemingly endless
moments of inexorable doom—

—which is exactly how it appeared to Chloe as she
writhed and squirmed in the chair, watching the two men
tumble across the loft. She wasn't even conscious of her
own voice anymore, which had now been reduced to a
single, broken howl. She had forgotten about her bruises,
and the cotton in her brain from the sedative, and the
liquid fire around her neck from the cable, and the horrible pictures that were wrenching her heart apart, and
even the terror that had incapacitated her from the moment she had been kidnapped from her own bedroom.
Her attention was focused with laserlike intensity on
the gun.

For a single, excruciating instant, Frank's weapon lay
in limbo on the tiles.

Then Frank came hurtling across the room, landing on
the gun with a grunt, grabbing at it with fumbling hands.
It slipped out of his gasp and skittered across the floor.
Frank slammed against the wall. He cried out inarticu-
lately, scrambling back to his hands and feet. Behind
him, Pope was struggling to his feet. Chloe could see the
doctor sucking in decrepit breaths, his body trembling
with pain.

Frank made another mad scurry for the gun. But Pope was moving again, and before Frank could get his hands on the revolver, Pope had pounced on him.

Chloe let out a caterwauling scream with the last of her vocal cords.

The two men went down hard, sliding across the floor, grappling. Frank shoved the old man off him and muscled himself back to his feet, scooping up the gun. But it was too late, because they were too close to the window, and Pope was putting everything he had into shoving Frank toward the cracked stained glass.

Chloe watched the next few seconds transpire over what seemed to be an eternity in her traumatized mind.

Several things were happening all at once as Frank spun around and tried to shoot: Frank's balance went all to hell, and his legs got tangled under him, and he cried out with a start as Pope lurched at him with big, calloused hands outstretched, shoving as hard as he could, and Frank careened backward, out of control toward the window.

The red glass erupted, and Frank went over the edge.

39

A couple of unexpected accidents prevented Frank from falling the equivalent of six stories to his death.

First, in some sort of wild, reflexive desperation move, his left hand shot outward right at the exact moment of impact, clutching at anything that would hold him as he careened over the ledge, ultimately finding purchase on a five-inch shard of broken glass jutting up from the edge of the window frame. The fragment pierced his hand just below the knuckles and held him like a game fish flopping on the hook.

Second, through some innate muscle memory, his right hand remained frozen around the beavertail grip of the Colt as he plunged through the window. The flash of the barrel had somehow drawn Pope's attention, and in that single frenzied instant elicited an instinctive gesture from the doctor. Pope's left hand clutched at the six-inch barrel.

And now, in the dying light and gusting winds, Frank dangled from the broken window, his left hand impaled and singing an aria of pain, his right hand still gripping the gun, caught in a tug of war with the doctor.

Pope was hunched over the sill, grimacing in agony, the dusky light reflecting off his grizzled face. He was holding onto the inner frame with his right hand, anchoring himself, his rheumatoid ligaments stretching like old rusty tow cables, keeping both men from falling.

The doctor's other hand was wrapped around the gun barrel, averting the muzzle away from him.

"Frank—!" Pope's voice was a harsh, strangled whisper above the winds.

"If I go, you're going with me," Frank hissed between clenched teeth, the pain like a banshee in his brain. His left hand was volcanic, the jagged glass protruding between two carpals. It looked like a rubber hand, like joke. Blood oozed down his arm and the side of the wall from the wound and the popped stitches in his wrists But Frank didn't care. The pain was keeping him alive He tried to swing the gun toward the doctor.

"GO TO SLEEP!" Pope boomed.

Frank froze, cringing at the burning pain, his legs dangling, his crotch warm and wet. He had pissed himsel and he hadn't even noticed it.

"Go to sleep, Frank," the doctor urged from inside the gaping maw.

Frank looked down and saw the construction site sixt feet below him, a circle of rubble and broken rocks. I wavered in and out of focus. Somewhere far in the distance, thunder rumbled.

"Kill yourself," Pope whispered, barely audible above the cutting breeze.

Frank gazed up at the psychiatrist. Pope's face was framed in a V of broken stained glass, a wrinkled death mask staring down at Frank. The pain was stitched across the doctor's brow, his eyes twitching, his flesh like gray elephant hide. "Go ahead, Frank," he uttered. "Put ar end to the pain."

Frank dangled helplessly, tears blurring his vision tracking down his face, drying instantly in the wind These were tears of pain, tears of anguish, tears of self-loathing. Frank's whole miserable life had added up to this single moment.

Wind buffeted Frank's pant legs, and he felt weak all of a sudden. Pope was right after all. A single blast to the cranium would fix everything. Frank glanced over at the gun and noticed it was trembling.

Pope's ragged wheeze from the window: "It's the only way, Frank. You're so tired."

Something glittered in the broken glass next to Pope.

"Go to sleep, Frank."

Frank noticed the shimmering ruby glass, and all at once he realized the answer.

It came flowing into Frank through his frontal lobe like electroshock, and he realized at once it was the only way he was going to win. The only way. And almost in that same instant he realized that he was going to have to act swiftly because the pain was draining him, taking the last of his adrenaline, and he would either collapse soon, or his hand would tear apart, and he would plummet.

The gun shuddered within the two sweaty fists, and the barrel started to move. Both men gaped at it as though it had a will of its own.

It was moving downward, downward toward Frank, away from Pope, and the sudden expression of hate and raw animal aggression burned in the doctor's eyes. "That's right, Frank," he whispered.

The barrel trembled toward Frank, and Frank watched it carefully. The wind whistled. Frank gazed up at the broken glass.

There was a huge triangular fragment next to Pope, a few centimeters to his immediate left, and Frank strained against the blazing agony of his left hand, strained to edge his body a mere couple of inches. That's all it would take. Just a few inches to the left.

Tears tracked down Frank's face.

"That's right," Pope uttered.

The gun barrel was almost pointing directly at Frank's temple now, and Frank's body was shutting down from all the pain and the shock. The blood was seeping down the stone wall like crude oil in the dim light, and Frank could hear his own heartbeat in his ears.

Frank looked up at the glass and decided it was indeed time to kill himself.

"Do it, Frank!"

Frank thumbed the hammer back, swinging the barrel toward the glass.

Kill yourself!

He fired at his own reflection.

The Colt barked, and the face in the glass shattered into a constellation of stars.

40

Pope's head was directly behind the reflection—in the path of two out of the three bullets—and sudden gouts of blood and tissue erupted as the rosettes of stardust blossomed, the slugs driving through the dark belfry tower and hitting the far wall. Outside the window, even in the noise of the wind, Frank could hear Pope's last surprised gasp.

The impact hurled the doctor backward, slamming him against the far wall, leaving a huge smear of blood.

Silence fell suddenly like a funeral shroud landing on the church.

Frank cried out in agony, still gripping the Colt like a life line.

He tried to lift his right leg over the ledge, his feet slipping and scuttling against the oily, blood-slick stone. He could hear Chloe's sobbing from inside the belfry, and the distorted whine of sirens in the distance. He dropped the gun inside the loft.

A wave of nausea and pain smashed into Frank, and he gasped. He was about to fall. He could feel the cartilage in his hand giving way, the fire inside him devouring his breath. The wind bullwhipped the side of the church, thunder rolling off the distant horizon.

Frank finally managed to get his right boot on the edge of the window sill. He let out a momentary sigh of agony. Just a few inches more. He tried to pull himself over, but his body was dead weight now. Dizziness crashed over him, his vision wavering, the side of the building swimming into multiple images. His brain was a cracked lens.

Just a couple of inches.

He put everything he had into wrenching his free leg over the ledge, but he couldn't make his joints work. His impaled hand was broadcasting fire into every cell, and the pain was radiating down his arm like a bass string being plucked. His body was completely inert. He couldn't breathe. He wondered if he was going to die like this: pinned to the spire of an abandoned church like some forgotten gargoyle.

Finally, he was able to work his boot over the ledge until he was straddling the sill. The added leverage allowed him to slide the rest of his body up and over, almost as though he were mounting a horse. His heart was hectic in his chest, and a cold fever-sweat had broken out on his face. He was summoning every last scintilla of strength. He knew what he had to do next, and he knew that it was now or never.

He sucked in a breath.

Then he yanked his wounded hand off the spindle of broken glass.

The pain drove him the rest of the way over the ledge and into the belfry, and he landed on the floor with a thud. His hand was shrieking. He let out an involuntary cry, curling up on the floor, cradling his bloody hand. His head was spinning, and he couldn't see very well. But he could hear another voice across the room.

Chloe sobbing breathlessly in her chair, the duct tape dangling from her chin.

Minutes passed.

Frank wasn't sure how long he had lain there, shivering in the shadows, clenching his wounded hand. It was almost completely dark outside now, and it was getting more and more difficult to see in the dim light of the belfry tower. Frank could barely make out the silhouette of Pope's body in the opposite corner. The gangly doctor had fallen against the baseboard, his back to the room. A puddle of blood was spreading underneath his head.

"F-Ff-Frank?"

Chloe's broken voice yanked his attention to the other side of the room. She was sitting forward in the armchair, straining against the duct tape wrapped around her midriff. Her face was a battle zone of creases and tears, and her bony shoulders were shivering.

"I'm okay, Chloe," Frank said, managing to sit up, breathing hard, holding his ruined hand. He yanked his shirttail out of his pants, tore a hank of fabric off it and wrapped it around his throbbing hand.

"Oh God, oh God," Chloe was murmuring, gaping at Pope's body.

"It's okay, Chloe, I'm here," Frank said, straining to stand up. His body was a rag doll. Every muscle seemed to be cramping fiercely.

"Oh Jesus," Chloe sobbed.

Frank went over to her, knelt down by the chair, wrapped his arms around her. "It's over, it's over, it's over," he murmured under his breath.

"Jesus!—JESUS GOD!" Chloe jerked her head violently forward.

Frank reared back. "Easy, Chloe."

"Easy?! Easy?! What the fuck is happening?! What is going on?!"

Frank reached out for her, but she butted her head at him, shaking furiously. Her eyes were wild now, blazing with narcotic shock and outrage. "Get me outta here! GET ME OUT!—please get me out, please, get me outta here!"

"Okay, okay," Frank said, reaching for the bands of silver tape wrapped around her torso, her arms and shins. The tape was like iron, and Frank's hands were numb with pain and trauma. It was impossible.

"Please, Frank," Chloe was saying under her breath, starting to sob again.

Frank fiddled with a leather snap on his belt. Cradled inside it was a Swiss Army knife that Frank had always kept for emergencies while on patrol. Frank yanked the knife free and fumbled its large blade open.

"Please . . ." Chloe was losing her voice.

Frank carefully sawed through the first layer of duct tape around her tummy, cracking open the tape and allowing Chloe to wriggle partially free. Next he sliced through the tape around her right wrist.

"Frank?"

Chloe's voice was low and steady all of a sudden, even measured.

"Almost done," Frank murmured as he worked on the left side, slicing through layers of sticky gray plastic tape. He was concentrating on his work, and wasn't paying any attention to Chloe's face, or the fact that the drugs were most likely affecting her reactions.

"Too late," Chloe said.

Frank looked up at her face, and saw her eyes glittering with fear.

Frank glanced over his shoulder.

Henry Pope was standing there with streamers of blood on his face and the .38 gripped in both arthritic hands.

41

The secret place in the human brain where voluntary movement becomes involuntary is known as the frontal lobe of the cerebral cortex. In this microscopic ocean of swaying ganglia and efferent fibers, neuroelectrical impulses pour in from the intrinsic muscles of the eyeball, signaling an emergency, flowing instantly down the axonal pathway, then into the ciliary ganglion, then on through the preganglionic fibers to the parts of the brain that fire movement.

It's a process that occurs virtually at the speed of light, and in many cases happens automatically.

And Frank Janus wasn't even aware of it as he whirled in the darkness of the belfry to face the trembling figure standing over him.

"Such a pity," Pope uttered over cracked, bloody lips, his scalp gouged on one side, the hair matted and sticky with blood. He was aiming the gun at Frank's forehead.

"No!" Frank's hand shot up on its own accord, completely involuntary.

The knife sank into Pope's belly just below the sternum at the precise same moment Pope pulled the trigger.

The gun roared, thrown off-course by the sudden attack, the muzzle flickering upward, the blast devouring a chunk out the ceiling, a spray of dust and debris erupting as Pope staggered backward, the hilt protruding from his gut. Frank was still gripping the handle as the two men lurched across the room with the doctor's movement.

Chloe's scream pierced the air.

The two men slammed into the adjacent wall.

Frank yanked the knife upward with his last bit of energy, severing major organs, and the two writhed against the wall for a moment, a tide of warmth oozing out of the doctor. Pope tried to speak but the shock was gripping him. He shuddered in his death throes, sliding down the wall finally, leaving a leech trail of deep red.

Pope landed on the floor and bellowed a death cry, and it sounded like a rusty exhaust stack vomiting pollution into the air.

Chloe covered her ears with her hands, sobbing uncontrollably now.

Frank refused to let go of the knife, refused to back off. Straddling Pope like some psychotic rodeo cowboy, taking big wheezing breaths, Frank was responding to some deep rooted, lizard-brain fight instinct that he had no hope of controlling. He was covered in blood, his own and Pope's, and he was gazing down at the old man in equal parts horror and fascination as Pope expired.

The old man shivered for a moment, then sagged against the floor.

Silence fell on the room.

Frank finally let go of the knife, sliding off the psychiatrist and slumping down on the floor next to the body. Frank was a jumble of pain. His own body weighed a million pounds. His pulse was fluttering irregularly, and his piss-sodden pants felt like ice. Was it over? Was it really over? The room was spinning.

Frank felt the darkness closing in like a warm fist.

He turned back to the doctor and stared down at the body in wonder.

Pope was lying there, frozen in death, curled into a semi-fetal position against the wall. His abdomen was ravaged by the knife, his yellow eyes still open. And yet, just for a moment, in the delicate red light, the doctor looked almost tranquil. His left arm had fallen at an awkward angle under his body, and his right arm was folded against his chest. He looked as though he were sleeping.

Just a few more inches, Frank mused feverishly, staring at the old man's gnarled thumb, *and it would have ended up in his mouth.*

42

Frank heard a noise across the room.

Chloe was standing up, the chair still attached to her left wrist and part of her leg.

Her gaze smoldering, her mouth working, she dragged the chair toward Pope, the wooden legs scraping the tile, making an awful racket, her feet crunching through broken glass. Her face was a mask of fury, her eyes laced with hate and barbiturates. Frank didn't have the energy to stop her.

Chloe yanked the chair over to where Pope lay cold and silent on the tiles, and she started howling at the corpse, "Fucking psychopath!"

Frank decided to intervene, but he couldn't reach out for her in time.

Chloe's right leg shot out at the body, her boot striking the dead man in the gut with incredible force. The body slammed against the wall, spattering blood, and the chair tore free, overturning on the floor. Chloe kicked at Pope again, and again, crying, "Fucking monster, monster, monster, monster—!"

Frank struggled to his feet and tried step in between her and the body.

Chloe was out of control. She shoved Frank out of the way with all her might and continued driving her boot into the flaccid remains of Henry Pope. The body was dead weight now, absorbing every blow with a muffled thump. "Touch me with those disgusting, filthy hands—!"

"Chloe—!"

"I'll show you crimes against God!"

"Chloe!—Chloe!—stop!" Frank finally gave her a bear hug, driving her away from the body.

She fought for a moment in his arms, but she was running out of steam. Frank shuffled her away from the body, pressing her against the opposite wall, whispering that it was over, it was over, let it go, let it go, and soon the rage turned to tears. Chloe started to sob, and she shuddered in his arms, and Frank held her and let her cry it out.

The loft was almost completely dark now, and outside, the dissonant harmony of sirens was approaching. Frank felt his own emotions giving way like a twisted rubber band finally snapping, and he too began to weep.

And they wept in each other's arms for quite a long moment in that dark belfry room amid the spiderwebs and broken glass and graphic photographs of aborted fetuses. Something was happening to Frank. It was like a shade being slowly drawn. He could feel it tugging at him, pressing down on him, making his eyes burn. He slid down the wall with Chloe still in arms.

They both landed on the floor in sitting positions, their tears drying on their drawn, exhausted faces.

Across the room, Pope's body lay in the shadows.

"He's gone," Frank whispered, his eyelids heavy, his brain shutting down. "He's gone."

Chloe nodded and didn't say anything, just sat there staring at the gaping window.

In the blessed stillness, Frank realized that a part of him was gone as well. And he would never be the same, never. A shade was slowly being drawn over his eyes.

He collapsed in Chloe's arms, falling into a deep, profound sleep.

A sleep without dreams.

EPILOGUE

The Dark Inside

"To know thyself is to be known by another."
—PHILIP RIEFF, *The Hidden Self*

The hearing took place in the federal court building in Daily Plaza, almost exactly a month—to the day—after Henry Pope's death. It was a closed proceeding, officially the final stage of a three-week inquest. Only the immediate players were involved. The Honorable Judge Margaret Vincent; two attorneys from the DA's office by the names of Maloney and Nava; a representative from Internal Affairs, Sergeant John (Jack) Musso; a court-appointed psychiatrist named Sebastian Kolh; Detective Sullivan "Sully" Deets; Chloe Driscoll; and Frank. The proceeding took place on the fifteenth floor of the federal building, in the judge's chambers.

The adjacent waiting room was a bland, high-ceilinged affair with institutional green walls and tall windows overlooking the giant iron Picasso hunkered down on the plaza. It was a hot day for September, and the sun was blazing down through the blinds, slanting through dust motes and painting fiery stripes against the sofa on the opposite wall.

Frank was sitting alone at the end of this sofa, impeccably dressed in a Ralph Lauren jacket of autumn browns, pretending to look through a *Time* magazine. His mind was elsewhere. It had been a crazy month, a month full of endless interviews, court proceedings, formal hearings, and oceans of grief. What did Henry Pope once say about this kind of stuff? *"Reexperiencing?"*

Frank had been reexperiencing the horrors of August over and over again, for IAB guys, for shrinks, for the court. But the worse day of all was Kyle's funeral.

They had buried Kyle Janus two weeks earlier at the Greek Orthodox cemetery in Franklin Park, and hundreds of mourners showed up. Kyle was one of those magic people who was simply liked by everybody. Even Helen Janus was allowed to make the trip south for the funeral, ensconced in a wheelchair and wrapped in a blanket—although Frank was skeptical that his mother knew what was going on. Frank spoke the eulogy, and he broke down halfway through it. No one in the congregation knew just how responsible Frank felt for Kyle's death.

Now Frank sat in the morning sunlight just outside the judge's chambers, feeling much older than he looked, awaiting the final word on the Pope case. His superficial wounds had healed. He was rested for the first time in his life, and he just wanted to go back to work.

He wanted to be a detective again.

"—Bambi?"

The voice shook Frank out of his ruminations. He glanced up and saw the big man standing just outside the door to the judge's chambers, his portly figure silhouetted by the glare of sunlight. "They're ready for you, Bambi," Sully Deets said with a sheepish nod.

Frank walked over to the doorway. "Hope this is the end of it."

Deets shrugged. "It better be. I got a bus load of open files back at the Twenty-fourth burning a hole in my desk. I need you back on the job."

"I appreciate all you've done for me, D."

The big man smiled. "Hey. You woulda done the same for me, right?"

"You bet your ass."

It was true, Frank would have done the same to help his partner, even in the midst of seemingly indisputable hard evidence—as Deets has done. But Frank was not so sure he could have come up with the same kind of gold that Deets had found. During the days following Pope's death, Deets's detective work became the key to exonerating Frank.

It had started the night of the frantic phone call from the "El" station, the one in which Frank had begged his partner to reopen the thumb sucker files, to look hard at Henry Pope. Deets had been unable to fall back to sleep that night, brooding on the possibility that his partner had been diabolically framed and driving his wife Margie batty with his tossing and turning and mumbling.

By the time dawn had driven away the night, Deets was up and dressed and making phone calls.

Over the next five days, Deets had singlehandedly built a framework of evidence that not only proved that Frank had been programmed under hypnosis, but also that Pope had possessed the motive and opportunity to commit the murders. Discrepancies in Pope's work schedule logs, contradictions in alibi witnesses, under-the-counter procurement of deadly sedatives and hypnotic drugs, and residues found in Pope's work locker and closet at home, all pointed toward Pope's guilt. But perhaps the most interesting discovery was a little-known bust that Pope had plea-bargained out of years ago: assault and battery during a pro-life rally outside an abortion clinic. When this fact was bolstered by Chloe's eyewitness testimony, and ultimately driven home by the revelation that every thumb sucker had undergone multiple abortions, the case was iced.

"Anyway, I better get in there," Frank said finally, smoothing out his lapel and turning toward the door.

"I'll be waiting for ya," Deets said.

Frank nodded, then walked through the doorway and into a small, windowless antechamber. There was a skinny black security guard sitting behind a card table next to a massive oak inner door. The door led into the judge's chambers. "Detective Frank Janus?" the skinny man asked, looking up at Frank through thick bifocals.

"That's me."

"Sign in, please."

Frank signed the register, then went over to the door and grasped the huge brass doorknob.

For most of his adult life, he would have paused in a situation like this. He would have lingered outside the door for just a moment, fearful and neurotic and full of dread, chewing on a straw, or biting a fingernail, or doing any one of the dozen nervous habits he had developed over the years. He would have felt that cold weight in his gut, and he would have braced himself for the worst.

Not today.

Today there was a new Frank standing outside the judge's chambers, with a new consciousness flowing through his mind at all times. It wasn't anything pathological. Like a multiple personality. He wasn't hearing voices. There was simply a new personality awakened within him, like a phoenix out of the ashes of all the death and destruction, driving his thoughts, getting him through the pain. The new and improved Frank Janus. Telling him: *You've done nothing wrong, Frank, you have nothing to be ashamed of, so get your ass in that courtroom and let them ask whatever they have left to ask.*

Frank opened the door and walked into the plushly appointed room, and the door slammed shut behind him with a decisive click.

PENGUIN PUTNAM INC.
Online

Your Internet gateway to a virtual environment with hundreds of entertaining and enlightening books from Penguin Putnam Inc.

While you're there, get the latest buzz on the best authors and books around—

Tom Clancy, Patricia Cornwell, W.E.B. Griffin, Nora Roberts, William Gibson, Robin Cook, Brian Jacques, Catherine Coulter, Stephen King, Jacquelyn Mitchard, and many more!

**Penguin Putnam Online is located at
http://www.penguinputnam.com**

PENGUIN PUTNAM NEWS

Every month you'll get an inside look at our upcoming books and new features on our site. This is an ongoing effort to provide you with the most up-to-date information about our books and authors.

**Subscribe to Penguin Putnam News at
http://www.penguinputnam.com/ClubPPI**